Praise

'*Ice Apprentices* is an extraordinary fantasy debut. Oswin is endlessly curious, hilariously funny and wonderfully kind – he became my new favourite hero within a few sentences.'

A.F. Steadman, author of the Skandar series

'Spine-tingling monsters, unlikely friendships and a hero to root for from page one. North's debut is bursting with adventure and vivid characterisation.'

Fran Gibbons, author of *A Clock of Stars*

'An enchanting debut, sparkling with adventure and magic.'

Natasha Hastings, author of *The Miraculous Sweetmakers*

'Oswin is brave, curious and seeks to uncover the mysteries of his own past and the skills he has been born with. Such an exciting novel, I can't wait for the next book!'

Nazima Pathan, author of *Dream Hunters*

JACOB NORTH

ICE APPRENTICES

SIMON & SCHUSTER

First published in Great Britain in 2025 by Simon & Schuster UK Ltd

1 3 5 7 9 10 8 6 4 2

Simon & Schuster UK Ltd
1st Floor
222 Gray's Inn Road
London WC1X 8HB

www.simonandschuster.co.uk
www.simonandschuster.com.au
www.simonandschuster.co.in

Simon & Schuster Australia, Sydney
Simon & Schuster India, New Delhi

A CIP catalogue record for this book
is available from the British Library.

ISBN 978-1-3985-3393-6
eBook ISBN 978-1-3985-3395-0
eAudio ISBN 978-1-3985-3394-3

This book is a work of fiction. Names, characters, places and
incidents are either the product of the author's imagination or are used
fictitiously. Any resemblance to actual people living or dead,
events or locales is entirely coincidental.

Typeset in Palatino by M Rules
Printed and bound in the UK using 100% renewable
electricity at CPI Group (UK) Ltd

To Mum, Dad and Sophie

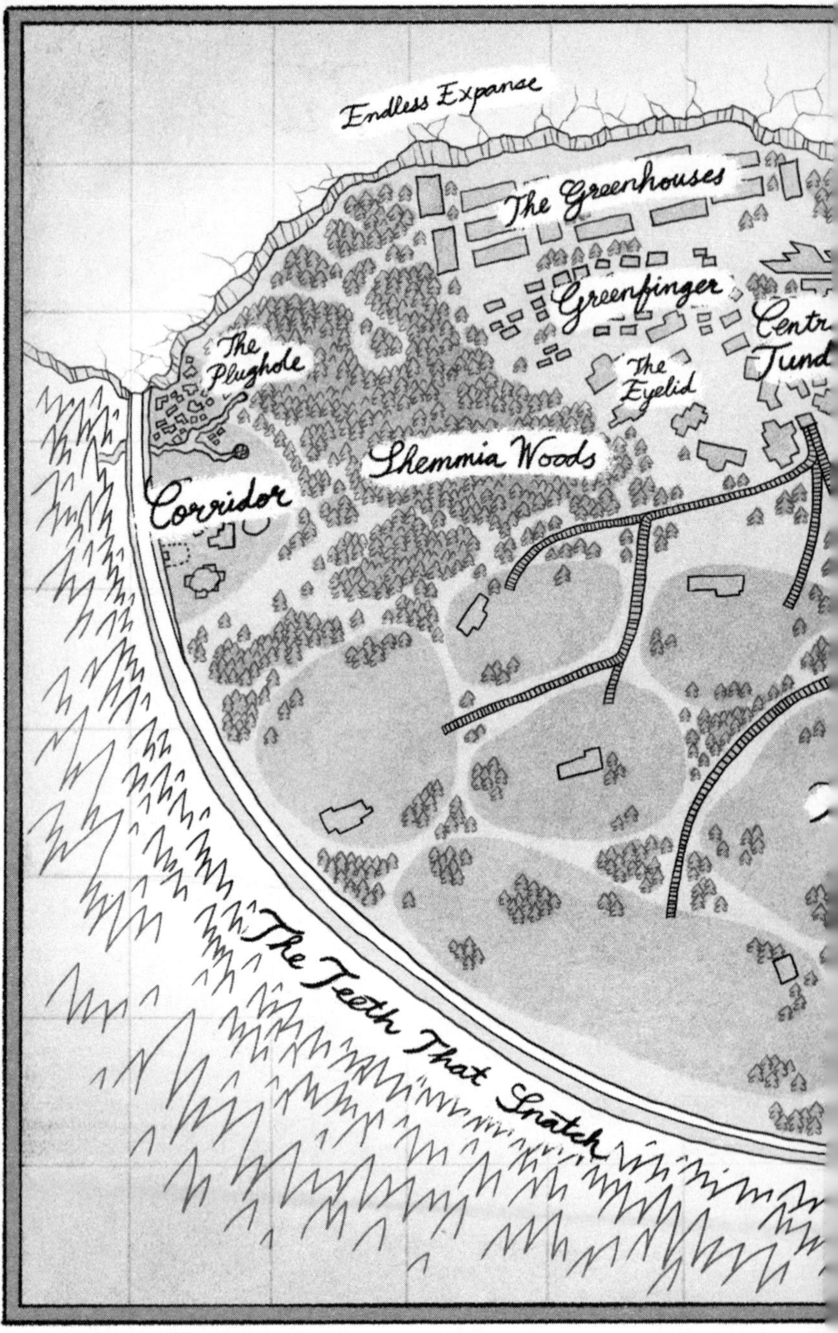
Endless Expanse
The Greenhouses
Greenfinger
The Plughole
The Eyelid
Shemmia Woods
Corridor
The Teeth That Snatch

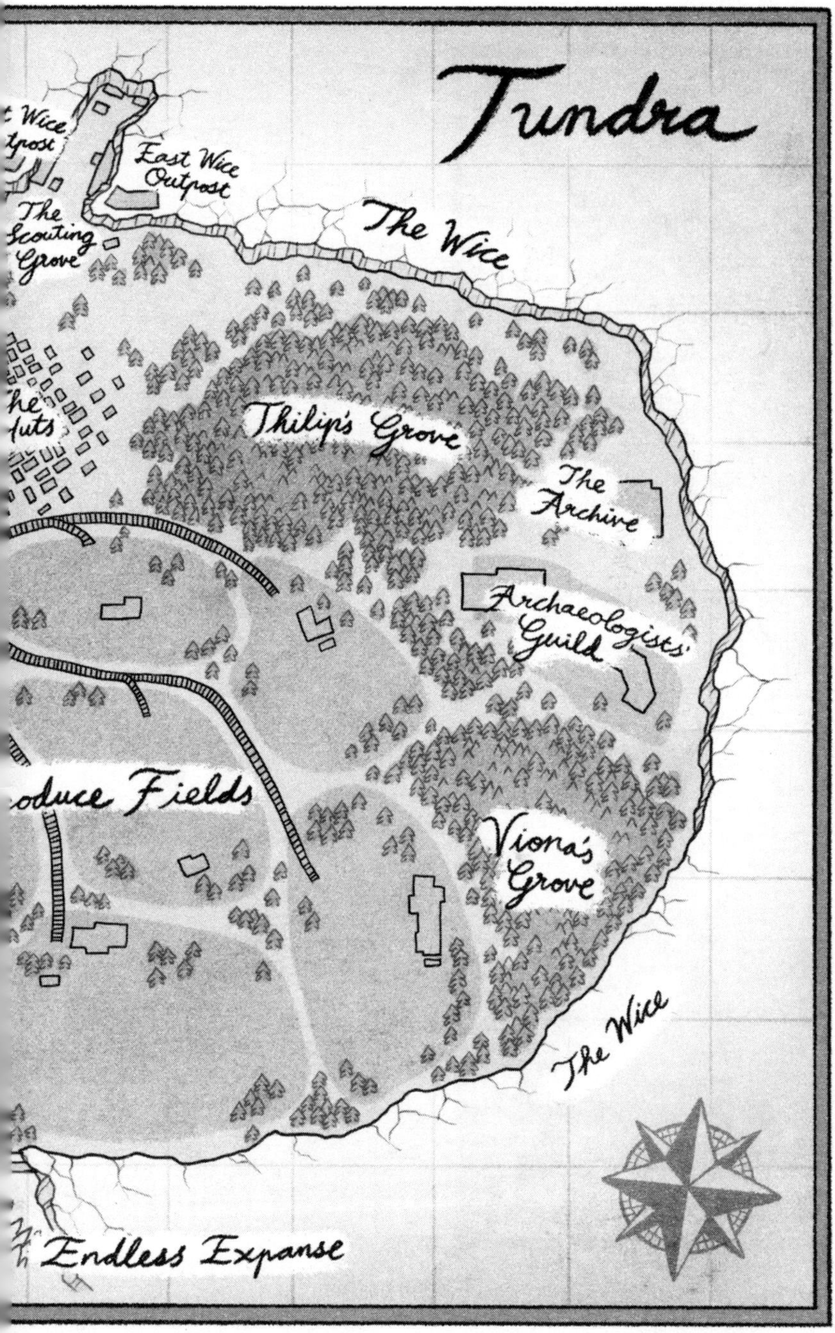
Tundra
t Wice
tpost
East Wice
Outpost
The
Scouting
Grove
The Wice
he
uts
Thilip's Grove
The
Archive
Archaeologists'
Guild
oduce Fields
Viona's
Grove
The Wice
Endless Expanse

Oswin

Maury

Ennastasia

Gale & Philomena

Zylo

Cathy

CONTENTS

PROLOGUE

Dear Oswin,

My name is Penny Yarrow, Grandmaster of Corridor. You won't know who I am, but I know you. I fought hard so you wouldn't be thrown back to the ice where you were found. Unfortunately, my efforts to get you a different guardian were unsuccessful. Lullia can be difficult, but I hope she will find it within herself to give you a proper upbringing.

There are a few things you should know, and I felt I should be the one to tell you as, knowing Lullia, she'll refuse. Unlike your Tundran brother, you are a stray: you were not born in Tundra or to Tundran parents. As the first stray who has been allowed into Tundra in years, you will face a resentment no one has dealt with since the Great Freeze. The hatred many felt for non-Tundrans who were using scarce resources hasn't disappeared, only lain dormant while there were no strays to direct it towards. As the only stray here, all this bitterness will fall upon your shoulders.

To lessen your difficulties, I wanted to explain the basics. You were found on the endless ice that surrounds our settlement. Given the dangerous nature of the Endless Expanse, your parents are certainly dead. Bleak as this is, remember you have a home in Tundra, and will one day find your place in our fight for survival against the cold.

On a brighter note, I've sent some welcome gifts. The tokens can buy a few goodies at the Token Exchange, the enchanted boots will keep your toes toasty in the coldest Freeze and the paper bag contains raisins grown from iron-transmuted seeds (far tastier than the ones transmuted from copper, in my esteemed opinion).

I have written a return address on the back. If you need anything at all, you only have to let me know.

May the Thaw be warm and the Freeze be swift,
Grandmaster Penny Yarrow

1

PLANTING SPLINTERS

Six years later

The first step of growing a log was to plant splinters. Oswin Fields *could* have thought it the most difficult step. After all, the ground of the produce field was hard-packed below the snow. But the second step was also difficult: lugging the logs, now grown to the surface, to the barn. It left his scrawny limbs sweaty, and his white face flushed peach-pink. The third step – to magically charge the logs by tucking them under duvets, reading them bedtime stories or making ticking noises while moving his hands like a clock – was more amusing

3

than difficult. By the time the fourth step arrived, and Oswin rolled the completed logs onto a rickety cart, he barely had the strength to kick the wheels to start the self-moving charm. He'd stand, his sickly lungs huffing, as the cart rattled along iron tracks towards Central Tundra. Thirteen years of life, and all he'd seen was the produce field. Rows of logs and stretching snow were burned into the backs of his eyelids. He'd watch the cart, weighed by the fact the timber would see more than he ever would. It was *that* step, unquestionably, that was the hardest.

When he traipsed into the family cabin, forcing the door closed against the wind's onslaught, his adoptive mother was waiting with a small roast potato. Oswin stamped the sleet from his boots before noticing sunflower seeds sprinkled on top. A treat.

'Decent work today,' said Lullia, her haphazard hair a fiery mess around her white, freckled face. She made him think of melting candles.

Oswin's misery boiled into pride. He'd pleased Lullia enough to get seeds with dinner. Today was a good day, then. He may not get to see the rest of Tundra, but he had to remember how lucky he was. He'd be dead without Lullia's generosity. At least, whenever he *did* forget, Lullia was quick to remind him the debt he owed her.

He ate, licked his plate clean, then waited expectantly in case Lullia had anything else for him to do.

'Sleep,' she said, her tone matching the harsh weather. 'We've got a long day tomorrow.'

Every day felt like a long day to Oswin, when splinters infested his hands and his muscles ached yet never had the decency to grow strong. 'When isn't it?' he teased, a smirk clashing with his permanently downturned eyes. Lullia glared at him and he ducked his head apologetically. He should have known she hated teasing by now.

'Goodnight,' said Lullia sharply.

She was always cagey, but something felt *extra* off this evening. 'Is something wrong?'

'I said goodnight.'

It was time to make himself scarce, so Oswin quickly retreated to his room. It was a squeeze; the door banged against the chest of drawers, the room was so small. He wasn't *entirely* sure what colour the floor was. He liked to think it was painted turquoise, like the lights he sometimes saw in the night sky, but it was probably the same dull wood as the rest of the tiny cabin.

It was the time of year when the snow was nasty, the sun coy and the nights black. By the time dawn was an hour away, the world outside was still grasped in choking darkness. Oswin was at his bedroom window, working on the locks that Lullia had installed. He could easily pick the two on his bedroom door, but the further three on the front entrance made it impossibly difficult. His bedroom window had just one lock, so was by far the easiest way out to enjoy the quiet night.

Except, as he was halfway out of the window, his mother's door creaked. It took him two silent seconds to relock the window and duck back below his blanket. With a click and a clank, his bedroom door opened. Candlelight spilled into the room. Oswin hoped the horrid glow would stay away from him.

'Get up.' Lullia sounded angrily conflicted, which was a first. She was usually just angry. Oswin peeked out from under his blanket. She stood in the doorway – half shadowed-silhouette, half candle-lit displeasure. 'Pack your things.'

Oswin sat up fully, eyeing the candle's flame. 'I'm already packed.' His only belongings were what he wore. He had stones and fallen buttons that he'd found and collected from the snow, but those fitted into his pockets.

'We leave now.' Lullia grabbed a travelling cloak from a hook. 'I told you: it's going to be a long day.'

'Leave?' Oswin half-tumbled into the corridor, the blanket left messily behind. 'For where?'

'No questions. Just walking.' When Lullia pushed open

6

the front door, the wind outside shoved Oswin's shoulders as he tried to pull on his cloak.

And it *was* a long day. They walked in darkness, following the iron tracks until the sun inched over a distant towering wall of ice. When Oswin asked Lullia where they were going, she told him to be quiet.

They followed another set of tracks in a different direction. By the time they were traversing empty fields of snow, the sun was overhead and Oswin's stomach was grumbling. He asked where they were going for the twenty-second time. 'If you tell me, I'll shut up.'

Lullia, worn down, turned her eyes skywards. 'Corridor.'

Oswin stopped abruptly. Lullia didn't bother to slow. With hurried footsteps, he caught back up. 'Corridor? *Really?*' Lullia's silence was confirmation enough, and Oswin's breath was stolen, he was so stunned. He'd never imagined it possible that a stray could go to Corridor, where ice apprentices were trained to contribute to Tundra's survival.

'I've answered your question; now shut up.'

Oswin only lasted three paces before bursting out, 'Why, though?'

Lullia's shoulders sagged.

By the time the sun was drooping, they were following a snow path that ribboned through the ice-floor of Shemmia

Woods. The woods lay between the Produce Fields and Corridor, the trees reaching out of the ice and scraping at the sky. By then, Oswin had lost count of how many times he'd asked Lullia why they were going to Corridor. (That was a lie. It was eighty-seven times.) She'd always maintained he could never be an ice apprentice, so the frail hope that he *might* become one was hingeing on her answer.

Lullia's response was a rant of all the things Oswin was *not* to do until they arrived. Mainly, *not asking questions.*

'But *why* are we going to Corridor—?'

Lullia growled. 'Repeat what I just said!'

'You said a *lot.*' He'd meant it as a joke, but Lullia clearly didn't care for his grinning humour. That was true even on a good day.

'I *said*, I've had enough of your questions. Stop tossing that stone you picked up and keep your mouth shut. No "How long until we get there?" or "Does Corridor have indoor toilets?" or "Will a stray like me be treated well?" What a ludicrous question. You're the *only* stray in the settlement. You should be grateful that Tundra took you in in the first place, regardless of how you're treated.'

'But I really would like to know about the indoor toilets. Walking to the outhouse on the produce field nearly froze off my—'

'Be quiet, you insolent boy!'

8

Oswin hung his head. Even if he felt warm at being called a *boy*, he felt guilty for upsetting his mother. He *was* a stray after all. He should focus on being valuable, not getting Lullia to joke with him.

'I'll say it once more: keep your mouth shut. Don't even *look* at me until we reach Corridor. Understood?'

Oswin didn't need the repetition. He'd already memorized her words. Not because she'd said it before (though she had; the journey had been long and Oswin was nothing if not an asks-too-many-questions fidgeter), but because his mind hoarded information.

Lullia put her hands on her hips. 'Repeat it.'

He attempted just *one* more joke. '"It."'

Lullia's irises flickered with outrage. She stepped off the snow and onto the ice floor of the woods, marching away. It wasn't the amused reaction he'd hoped for.

'I'm sorry,' he called. Nothing. 'Where are you going?'

'Away from your resting-sad-face and *incessant* babbling. Stay there.' Lullia disappeared between the trees.

Oswin tossed the stone he'd found. Despite his itch to explore, he intended to do as she asked. He knew better than to break Lullia's rules when she could find out – he preferred to break them when she *couldn't*. But then he caught a murmur of voices coming from the opposite direction Lullia had gone.

A voice said in an unsettling rumble, 'I'll be there when you plant it. I'll ensure all goes according to plan.'

Oswin stepped off the snow path towards the voices. His boots slid on the ice, forcing him to grab a tree for balance. But he didn't slow – he wasn't going to let a few tumbles stop him. Bruises faded. Unanswered mysteries would bother him forever. He hated himself for disobeying Lullia. She'd only *just* told him to stay on the snow path – and who knew when she'd get back – but not investigating wasn't an option.

He travelled deeper into Shemmia Woods, unused to the feeling of trees and pine needles, having spent six years in a field of snow. He didn't hear the voices again, but he did gain a heavy sense of *wrong*. It settled over his shoulders, constricting his neck. He glanced behind himself. He could have sworn some of the trees' roots had moved. Were they resting in different formations than before? He thought back and grew certain of it.

Pushing down his unease, he hurried on, hoping to overhear more of the mysterious conversation. This wasn't the same as when he'd sneaked by the neighbouring field's gristles – thistle-like alarm creatures who growled when approached. This was different. Someone was up to no good, but as he trekked through the ice-floored woods, his only companion was silence.

He *did* find lines on the ground, though, as if someone had scored knives across the ice. He was so busy peering at them that he almost missed the root snaking for his ankle. At the last second, his eyes caught the movement, his heart freezing. Quickly, he lifted his boot, just as a root speared the place his toes had been.

'Splitting splinters!' he breathed in disbelief. He knew wood could be magical. He planted splinters that bloomed into logs after all, but he'd *never* seen the logs *move*. It wasn't just one root, either. As far as he could see, tendrils were inching towards him. He jumped to the only reasonable conclusion.

The roots were going to eat him.

2

CARNIVOROUS ROOTS

Oswin hurried to a tree and grabbed it, but a root coiled around his ankle, dragging him down. More roots writhed hungrily forward. 'Help!' Another root trapped his arm to the ice. He tried to pry it free, but a third seized his other arm. His eyes darted between his restrained hands in panic. 'Help!'

'Oswin?'

The roots stilled.

Oswin checked the voice against a three-year-old memory, not believing his luck. 'Zylo?' The roots retracted, the ice sealing over them, leaving no evidence they'd attacked. A shaky breath rattled out of Oswin, relieved even if the echo of the roots still stung around his ankles and wrists.

A boy skated over, drinking up the metres like meltwater. He was the ingredients of a mountain condensed into the body of a boy: tall, muscular, rugged. He had black wavy hair, growing a bit beyond his large ears, and pale beige skin dusted with frost. Reaching Oswin, he hefted him into a spinning hug. 'Ozzy! You're finally here!'

'Careful,' wheezed Oswin. 'My chest compressor.' His binder pained his ribs, but having a flat chest was worth the discomfort, and his lungs were sickly whether he wore it or not. He'd been born fragile.

'Splinters, I'm sorry.' Zylo put him down and checked him over as the world spun around Oswin. 'Did I break anything? Can you breathe? Cindering coals, I'm so, *so* sorry!'

Oswin shook off his disorientation. 'I'm fine. You can stop worrying.'

'Fat chance of that.' Zylo spent a few minutes double-checking. 'Still, it looks as if you're in one piece.' He stared at Oswin, who stared right back, before they hugged again, Zylo squeezing gently this time.

After three years of being apart, Oswin was back with his brother. He beamed as he buried himself into the fabric of Zylo's doublet before pulling away, taking in how strong Zylo had grown, and feeling both proud and jealous. 'What are you doing here?'

Zylo helped him back to the path, floundering for a second despite the simple question, then forced a smile. 'Meeting you and Lullia, of course. I knew you'd be arriving soon. What were *you* doing off the snow path?'

Oswin glanced at the now motionless roots, the sensation of their grip fading. At best, Zylo would worry and refuse to leave his side. At worst, he'd think Oswin was seeing things and unfit to become an apprentice. Oswin wasn't even certain he was going to be an ice apprentice. He didn't want to hurt his already slim chances. 'I got curious.' It wasn't *entirely* a lie.

'You've not changed a bit, then.'

'Why do you call her "Lullia" and not "Mum"?'

Zylo flinched from the whiplash of the question. 'Because I don't want to.'

'But she's our mother now.'

Zylo cleared his throat, clearly wanting to change the topic. 'I notice you kept my parting gift.'

Oswin straightened his trapper hat. Wearing it made him feel as manly as Zylo. 'I did! The person who gave it to me isn't *totally* brainless.'

'Oi! You're meant to respect your older brother.' He rocked Oswin's head affectionately as their shoes

14

crunched on the snow path, Zylo having swapped bladed shoes for a normal pair. 'You didn't lose it, then.'

'Wouldn't dream of it.'

Lullia was waiting on the path, and though she was clearly surprised to see Zylo from the wide-eyed look she gave him, her anger soon replaced her shock. 'What did I say?'

Oswin grimaced, averting his blue eyes. 'To stay here.'

'You *can* remember my orders, then. Did you stop to think how I'm feeling? You're becoming an ice apprentice, which means *I'll* have to work the produce field alone. I'm *devastated*. Yet here you are, ignoring the simplest of instructions. What kind of son does that?'

Oswin swallowed the lump in his throat. For a moment, he'd been excited at Lullia confirming what he'd hoped – he *was* going to be an ice apprentice. But his excitement had been snuffed by what he'd been too selfish to realize: Lullia would have no one. 'I'm sorry.'

'I know a stray has no place at Corridor.' Lullia threw her arms up, frustrated. 'But who am I to say? I'm only your *mother*.' Oswin got the sinking feeling that, if she were able, Lullia would drag him back to the produce field, never to become an apprentice, learn magic and help the settlement survive.

Zylo squared his shoulders. 'Oswin does belong at Corridor – the Grandmaster requested him.'

A stillness fell, deadlier than the ice surrounding Tundra. Zylo had never questioned Lullia when they'd all lived on the produce field.

'Remind me who gave up years of her life raising you?'

Zylo stared her down, unwavering, and Lullia's fury faded. Oswin had never seen *that*, either.

'Fine,' she spat, then crouched in front of Oswin, but not to take him away. Roughly, she adjusted his cloak until he felt like a prized doll she was being forced to share. 'If you insist on becoming an ice apprentice, at least avoid being so pitifully unkempt.'

'You're not coming the rest of the way?'

Lullia's mouth pressed into a thin line.

Oswin said, quietly, 'How long have you known I would be attending Corridor?' Lullia didn't answer. Clearly, she'd known a while. Oswin's vision misted. 'Why didn't you tell me?'

Lullia looked him dead in the eye. 'Because I couldn't bear to lose you.'

She had never said anything so kind. Oswin felt like marching right back to the produce field with her. His heart burned with a painful happiness, and then shame when he realized he couldn't give up the opportunity to attend Corridor.

Lullia must have noticed his elation, because she

crushed it quickly with a snarl. 'I only mean that running the produce field alone will be impossible.'

The happiness melted. Lullia couldn't bear to lose a *worker*. Being her son was inconsequential.

Lullia stood back up. 'Now, *don't* go poking your nose where it doesn't belong.'

That was it, apparently. Without another word she walked off.

'Bye, Mum.' Oswin's heart sank deeper the further into the distance she went. He didn't know when he'd see her again and couldn't remember a time without her. He could recall everything, except his life before Tundra.

'Come on,' said Zylo. 'Corridor's this way.'

Oswin heard Zylo's boots in the snow, but he took a few seconds longer to watch Lullia's retreating silhouette. Then he drew in a deep breath and followed his brother.

The remainder of the journey was considerably shorter. By the time it was mid-evening and Corridor was in view, fluffy snowflakes had birthed a hill on Oswin's trapper hat. From the look of the cabins ahead, roofs buckling below icicles and oak walls succumbing to white mounds, Corridor wasn't faring much better than his hat. A charmingly uneven fence sat between them and the lodges behind it. At the back of the training grounds was a long, curved building buffeting up against a cliff of ice. Extra floors had been built on top, supported by beams that grasped the cliff like the gnarled fingers of an old man steadying himself. Back before Zylo had left to start his own ice apprenticeship, he'd told Oswin that the training ground was named after *this* building. It really did look like one long corridor. He could hardly believe he was finally seeing it in person. He only wished Lullia was there to see it, too.

Oswin wriggled his fingers, unable to stay still, he was so excited. 'You've never spoken to Lullia that way before.'

'I wasn't going to let her treat you like that.'

'She raised us. We have to respect—'

'You're going to be an ice apprentice. You don't have to deal with her any more if you don't want to.' At Oswin's expression, Zylo quickly added, 'Look – let's not talk about this right now. Today is too exciting.'

At the back of Oswin's brain, behind the painful stab of leaving his mother, was a frustration that the roots had stopped him from getting to the bottom of the mysterious conversation he'd overheard. It was the same feeling he'd experienced whenever Lullia had refused to answer his questions about what Tundra was like. The trouble was, thinking about her like that gave him an uncomfortable guilt. Competition was a great distraction, so he said to Zylo, 'I bet I can make it to the fence before you.'

'Not if your running is as poor as your timber hauling.'

'I got better after you left.'

'With *your* lanky arms?'

'I've been rolling the logs up a ramp onto the cart instead of lifting them.'

Zylo quirked an eyebrow, impressed. 'Can't believe I didn't think of that.'

Oswin nudged him. 'Thinking isn't your strength, is it?'

'Because ...' He grabbed Oswin, stole his hat and ruffled his short brown hair. *'Being strong* is my strength!'

'All right! All right!' Oswin escaped, laughing.

Zylo chucked his hat back. 'You want a race? You got it.' He sprinted for the fence. Oswin rushed after him, but only made it halfway before he fell to his knees, cursing his paper-fragile lungs.

Zylo returned in a second. 'Too much for you?'

Oswin nodded as he squeezed in a breath.

'Sorry – I forgot about your lungs.'

'It's okay.' Oswin clutched his side as he staggered to his feet. 'I did, too, and they're *my* lungs.'

When they reached the fence, Oswin was breathing easily again. His eyes drifted to giggling apprentices, as they ducked below ice bridges and hurled snowballs at each other. Despite his aching lungs, he couldn't stop a smile. He'd never seen anyone else his age – the children of the neighbouring Produce Fields had been significantly older, and he'd only ever seen them from afar. Even the air smelled fresher here. Sharp with dew.

Zylo knocked the back of his knuckles against the fence. 'Open up, please.'

Oswin cast him an odd look. 'Why are you asking a fence to open?'

'Because he's lazy.' Zylo unclasped a spellbook from his belt and banged it on the posts. 'Come on, Reginald.'

'Reginald ... ?'

'Ow!'

Oswin tried to spot who'd spoken, but he couldn't see anyone. Zylo gave the fence another rap.

'All right!'

Oswin looked down. The rails of the fence moved like a mouth. 'Reginald is the fence?'

'Reginald is right here.'

'Where are your ears?' asked Oswin.

The rails moved into a frown. 'How rude. You realize Ferdinand and I were having a nap before you disturbed us?'

Zylo said, 'Can *Ferdinand* let us in?'

Oswin was *very* confused. '*Ferdinand?*'

'The gate,' said Zylo, as if it was obvious. 'Either of them could let us in if they'd be kind enough.' He raised the spellbook threateningly.

'All right!' The gate swung open. 'Petulant apprentices . . .'

'Thank you.' Zylo walked through, whistling.

Oswin followed, a hand inching towards Zylo's spellbook. 'May I?'

Zylo snatched it out of reach. 'Spellbooks aren't toys. I wouldn't be a good big brother if I let you hold this before you'd started training.'

Oswin held back a whine as they passed apprentices climbing vertical floating ice panels. Their axes and spiked shoes dug into the frozen sheets, some apprentices even leaping from one hovering section to another. The height made Oswin feel unwell, but he couldn't ignore the thrill of what else Corridor could have in store.

'I know Lullia refused to speak about it, as she did *everything*, but magic's everywhere. Now you're at Corridor, you'll get to see it.'

Oswin frowned. 'Mum let me see magic. She read bedtime stories about how sewing the logs' bark channels magic into them, so transmutationists can turn them into coats.'

'Those were *instructions*. Not stories. She let us conduct magical processes on the timber because she needed to make tokens from selling the logs. She kept the *real* magic hidden.' Zylo shook his head. 'Look, if you're interested in casting spells, don't worry. You'll get your own spellbook next year.'

'Why not *this* year?'

'Because spellbooks aren't toys.' Evidently anticipating Oswin's *Why not?* reply, Zylo said, 'I saw a kid's hands swell to the size of a cabin, and one of my friends lost the ability to say words with the letter O for a week after using their spellbook before being properly trained. They're powerful things.'

All the talk of magic made Oswin think of carnivorous roots, which in turn made him recall what had led him into their clutches in the first place. 'What about mysterious conversations someone might overhear in Shemmia Woods?'

Zylo froze. It took him a second to thaw. 'What?'

'I overheard a conversation. That's why I left the snow path – to eavesdrop.'

Zylo's eyes bulged. 'What did you hear?'

'Only a sentence. Something about planting and plans.' Oswin could have repeated the sentence verbatim if he had wanted to. He didn't.

There was a long pause. Eventually, they started walking again.

'It's not uncommon to think you hear whispering in Shemmia Woods,' said Zylo. 'But it's always the wind. It can make odd sounds.'

Oswin side-eyed him. 'If you say so.' He was certain

that what he'd heard hadn't been the wind. Maybe it had been a trick from the roots, luring him to an ambush? Either way, something sinister was lurking. If he could uncover it, maybe he could prove Tundra hadn't been mistaken in taking him in.

They reached the curved building, a river lapping at its wooden stilts.

'What now?' said Oswin.

'You're meant to gather with the new apprentices for introductions, but I don't know where that is.' Zylo's eyes grew suddenly serious. He grasped Oswin's shoulder. 'Just remember, whatever you do at introductions, do not, under any – and I mean *any* circumstances – tell anyone—'

'I can show you to the introductions!' a boy with warm brown skin interrupted them. His dark brown hair was in a messy bun, with one of his eyes missing and the other glinting behind a monocle. He had the expression of an old scholar, zealous to experiment with magic, but on the face of a teenager.

Zylo managed a nervous smile, letting go of Oswin's shoulder. 'That would be helpful. Thanks, Maury.'

The boy indicated they follow, pocketing a clanking contraption he'd been fiddling with. 'It's the least I can do after ... you know ...' He held a meaningful look with Zylo.

'What?' said Oswin.

'Oh, nothing,' said Zylo quickly as they set off.

Oswin whispered, 'Can you at least tell me what you were going to warn me about?'

Zylo glanced at the boy. 'Another time.'

Oswin bit back his frustration. First the conversation, then the roots, and now this. There was little worse than not getting answers.

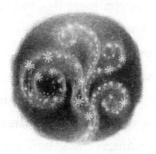

3

A STRAY AMONG TUNDRANS

'I'm Maury Craftwright of the Huts,' the boy said. He held an eager hand to Oswin, who stared at it. Zylo quickly explained the concept of a handshake. Oswin did as Zylo had described, surprised at how enthusiastic Maury's grip was.

'What are the Huts?' Oswin deepened his voice, hoping Maury would see he was a boy.

Maury looked at him as if he'd asked what food was. 'An area of Tundra. Like the Eyelid or Greenfinger.' Oswin's mouth parted more with every unfamiliar word. 'The Huts are more ramshackle than the fancier places like the Eyelid, and they don't have the steady work from the

Greenhouses like Greenfinger has, but anything's better than being in the snow.'

Oswin felt a prickle of annoyance for all the times Lullia had insisted on not explaining the layout of Tundra. She'd said he'd always work the produce field so shouldn't bother wondering what lay beyond the perimeter fence. 'What are all *those* things?'

Zylo said, 'Once you see a map you can memorize it.'

Oswin swallowed his questions like an apple full of nails.

Maury said, 'I tell most people this when I first meet them to avoid confusion so, just so you know, I'm a boy when my hair's in a bun, but a girl when it's down.'

A wave of relief washed over Oswin. There were apprentices like him at Corridor. He'd worried he'd be the only one. When Oswin had first woken up in Tundra, almost everyone had assumed he was a girl. It had taken him a few years to realize this wasn't the case, and that being mistaken for a girl was infinitely worse than all the times Lullia had called him 'mismatch face'. She was right: his cheeky grin clashed with his permanently sad-looking eyes. Oswin always looked both a second away from crying and a second away from snickering. It was an unpleasant face, but the second he'd started to think of it as a boy's, it had improved tenfold.

Maury adjusted his monocle and smiled, revealing a

charming gap between his front teeth. 'Who's this with you, then?'

'This is Oswin, also of the Produce Fields.'

'What about a surname? You've never mentioned yours before.'

Zylo floundered, remaining peculiarly silent.

Oswin said, 'Fields.'

Maury's steps faltered. *'Fields?'* He looked, wide-eyed, at Zylo.

'Yes.' Oswin was already nervous about the upcoming introductions, and the way Maury's expression had gone from pleasant to horrified made him feel worse. 'What's so important about our surname?'

'Where are the introductions going to be again?' Zylo cut in.

Oswin didn't understand the shift in the air. 'Did I say something wrong?'

Maury said, 'They'll be over by the Atrium. We're almost . . . there . . .' He got out his metal contraption, using tiny tools to tinker with it and avoiding eye contact at all costs.

Oswin couldn't figure out what he'd done wrong. 'Sorry,' he muttered.

'It's not your fault,' whispered Zylo. 'Our surname isn't liked.'

'Why?'

'Because—'

'Here we are,' said Maury.

Ice columns loomed around a hundred plush armchairs that were filling up with apprentices. Some of the apprentices wore thick grey garments to combat the chill, but others stood out with red doublets or golden cloaks. Oswin had never seen so much vibrancy poured into fabric. He felt suddenly underdressed in his grey clothes.

'Good luck, little bro.' Zylo gave him a final hug before pushing him towards the Atrium.

'When will I see you next?' Oswin would rather not be left alone. He was sure to put his foot in his mouth as soon as he started speaking.

'Dinner. Now, go on!' Zylo looked as if he had something important to rush to. With an uncertain nod, Oswin walked between the pillars and found a seat. Maury, untying her hair, moved timidly away. He tried not to feel sad about that.

At the front was an ice stage where a woman in a creaking wheelchair waited. Her torso was drowned in scarves, so that she looked like a rodent peeking out of a cinnamon bun. She had wrinkled white skin, large ears, straw-like hair and spectacles. She looked like an *old* rodent peeking out of a cinnamon bun, Oswin amended.

A hush fell over the apprentices, and the woman beamed. 'Welcome to Corridor!'

The apprentices cheered and whooped. Right then, Oswin didn't care about his mismatched face. He smiled ear-to-ear.

When the cheers died away, the woman with the scarves said, 'I am Grandmaster Penny Yarrow. I'm in charge of Corridor where, over five years, you'll learn to delve frost caves, invent items to help navigate our cold world, survive beasts and cast –' she unhooked a spellbook from the side of her wheelchair – *'magic.'* Snow spiralled into the air, turning turquoise then crimson. Oswin gaped. 'There are three kinds of magic: fog, timber and coal. Each distinct in its uses and requiring its own set of skills and knowledge to master.' Yarrow closed her spellbook and the snowflakes began to fall. Apprentices stuck their tongues out to catch the snowflakes, receiving harmless zaps when they succeeded.

Yarrow indicated a stiff-postured woman with scarred brown skin and a fluffy grey hat that looked like a bird's nest. 'Behind me is Secondmaster Sabel Rochelle, who is second in command.'

Rochelle lifted one of her hands, scarred like her face, to give an efficient wave. Oswin tried not to squirm under her intense gaze as she raked it over the apprentices. She looked like the type of person who didn't stand but *loomed*. Her presence eroded bravery.

'And this –' Yarrow nodded at a mammoth man with tawny skin and black hair that flowed above his head like reeds in a river – 'is High Watcher Greyheart. He's kindly taken an evening out of his busy schedule of governing Tundra to come here and celebrate your ice apprenticeships. Do give him a warm welcome.'

Greyheart stepped forward, the thuds of his massive boots making the snow on the stage jump. He spoke in a grumbling drone. 'Some of you may grow to be delvers, searching the frost caves for splinters on which produce workers rely to grow timber. Others may venture to the Endless Expanse to gather precious metals – the only known material that can be turned into seeds. Some may nurture those seeds into food, transmutate that timber into building materials and clothes, or invent life-saving magics. Whatever it is you end up doing later in life, it is *here* where you will learn to be useful. Here you will find what role you'll play in our battle for survival. If not, well . . .' He pointed at the glistening cliff that stretched into the horizon. 'The ice is right there.'

'What do you mean by that?' blurted Oswin, because of course the ice was right there. It wasn't going to walk away. When he realized dozens of apprentices were shooting him judging looks, he ducked down.

'It means,' said Greyheart, 'that if you can't be bothered to make yourself useful to Tundra, you might as well leave. This settlement won't feed dead-weights. One log too many and the cart gets stuck.' He dragged entirely black eyes over the gathered apprentices, and there was an uncertain fizzle of applause as he stepped back on the stage.

Oswin bounced a leg, questions whispering in his head, mainly about why Grandmaster Yarrow had requested he become an apprentice, but it was clear now that he couldn't simply yell out his questions. He wrestled them back, avoiding thinking about the impending introductions he'd have to make with the other apprentices, or the dread that he'd *still* be useless at the end of his apprenticeship.

Yarrow said, 'Be swift with your introductions. You'll have three minutes in each group.'

'Group?' murmured Oswin, then his hands gripped the armrests as the floor abruptly dropped. The armchair stopped only two metres from the ground, but it was enough to make unease weigh in his belly. He *hated* heights.

His armchair zoomed, spun and stopped by three others. As if a bucket of water had been upended above them, a thin sheen of liquid wobbled into a giant bubble. It froze until the armchairs were hovering in a sphere of ice. Oswin looked at the others, no one speaking for several seconds. One had wings poking out of their hair, another antlers. He tried not to stare – none of the neighbouring produce workers had had wings or antlers – then he noticed Maury also in the sphere.

She smiled her gap-toothed smile, breaking the long-stretching silence. 'I'm Maury Craftwright of the Huts. It's nice to meet you all.'

As the apprentices introduced themselves, Oswin watched, his tongue an immovable glacier. One of the apprentices was bragging about how, if it wasn't for his family's magic, healing in Tundra would be 'a few icicles short of a stalactite'. Another explained how their parents worked in the Greenhouses, and that the warmer weather meant they'd start growing seeds into food again.

Questions burned on the end of Oswin's tongue – he'd never heard of half these things – but before he could muster the courage to speak, the ice sphere shattered. The armchairs shot away from each other and Oswin squeezed his eyes shut, trying to ignore the feeling of motion. When the armchair stopped, he was in an identical ice sphere with four different apprentices.

'No way!' said one boy. 'You're Ennastasia Barkmoth!'

A girl crossed her legs as her brow knitted into a fearsome frown. 'How observant.' Ennastasia had black skin and hair twists that curled around each other to form an elaborate pattern dropping no lower than her jaw. Oswin didn't think he'd ever seen clothes as grand as hers. Her red cloak alone looked more expensive than Lullia's house, not to mention the ruby earring hanging from her right ear. His hands twitched as he wondered how difficult it would be to pocket the jewel. It would look great in his collection of odd bits and bobs.

'Well?' Ennastasia's eyes landed on Oswin, who fidgeted with the hem of his shirt. 'Stop staring like mindless mamats and name yourselves. Ideally *before* I die of old age.'

Oswin whispered, 'What's a mamat?' to the apprentice next to him, who just managed to explain they were small rodents with icicle tails and manes of ears before one of the other boys spoke.

'Ennastasia, do let your grandfather know how much gratitude we all have for—'

'Yes, yes.' Ennastasia wafted her hand. '*Name*. Get on with it.'

In a flurry of names, the apprentices introduced

themselves. Oswin would have remained in awkward silence had one of them not mentioned how they worked on a produce field.

Oswin gaped at him. 'Me too!'

'What does your family produce?'

'Timber. Yours?' Oswin couldn't believe he was having a successful conversation.

'We're given the metal found on the Endless Expanse and prepare it so the Greenhouses can transmutate it into seeds,' said the apprentice.

Oswin didn't know what to say. He wished he had more mouths so he could ask multiple questions at once. 'Do trees usually try to eat you at Corridor?'

When the boy pulled a perturbed face, Oswin cursed whatever blunder he'd made.

For the next few minutes, the other apprentices politely expressed their gratitude to Ennastasia and her grandfather, while Ennastasia glared at them. Then, with sharp jerks, the chairs moved apart, the ice spheres evaporating and new ones forming. In a whirl of faces, Oswin soaked up names, while quietly observing the apprentices. Learning the torrent of information felt as satisfying as stretching his legs. Lullia had never taught him so much, let alone in one go.

Eventually, Oswin was grouped with Ennastasia again.

She snapped her fingers. 'Hurry. We don't have much time.'

A boy with a black, bobbed haircut and a fringe that fell over his eyebrows said, 'Why don't you go first?'

'Because I don't want to.'

'Okay ... I'm Gale Residuan of the Huts.' Gale leaned towards one of many lilac orbs floating around his shoulders, as if listening to a hushed whisper. He looked curiously at Ennastasia. 'My orbs tell me you're important ... Who *are* you?'

'I wouldn't care if your orbs said my head was about to be detached from my body. I'm not a cave delver; I have no use for prophecy. And even if I were, I wouldn't believe a word of that nonsense.' Ennastasia pointed at a girl with pinkish skin and a ponytail so blonde it was almost white. 'You. Next.'

'Cathyquizzia Montmurmur of the Eyebrow.'

Gale leaned towards one of his orbs, nodding in sage agreement with its indecipherable chittering. 'The Eyebrow is geographically above the Eyelid but below Greenfinger,' he said cryptically, as if prophecy infested the air. 'The inverse of its rank and importance. Isn't that so, Cathyquizzia?'

'Unless you want a punch, you'll all call me *Cathy*.' Cathy's smile showed far too many teeth. 'Except you, Ennastasia. I can't express how lovely it is to meet you.'

'Yes. How *lovely*,' Ennastasia drawled, while Gale gaped at the revelation of her name. Oswin had no idea why it was such a big deal. He was about to ask when Cathy turned to him, the blue glass shards hanging from her ponytail clinking.

'And you?'

Nerves wriggled in his skin. 'Oswin Fields.' There was painful silence. 'Of the Produce Fields,' he added hurriedly. 'My family grows timber. Really good timber. Planted most of the splinters myself. I was great at moving logs. Very useful. I don't know what Tundra would do without—'

'Your surname's *Fields*?' said Cathy.

Oswin's words were icicles that took a second to melt. 'It is.'

Cathy snarled, Gale's orbs hid behind him and Ennastasia narrowed her eyes.

Oswin thought back to what his older brother had said about their surname. 'Is something wrong with that?'

Cathy said, 'I thought it was a silly rumour. Something the other Eyebrow kids made up to make playing Feasters and Starvers more fun. In our version of the game, instead of only the starvers stealing the feasters' food, someone would pretend to be a stray and poison all of us so they could take the food for themselves.'

'I'm ... confused.'

Cathy grinned nastily, two wisps of blonde hair breaking free from her ponytail to frame the disgusted crinkle of her nose. 'You're *actually* a stray. *The* stray.'

Oswin's heart stopped. His mind replayed their conversation in a panicked flurry, accurate to the syllable. He'd mentioned *nothing* about being a stray. 'How do you know that?'

'The rumour said a stray was in the Fields family. It's not Zylo, so who does that leave?' Cathy shook her head. 'Not only did they let a stray into Tundra, but into *Corridor*, too.' She spat over the side of her armchair. 'We managed to rid ourselves of strays. I can't believe they'd let another one get their fingers on our resources. And into the Fields family, too. The irony! At least now the *smell* makes sense.'

Oswin wanted to say sorry, or at the very least ask why it was ironic that he was a Fields, but forming words was proving difficult.

When Gale said, '*I* can't smell anything,' Oswin shot him a grateful look.

Something snapped in Cathy. 'My aunt's family starved in the Great Freeze, and my father didn't have enough fat to fight off sickness, because strays used up resources. You're an extra mouth to feed. An unneeded log weighing the cart.'

Oswin knew that now wasn't the time to demand answers, but he couldn't stop himself. 'What's the Great Freeze?'

The question had been a mistake. Furious, Cathy prepared to leap at him. Oswin would have been more scared, but something else caught his attention.

'Wait!' He held out a hand, looking at the glistening walls of the ice sphere.

Cathy bared her teeth. 'Words can't keep you safe.'

'Seriously!' He pointed. 'Haven't you noticed?' The ice sphere looked thicker than the previous ones, as if even a battering ram couldn't break it, and it was closing in.

Cathy's anger waned. 'Noticed what?'

Ennastasia stiffened. 'The sphere . . .'

She looked at Oswin.

He looked right back.

At the same time, they said, 'It's shrinking.'

4

THE SHRINKING SPHERE

The sphere was going to crush them.

'Oh, no, no, *no*.' Gale made frantic motions as if that could stop it, his hovering orbs trembling.

Ennastasia stood on her armchair and punched the ice surrounding them, then cursed under her breath as she cradled her hand. 'Do any of you have something sharp?'

Cathy grabbed one of the glass charms from her ponytail. 'Would this work?'

'No idea,' said Ennastasia. 'But it's the best thing you half-brained mamats have come up with. Chuck it over.' Cathy did, Ennastasia wincing when the glass cut into her palm, but still jabbing it at the ice, digging through it.

Oswin took a different approach. 'Help!'

Gale was inspired. 'HELP!'

The sphere grew smaller.

Ennastasia pointed at Cathy. 'Use another of your charms to scrape at it, or did you forget you had more than one?'

Cathy blinked, then yanked another shard from her ponytail to stab into the ice.

To Oswin's relief, he heard panicked shouting outside. 'They heard us – the masters.'

Cathy glared at him as she kicked at the shard she'd jammed into the wall. 'Shut it, stray.'

Gale said, 'H-How do you know they heard us?'

'I can hear them. They're trying to get us out.' Oswin closed his eyes, focusing on the heated conversation outside.

'Attack this section. Combined, our spells might break it,' Oswin heard a voice say.

'You're not the boss of me, Rochelle,' someone else said, but a moment later there was a creaking in the ice.

'I very much am!'

Oswin opened his eyes. 'They're using magic to break the sphere.'

Cathy snarled. 'I can't hear anything. Now isn't the time for lying.' She returned to kicking the shard, but it was getting harder as the sphere shrank. The space had grown so tiny, the armchair frames buckled against each other, splinters bursting in small explosions.

Oswin didn't bother proving what he'd heard. He'd realized his hearing was abnormally good growing up. He'd easily eavesdropped on produce workers when they'd argued in the neighbouring fields. They'd bickered over who grew the best timber. Right then, stuck in a shrinking sphere of death, wasn't the time for Oswin to explain that.

They contorted themselves to fit in the tiny space, the armchairs crunching to pieces. Oswin felt warm bodies and soft fabric pressing against his front, and the cool surface of the ice sphere on his back. Gale was crying, Cathy was shuddering, and even though Ennastasia kept hacking at the walls with the glass charm, her eyes were stretched wide. They had seconds before their spines would snap like the armchairs had.

There was a cracking sound. Thankfully, it wasn't their bones. The sphere splintered, starting at the place where Ennastasia had been hacking. Oswin wondered if this was what it felt like to be a hatching bird. The curved sheets of the sphere fell into the snow, shattering into smaller fragments. Sunlight surrounded them as the decimated armchairs fell, and the apprentices landed with soft thuds in awkward angles among the wreckage.

Secondmaster Rochelle *loomed* over them. Oswin had been right. Someone as imposing as Rochelle couldn't merely stand. Her presence was that of a stormy mountain.

'Well . . . ?' one of the masters asked, taking a stumbling step, their beard unkempt and their hair long and scraggly. They were scrunching a handful of dry leaves in one hand.

'They're all right, Master Tybolt,' Rochelle said as she checked each of the apprentices, her eyes two abysses. 'Yarrow, they're all right,' she added, turning to the Grandmaster.

Gale gave Secondmaster Rochelle a teary-eyed hug – which Rochelle didn't look as if she knew what to do with – before hurrying to the other apprentices standing to the side. Cathy cast a glare at Oswin as she stalked off, as if it had been *his* fault, while Ennastasia dusted her shoulders, giving the impression ice spheres tried to crush her every teatime.

Ennastasia said, 'I had that under control.'

Secondmaster Rochelle raised an eyebrow, opened her mouth to say something, then smiled thinly. 'I was merely eager to assist a Barkmoth. Send your grandfather my regards.'

Ennastasia huffed, then stormed in the direction of Grandmaster Yarrow, demanding to know why her life had been put in jeopardy. Yarrow's assurance that she'd look into the matter didn't placate Ennastasia.

Oswin appreciated being back on the ground, but also wanted to know why the sphere had shrunk. Yet his thoughts stalled at the sight of Maury lying in the snow, away from the other apprentices. She was motionless. 'Is she okay?' he said.

Secondmaster Rochelle saw where Oswin was looking and set a brisk pace towards Maury through the sun-glistening snow. Oswin followed. Maury looked frail, her breaths frosting in weak puffs. Oswin's throat constricted as Rochelle muttered a series of spells. She checked Maury's pulse, then said, 'She's only fainted.'

Oswin caught sight of a translucent glow around Maury's right hand – perhaps from the contraption she'd been fiddling with – but it vanished as she awoke.

'What happened . . . ?' Maury asked groggily.

Grandmaster Yarrow moved over to them. 'You fainted.' Maury looked alarmed, and Yarrow held up a comforting hand. 'Everything's fine.'

'This is like when I tried to build a spinning ladder,'

Maury complained, to a raised eyebrow from Yarrow. 'I thought it'd make climbing less boring.'

'Maury Craftwright, isn't it?' Yarrow asked as Rochelle helped Maury sit up.

'Yeah.'

'Do you know what happened, Maury?'

'One minute I was watching the shrinking sphere and then . . .' She squinted her eye. 'Then nothing. That's when I must have fainted.'

Oswin had come to Corridor expecting to be safe, but already his life had been at risk twice. He *should* have been scared, but he wasn't. He was just painfully curious.

The shrinking sphere stuck in his mind as the apprentices were shepherded to dinner. Cathy asked Master Tybolt why the sphere had shrunk, but they only looked uncertain before telling her to focus on dinner. When she pestered them again, Tybolt threw a handful of dying leaves at her.

It became clear that even Ennastasia's threats couldn't squeeze answers out of masters who didn't have any. None of the apprentices seemed pleased with the lack of clarity, but when Secondmaster Rochelle *loomed*, no one dared pry further.

If the masters didn't know what had happened, Oswin would have to do his own digging.

Rochelle boomed, 'You're all to eat your dinner. Then you will be escorted to your dormitories, where you shall remain until tomorrow morning. Understood?' Her authority was an almighty shove.

'Understood!' the apprentices said, healthily afraid.

They were led to the Alchemy Lodge, where food was served, and Oswin took a sharp intake of breath at the sight. On its first floor the Alchemy Lodge had a mammoth three-panelled window in the shape of a mountain peak and a balcony so laden with snow you could have swum in it. On the ground floor glass doors led to a cafeteria. Rochelle herded them inside and Oswin let himself be pushed along by the tide, the sensation unfamiliar. Lullia had never let him leave the produce field, so the only times he'd sneaked out of it had been under the cover of night. He'd never been around so many people before.

Corridor's cafeteria was a sprawling low-roofed room. Swaying lampshades glowed onto oak tables. There was the clink of cutlery, chatter of apprentices and scrape of rattan chair legs. Memories of the shrinking sphere put a dampener on what Oswin imagined would have been a joyous meal, but only for a short while. As apprentices found their seats, conversations started to hum, rising in confidence as conspiracies about the shrinking sphere bloomed.

Oswin found a seat in the corner, his mind soaking in what he could see of the stretching room. The smell of roasted vegetables, pastry and gravy washed over his tongue, and he relished it. The best he'd smelled before then was burnt porridge.

'How'd it go?' a voice broke him out of his food-induced trance.

'Zylo!' said Oswin.

'Hungry?'

'No, it's Oswin.'

Zylo barked a laugh. 'But seriously, do you feel hungry?'

Oswin shot to his feet. '*Yes.*'

Zylo guided him to a buffet of steaming food, handing him a bowl. 'Don't worry if you can't fit in everything you want – you can always come back for seconds. There's plenty of food right now.' He sighed happily. 'I'm so glad the Freeze is over. The Mirristical Wall can't reflect sunlight onto the Greenhouses if there isn't any sun to begin with, and then how can anyone expect the seeds to grow?'

'Where do the seeds come from?'

'Metal. Obviously.'

'Oh, yes, obviously,' said Oswin sarcastically.

'You can't very well transmutate seeds from timber, can you?'

'You *can't?*'

Zylo thought deeply. 'Timber can be made into inedible stuff. It's good for lots of things – making building materials, cloaks, paper, weapons. What did you think all the timber we grew was for?'

'I know *that*,' said Oswin. 'But why can't timber be transmutated into seeds? Why does it have to be metal? And how did anyone figure this out in the first place?'

'Whoa, whoa.' Zylo put a hand on Oswin's shoulder. 'One question at a time. I've only got so many wrong answers in me. Firstly, no idea. Timber simply can't be made into seeds. Anyone who tries fails. Secondly, also no idea. Just has to be metal, plain and simple. Thirdly—'

'"Also no idea"?'

Zylo thumped Oswin's shoulder. It nearly knocked him over. 'Now you're getting it!'

Oswin shook his head, amused, but his amusement soon turned to awe when he saw the buffet. There was beetroot tart, leek pie, noodle broth, chickpea curry and an assortment of hot teas. He bathed in the warm smells. 'I can eat as much as I want?'

'It's the start of the Thaw; if there's a time to fatten up, it's now.'

'The Thaw?'

Zylo put a hand to his forehead. 'Splitting splinters, I forgot how little Lullia explains. There are two seasons.

Even *I've* learned that much.' He gestured encouragingly at the food. 'It's the Thaw right now, so there's a lot more food. Eat your fill. When the Freeze arrives, you'll need the reserves.'

'Shouldn't I eat after everyone else?'

Zylo's expression drooped. 'We're not back home. Stray or not, you eat at the same time as everyone else.'

'Really?'

'Really.'

In a rush of limbs, Oswin piled his bowl high. Though Zylo had said he could come back for seconds, Oswin was worried the food would disappear. Protectively, he hunched over his prize as they returned to their seats. He practically inhaled his food, taking turns between shovelling leek pie and gulping tea. It was the best-tasting meal he'd ever had.

'You're acting like a starved mamat.' Zylo reached forward jokingly, as if to steal the food.

'Don't!' Oswin cradled his bowl, continuing his flurry of eating with a safe distance between himself and his brother.

Zylo's eyebrows lowered. 'You *are* starved, aren't you?' Oswin chose furious eating over responding. 'Lullia can be like that, huh?'

'I don't know what you mean. Mum gave me food.'

Oswin finished and his eyes darted covetously to the buffet. 'When I behaved.'

'Take it slowly. You don't want to eat too much at once if you're not used to it. You'll make yourself unwell – *and there he goes . . .*'

Oswin rushed back to the buffet. As he grabbed slices of leek pie, he heard a faint chime and turned to see Cathy and her glass-charm ponytail. He glared at her flint eyes and turned his body to shield his food. A boy was with her this time. He had horns growing out of his shoulders, a sharp jawline and tawny skin.

'Who are you?' Oswin asked, despite knowing it was unwise.

The boy said, 'Frank Seedson of Greenfinger—'

Cathy cuffed him. 'You don't have to answer.' Frank nodded seriously, seemingly trying to *loom* like Secondmaster Rochelle. But where Rochelle looked like an ancient beast guarding her hoard, Frank looked like a tiny sticeling puffing its unkempt feathers.

Cathy said, 'Don't get comfortable, stray. We're making sure everyone knows what you are.' Twirling one of her wisps of hair, she leaned forward. 'Stay away from us or things will get nasty.'

Oswin's fingers dug into his bowl, and Cathy's eyes dropped to it.

She asked, in a mockingly innocent tone, 'Should a stray take that much?' then sauntered off, Frank following.

When Oswin sat down again, his appetite was curbed.

'What's wrong?' Zylo gestured at the food Oswin was staring at instead of devouring.

'Nothing.' He didn't tell him what the others had said, or that Cathy was right.

'If anyone's mean to you, send them to me. Even the hardiest of the Endless Expanse scouters wouldn't dare mess with these arms!' To make his point, Zylo flexed, and Oswin wondered if the doublet he was wearing would tear.

'Scouter?'

'A scouter's job is to scout the Endless Expanse for metal. If I can intimidate *those* tough Tundrans, a few mean-spirited apprentices will be nothing.' He flexed again, striking a rather ridiculous pose.

Oswin couldn't stop a weak smile. 'All right.'

'There's my Ozzy.' Zylo grabbed Oswin's trapper hat and jostled his head.

'Stop it!'

'Make me,' Zylo teased, but let go.

As Oswin ate, now at a more subdued pace, he couldn't help noticing another apprentice sitting alone. Ennastasia. She hadn't been nice to him, but she hadn't been mean.

Besides, seeing someone on their own made him feel like a bag of rocks was sitting in his stomach. He was about to ask Zylo if they could join her when he spotted Cathy and Frank striding around the room. Each group they stopped by craned their necks in Oswin's direction. He shrank down, a lump in his throat. He shielded the lower half of his face with his neck scarf and pulled his hat low on his head.

Zylo glanced over, seeing the apprentices staring. 'I dealt with something similar when I first joined. It'll pass.'

'Why? You're not a stray.'

Zylo let out a low rumble. 'I suppose I didn't have that extra complication, but I'm still a Fields.'

'We're both adopted.'

'Doesn't matter. Non-blood relations are just as binding.'

Curiosity burned Oswin's lips. He put his cutlery down. 'Why does being a Fields matter so much? I know why being a stray is bad, but I don't see what's wrong with our family name.'

'Being a stray *isn't* bad.'

'It is!' Oswin protested hotly. 'I should have died. I should have frozen to death when my stray parents abandoned me. Tundra took me in and gave me a roof over my head, yet all I do is –' frustrated, he shoved his bowl away – 'drain its food. I'm useless. *Worthless.*' In truth,

51

there had been many nights when he'd considered leaving Tundra and freeing the settlement of the burden of taking care of him.

'You're *not*. Forget everything Lullia said. Ignore the nonsense some Tundrans spew. You're *not* worthless.'

Oswin shook his head. 'I just don't understand this Fields business.'

Zylo sighed. 'You don't stop snooping until you get answers, do you?'

'No. I don't.'

Zylo took a second to consider his words. 'I don't fully understand it myself, but I do know there was once, a decade ago, a cruel man who almost tore Tundra apart. His ideas turned brother on sister. Had neighbours at each other's throats. A lot of people died because of him.' He held Oswin's gaze. '*A lot.*'

Oswin ignored how many apprentices kept glancing at him as if he were some grotesque, half-collapsed snow sculpture. 'How does that answer my question?'

'After this man was stopped, and Tundra finished counting the dead, he was committed to the ice. That means he was exiled to the Endless Expanse without gear, food or a way back. That means being *sentenced to death*.'

'Why are you telling me this?'

'Because that man, who caused more Tundrans to die

than anyone else in history, who nearly toppled the only remaining human settlement in this ice-covered world . . .' Zylo's breath caught in his throat. 'He was Michael Fields. *Our uncle.*'

5

AN INSTRUCTION OF THEFT

Zylo hadn't known any more about Michael Fields than that. No matter how many questions Oswin asked, all he received were confused musings.

As Zylo led him from the cafeteria towards the corridor-like building, Oswin clenched and unclenched his fists. 'You've been at Corridor for three years, yet you've done nothing to learn about our *evil* uncle. Aren't you curious?' The questions in Oswin's head felt as if they'd explode his skull. He couldn't imagine *not* turning over every rock and nosing into every crevice until he had answers.

'I *was* curious ...' Zylo got a faraway look in his eyes. 'Of course I was, but more than anything I wanted to keep my head down, do my work and get a role as a scouter. Being Michael Fields' nephew hasn't done me any favours. Asking questions made people wary and led to ... unintended consequences. So, I stopped.'

Oswin threw his arms up and cried, 'You stopped asking questions?' He couldn't imagine anything worse.

'Yeah.'

Oswin dropped his arms, about to ask about the unintended consequences, but his brother spoke before he could.

'You've been through a lot today.' Zylo gave him a pat on the back. 'First days are nerve-wracking.'

'They are.' Oswin didn't mention the shrinking sphere or the carnivorous roots. Back when they'd both worked the produce field together, Zylo would worry endlessly if Oswin got so much as a graze. Oswin's quick healing had never stopped his brother fussing. Knowing about the incidents with the sphere and the roots would send him into an over-protective panic.

He glanced at Zylo, still amazed at how much larger he'd become. 'Will I get as strong as you now I'm an ice apprentice?' He imagined himself tall and muscular.

'Perhaps. I think I've bulked up so much because of the work I do on the weekends.' Evidently sensing Oswin's budding question, Zylo explained, 'I go into other parts of Tundra and repair houses. Gets me enough tokens to buy scouting books at the Token Exchange.'

'Why repairing houses?'

'Timber's what I know. Plus, it's interesting watching people enchant the wood to keep the interiors warm. That's if we're working on fancy lodges in the Eyelid. You won't catch magic like that in the Huts.' Before Oswin spouted a deluge of questions, his brother pointed at the corridor-like building. 'Those are the dormitories. That building was built so long and thin that it encloses all the parts of Tundra not surrounded by the Wice. Most of it's unused. Some buddies and I walked its entire length in our first year, and it took us the whole day to get to the end and back. But this section –' he gestured at the part surrounded by the other buildings of Corridor – 'is split into five dormitories, one for each year group. My dormitory, Hazel Dorm, is there.' Zylo pointed in the direction of the Atrium. Then, he shifted his hand to the part closest to the cliff of ice, where extra floors climbed up the side, a mess of rickety wood attached by unsteady beams. 'Yours is there: Spruce Dorm.' He must have noticed Oswin's unease at the height, as he quickly added, 'The ground floor, I mean. Those extra floors are mainly storage.'

Oswin pressed his fingers against each other. 'I have questions.'

'I'd ask who you were and what you'd done with my brother if you didn't.'

'What's the Wice?'

'That.' Zylo pointed at the looming cliff of ice. 'It's one big cliff that hugs Tundra. At the top of it is where the Endless Expanse begins.'

'And what's the Endless Expanse?'

'The ice, Oswin. *The* ice. What the rest of the world has been for thousands of years. The reason Tundra is the only safe haven.'

Oswin drew in a breath, freezing air travelling down his throat. One of the few questions Lullia had ever answered was what was beyond Tundra. 'Ice,' he said, echoing the answer she'd given him. *'Just* ice.'

'And death.' Zylo's eyes twinkled. 'Open skies. Space to stretch your legs. Winds so harsh they could rip the skin from your bones.' He looked starstruck. 'Scouting must feel so *pure*. Just you and your team. Marching for miles for the smallest fragments of metal hidden below the ice. I can't wait to be a scouter.' He winced. 'Well, except for the monsters – they're the downside – but we Tundrans are good at avoiding them. We're lucky that, when our ancestors escaped the frost caves, they emerged here and not onto the Endless Expanse. If the elements hadn't claimed them, the beasts would have.'

Oswin's gaze sank to the ground, miserable at the reminder that he wasn't a Tundran like Zylo. His ancestors, whoever they were, hadn't escaped the frost caves and founded Tundra. They'd wandered the Endless Expanse, barely hanging onto life in a miserable cycle of hunger, cold and beasts.

As they reached Spruce Dorm, Zylo must have read Oswin's thoughts. 'You're as Tundran as I am.'

'I'm not. I never will be.'

'You *are.*' Zylo put his hands on his hips and looked at him, then shook his head, defeated. 'See you in the morning. Get a good night's sleep and remember to wash behind your ears.'

'Only if you promise to wash at all.'

Zylo sniffed his armpit and made a face. 'Fair point,' he said, as Oswin laughed. 'Night, Ozzy.' He walked to Hazel Dorm. Oswin watched him leave before taking the steps to the front door of his dorm, eager to plan an investigation into Michael Fields, carnivorous roots and shrinking spheres.

Inside, the first thing Oswin noticed was a dedicated *indoor* toilet. He almost cried. Then it hit him that he was standing inside the building after which Corridor was named, and he did have to wipe away happy tears.

The corridor was curved enough to throw him

off-balance, but not enough to be obvious. He squeezed his eyes shut, then opened them again as he walked, feeling as if the hallway was stretching. Doors lined one side, while large windows stood on the other, each showing a break of snow stopped short by a thick cluster of endless stalagmites and stalactites, so dense he couldn't see what was above them from his current angle. They reminded Oswin of a face hidden in a cowl, light dying beyond the first rows where total darkness won. He shifted his position, looking up through the window, expecting to see the stalactites attached to an icy ceiling, but realized they were suspended in air. The dormitories marked the end of Tundra, which meant whatever he was looking at was beyond the settlement itself.

Oswin stepped closer to the windows, putting a hand on the glass. Something about the icy spikes felt off. He realized why. They moved. Every time he blinked, there was a shift so minute that, if he hadn't had such a sharp memory, he never would have noticed it. The stalagmites and stalactites were inching left and right ever so slightly, like slowly grinding teeth.

As if realizing he was staring, the ice stopped moving. Oswin blinked rapidly to check, finding the icy spikes now entirely still. He had a horrid thought that they didn't just move like grinding teeth but *looked* a bit like them, too.

For all his excitement about Corridor, Oswin had to admit that the Produce Fields had felt safer.

He walked away from the windows and to a huddle of apprentices at a noticeboard. Cathy and Frank were turning away from it, so Oswin took off his hat, pulled his neck scarf over his nose and hunched. The two walked by without noticing him. Oswin watched them go. Even if he strained his eyes, he couldn't make out the moment the corridor curved beyond his vision, it was so long.

Once Cathy and Frank were gone, he put his hat back on. Standing on tiptoes, he peered over the other apprentices and saw his name written next to the number four. Room four was a few paces away and five times the size of Oswin's room back home. There was a bunk bed with a desk below and a window with such a large windowsill a map could have spread across it. But, most unexpectedly, he found Ennastasia Barkmoth standing in the middle.

'Haven't you heard of manners? It's customary to knock.' She narrowed her eyes at Oswin. Her luxurious attire had been swapped for the Corridor uniform, but her ruby earring remained, catching the light in haunting shimmers. 'What are you even doing here?'

Oswin forced his gaping mouth closed.

Ennastasia crossed her arms. 'Are you really going to stare for ten more minutes?'

'Sorry! I've just been wondering what your earring is.' He'd also been thinking about how easy it might be to pluck it from its chain – it would go wonderfully with his collection of assorted items – but he wasn't going to say *that* out loud.

Ennastasia's expression didn't move, and now it was her turn to stare at him. Oswin cleared his throat.

She snapped, 'Where'd you get your hat?'

'It's just a hat,' he said vaguely.

'And this is just an earring. I presume you're here to clean my room? It's terribly small, but I suppose it will do.'

'"Small"? "Clean your room"?'

'You're my servant, correct? I see no other reason why a stray would so rudely barge in.' She looked him over. 'Or are they really meaning to make a stray an ice apprentice? Is there anyone they won't give magic to? Surely they realize how dangerous it is.'

'I'm not your serva . . . I *am* an ice apprenti—'

'If you're not here to clean, then kindly get lost.' Ennastasia took a few steps forward, Oswin a few back, then she slammed the door in his face.

Oswin gawked at the number four carved into the door. 'She's pleasant.'

Not sure what to do, he walked back to the noticeboard. Ennastasia was listed next to room five. He decided he didn't mind if they swapped. It was obvious to him that Tundrans should have priority when it came to choosing rooms, even if that meant going against what had been allocated.

Room five was identical to room four, but blessedly empty of sharp-tongued apprentices. Sitting in the middle was a beige pack with metal buckles. It was addressed to "The Distinguished Inhabitant of Room Number Five", which was now technically him. While he read the note – which explained the pack contained the equipment he would need for his apprenticeship – he put on a posh voice and muttered jokingly, 'Distinguished inhabitant,' to himself.

Next, he ran a hand over the coarse fabric. He'd never owned a pack before. He'd only ever had a few locks and scraps of fabric he'd nicked from the neighbouring Produce Fields. He felt odd, like how he imagined Ennastasia must have felt in the fancy clothes she'd worn before.

Biting back a smile, Oswin upended the pack's contents. He found workbooks for things he'd never heard of before, including 'Etymagery' and 'Scelving'. There were two sets of the Corridor uniform, enchanted to fit whoever wore it, a map of the apprentice grounds and some curious sticks that, when pressed to the pages of the workbooks, left thin lines. According to the word etched into their sides, they were 'pencils'. He only bothered to unpack a few items into the chest of drawers before dumping the rest on the floor.

He couldn't stop smiling at the fact he was unpacking into his own room *at Corridor*. Though one question (from his currently monumental pile) kept pestering him: why *had* the Grandmaster requested he become an apprentice in the first place?

It was late, so Oswin tried to climb into his bunk bed to sleep, but the height involved in clambering from the ladder onto the mattress made him nauseous. Instead, he grabbed the pillow and curled up on the floor. It wasn't much worse than his lumpy bed back home. The trouble was, his brain rattled with questions. This he was used to – his whirring thoughts often kept him awake – so he did what he usually did when unable to sleep: practised lock picking. He'd brought his locks and tools with him from home. Using metal instruments to move the interior pins was a soothing balm on his mind. When morning light seeped around the curtains, he felt refreshed, even if he hadn't slept a wink.

That was when something made Oswin's ears prick up. He sat bolt upright, the brittle floorboards creaking. The sound had been – quite impossibly – both distant and near at once. Just as he was telling himself it was his precise ears hearing a rodent snuffling outside, it came again. Humming in the back of his skull, it made his bones shudder, like the harsh blizzards that had battered the produce field cabin.

Oswin rose to his feet. He definitely *wasn't* imagining it. He wondered if it was some apprentices who'd sneaked out on their first night – he'd certainly been tempted to do so himself – but the noise hadn't sounded like apprentices, nor the mysterious conversation he'd caught snippets of in Shemmia Woods. In fact, it didn't sound human at all. The noise slithered through the air, dripping down his ear canal like viscous syrup. With a snap, his mind made sense of it.

'*Oswin Fields,*' the voice said.

That was him. That was *his name*. He didn't dare respond, staying perfectly still.

'*Oswin Fields, Steal The Ghost.*'

The sound melted into the air, mingling with the morning sunlight until it was abruptly gone, leaving emptiness.

Oswin breathed once, then twice, trying to calm himself. When someone knocked loudly on his door, he fell over from the shock.

'The welcome assembly is about to start!' the person called.

Oswin struggled to say, 'Right. Okay. Thanks!' As quickly as his adrenaline-filled limbs could manage, he got up and opened the door. He leaned out and checked both ways, seeing the smooth brown hair and gold monocle of Maury, who was about to knock on Ennastasia's door.

'Wait!'

Maury looked at him, her brown eye widening. 'Fields!'

'My name's *Oswin*,' he said with feeling.

Maury stammered, then smiled her gap-toothed smile. 'Sorry about yesterday. I got a bit nervous, is all. I know it's not fair to judge you because ... well ... ' She tapered off.

Because apparently my uncle was the evilest person in Tundran history? Oswin wanted to say, but instead went with: 'It's fine, but you probably shouldn't knock on that door.'

It was too late. Ennastasia threw it open to scowl at Maury. 'I heard you long before you knocked. You're stomping around like a vohoont! Hasn't anyone here heard of basic decorum?'

'Ennastasia! I didn't realize it was your room.' Maury bowed deeply. 'I'm terribly sorry. Might I add how charming you're looking today?'

Ennastasia's lips quirked down miserably. She shoulder-barged Maury, slammed her door and marched off.

Maury caught herself against the wall from the shoulder barge and glanced at Oswin. 'She's pleasant.'

Oswin pointed at her, feeling vindicated. 'That's what I said yesterday!'

Maury held out her hand. 'Let's start over. I'm Maury Craftwright of the Huts. Great to meet you.'

Oswin looked at her hand, smiled and shook it. 'Oswin of the Produce Fields.' He felt satisfied with how quickly he'd learned the customary Tundran greeting, even if he'd never *really* be Tundran.

'Shall we go to the welcome assembly?'

'Yes. Let's.'

6

A THEORY OF NONSENSE

Before Maury led Oswin to the welcome assembly she first pushed into his room, quite without permission. She grabbed his uniform from the bottom of the messy pile on the floor after having found his drawers empty.

'You'll need to change.' She handed him the uniform.

'Oh. Right.'

Maury turned to give him privacy, her attention landing on a loose drawer handle. Unprompted, she set to fixing it.

Corridor's uniform was a variety of greys, with extra undershirts and undergloves for warmth. The thick trousers came with braces and the doublet had puffy sleeves. The cloak was coal-coloured, with cotton fluff where it clasped to Oswin's shoulders, and as he wriggled his toes he swore the boots had been enchanted to warm his feet. He wasn't sure he'd ever worn so many layers and loved the rectangular silhouette it gave him, but what he loved even more was the fact he was wearing the Corridor uniform.

Once Oswin was changed, and Maury had fixed the drawer handle, they hurried outside, their shoes sinking into the fresh snowfall that glittered in the sunlight. It was one of Tundra's marginally warmer days.

'We're in the Thaw right now, aren't we?' Oswin checked, having to focus on his breathing as they rushed. The sky was clear, not plastered with clouds, and the snow was soft underfoot.

'The start of one, yeah.' Maury looked dubiously at him as she tied up her hair, and Oswin reminded himself that meant Maury was in boy-mode. 'First you don't know about the Huts, and now you don't know about the Thaw?'

'I had an isolated childhood.'

Sympathy tugged at the corner of Maury's eye. 'Me, too. But hey, at least I had lots of time for tinkering.' He pointed to where his left eye should have been. Instead, there was skin scarred over from an old injury. 'Lost this bad boy when one of my makeshift catapults went wrong.'

He smiled his gap-toothed smile. 'On the upside, I can only make that mistake one more time.'

'You built a catapult? All by yourself?'

'A makeshift one. It was rather small. My dad's a watcher, with no talent for inventing, but—'

'What's a watcher?'

'Someone who enforces the rules of Tundra,' said Maury. 'But my mum is an inventor. She's not as high up as my dad, but she makes impressive stuff. Even did some work at Corridor when I was little. Well, litt*ler*.'

'You got to see Corridor before you were an apprentice, then?'

Maury dodged his question, instead puffing out his chest. 'One day, I'm going to be just like my mum!' As they journeyed to the Atrium, Maury filled Oswin's brain with a welcome wave of invention knowledge, from how to construct cave-delving equipment, to an experimental flamethrower, to self-pulling carts.

'Self-pulling carts?' said Oswin. 'One stopped at the edge of the produce field. I'd load it with timber and from one kick it would rattle to Central Tundra. That was your mum's work?'

Maury winked, using an exaggerated facial expression to make it clear it *was* a wink. 'Yup. She invented those tracks so produce workers wouldn't have to trudge to

Central Tundra every harvest. Of course, the client she invented it for took all the credit *and* the tokens.'

'I owe your mother a huge thank you, then.' Oswin had barely managed to get logs onto the carts; he was sure his lungs would have imploded if he'd had to carry them to Central Tundra, not to mention the agony his ribs would have felt, constrained below his chest compressor. 'You seem to know a lot.'

'About invention? I sure do.'

'Do you know what makes trees try to eat you?'

Maury quirked an eyebrow. 'Trees? Trying to eat you?' When Oswin didn't break into a grin, Maury must have realized he was serious. 'No idea. Maybe it's an oddity.' His tone made it seem like a joke.

Oswin didn't get it. 'What's an oddity?'

But there wasn't time for Oswin to get an answer – as they passed between ice columns and into the Atrium, Maury pushed him ahead, saying, 'Quick. Those chairs are free.'

Before Oswin could protest, he was shoved into a seat. He looked at the armchair, firmly planted on the ground, and hoped it would stay that way. When the person sitting on his other side leaned forward, he very nearly jumped out of his seat.

'Ennastasia,' said Oswin.

'No, I'm a caveclaw attacking delvers in the frost caves. Yes, it's me, obviously.' She curled her upper lip. 'Are you following me?'

'No!' Oswin hid behind his neck scarf, leaving only his eyes poking out.

Maury stiffened like a wooden post. 'Hello again. How lucky to see you twice in one day! You must send your grandfather my regards . . .'

Ennastasia stewed in her sour mood, shifting her fiery glare from Oswin to Maury. 'Hello, Mary.'

Oswin looked at Ennastasia as if she'd slapped Maury.

'Don't worry,' said Maury quickly. 'She doesn't know I've switched to Maury yet. I used to be Mary in girl-mode and Maurice in boy-mode. I only recently changed to Maury for both.'

Ennastasia's glare faded. 'I'm confused. What ridiculous names shall I call you by, then?'

'As I explained,' Maury said patiently, 'just the one name, now. Maury, if it pleases you. I, of course, would never wish to inconvenience a Barkmoth.'

'Fine. Maury. I suppose it's adequate.'

Maury gave a small bow. 'I'm honoured a Barkmoth would think so. Your grandfather must have raised you with the utmost—'

'Ice below, won't you stop?' Ennastasia cursed, pinching

71

the bridge of her nose. 'Must I suffer this the entire welcome assembly?'

Oswin checked the other armchairs, all occupied. There must have been two hundred apprentices of varying ages crammed into them. 'I don't think you have a choice but to sit next to us.' His voice dripped with sarcasm. 'Sorry.'

Ennastasia eyes settled on him with interest.

Oswin's smug smile vanished as the floor fell from his feet. He *hated* the floating armchairs.

The chairs hovered into tiered seating around the stage. Grandmaster Yarrow and the other masters lined up, wearing cloaks of varying colours and embroideries. There was Master Tybolt, who'd helped destroy the shrinking sphere, their scruffy beard shorn back to scruffy stubble, their long hair unkempt. They still had a handful of leaves scrunched in one hand.

Oswin leaned towards Maury. 'Are they really a master?' They don't seem very official.'

'The one with branches stuck to their green cloak? That's Tybolt.'

'They look as if they don't want to be here.' Oswin would have described the master's expression as a firm alliance of boredom and disdain.

Maury hummed in agreement. 'They usually do.'

Yarrow was greeted by applause as she adjusted her

many scarves. 'Another year at Corridor begins. Let it be one of learning, filled with the precision of Etymagery, the adventure of Scelving and the mastery of Spellbookery.'

'What are all those things?' Oswin whispered to Maury, who put a finger to his lips. Oswin leaned towards Ennastasia. 'What's—?'

'Shut up and listen.'

Yarrow said, 'As I do at the start of every year, I must remind you all of the dire need to stay away from the Teeth That Snatch.'

Oswin frowned. 'Ennastasia, do you know what—?'

'I told you to shut it.'

Oswin fixed his gaze on her. Given he'd been cursed with eyes stuck in a permanently miserable expression, the very least he could do was get some use out of them by guilting people.

Ennastasia exhaled a defeated breath. 'They're the icy spikes beyond the dormitories. No one *ever* comes back from them. Walking into *the Teeth* is a death sentence.'

Grandmaster Yarrow adjusted her spectacles. 'I wish you all the best of luck in passing your Utility Provings this year. If you don't pass at least half, then the Watcher's Ring – those in charge of Tundra – require you be removed from Corridor.'

A tense stillness fell over the apprentices. Ennastasia

shot Oswin a pre-emptive silencing look before he could ask her what Utility Provings or the Watcher's Ring were.

Yarrow answered one of Oswin's questions anyway. 'Utility Provings are trials you must complete to prove your usefulness.' She wore a grim expression. 'There are two a year. One at the end of the Thaw and one at the end of the Freeze. The make-up of these trials isn't announced until nearer the time to ensure they are difficult to prepare for. They're dangerous, requiring swift minds and feet to pass.'

Yarrow seemed disappointed at the concept of the Utility Provings, which confused Oswin. She was the Grandmaster. If she didn't like the trials, couldn't she just cancel them?

Yarrow shook off her disapproval and said, 'I shan't keep you long; you have a full day of lessons ahead, and we've all yet to have breakfast.' She rubbed her hands together and looked at Secondmaster Rochelle. 'I believe there is fruit salad this morning, as a special treat.'

'With syrup,' Rochelle responded, with something that Oswin might have called a smile if he'd squinted his eyes and tilted his head in a darkened room.

Oswin fiddled with the white ribbon tying his doublet closed, holding back a dozen questions.

'Sit still,' Ennastasia muttered.

'Sorry.' Oswin forced his muscles to stop. It was surprisingly difficult.

Yarrow said, 'But we can't begin the year without our welcoming tradition.' She placed a hand on her spellbook. *'New Apprentices Approach.'*

Oswin had no intention of going to the front, but his chair had other ideas. It looped through the air in a gut-wrenching motion and stopped by the podium. With whooshing movements, Ennastasia, Maury and the other first-year apprentices found their chairs hovering at the front alongside him.

Yarrow wafted her hand, the pages of her spellbook turning on their own. *'The Snow Rises.'* Snowballs hovered into the older apprentices' hands.

Oswin swallowed.

Yarrow, having finished casting spells, said, 'From A to B, nothing but nonsense, yes sirree!'

The older apprentices loudly chanted the same line, then loosed their snowballs. Oswin caught sight of Zylo grinning, aiming directly at him. Oswin held his hands in front of his face as a deluge of snow crashed over him, the jolts of cold making him jump. The masters shielded themselves with spells as the first-year apprentices squealed with every snowball. All except for Ennastasia, who remained miraculously unscathed. No one had dared aim a snowball at her. Oswin thought that would please her, but she looked even angrier than before, if that were possible.

'Let the year begin.' Yarrow snapped her spellbook shut and the floating armchairs lowered.

'*The Apprentices Dry,*' said Secondmaster Rochelle. Puffs of steam rose as the apprentices' cloaks dried. Oswin sighed at the pleasant warmth of the magical drying and hopped off his armchair, resisting the urge to kiss the ground. He shook his head, clumps of snow flying off, and dusted his hat.

With roars of excitement, apprentices rushed between the pillars, bound for the Alchemy Lodge. Some opened spellbooks and summoned ice paths to slide along. Masters followed, trying to calm the overjoyed clamour, but they didn't seem to mind, exchanging *What can you do?* shrugs. Cathy and Frank were already speeding off, whooping, while Ennastasia looked so furious that Oswin was sure, if she *had* been hit by snowballs, she wouldn't have needed Secondmaster Rochelle's spell to dry off. Her anger alone was so intense he'd expect a burn if he touched her.

Knowing it was unwise, but too curious about what her reaction would be to stop himself, Oswin formed a soft snowball in his hand, took aim and thwacked Ennastasia in the face with it.

She stiffened, her eyes squeezed shut, face scrunched and mouth gaping. She stayed like that for a second, as if her brain couldn't comprehend what had happened and needed to double-check it. When she finally opened her eyes, they stretched wide. With anger or confusion, Oswin couldn't say. All he knew was that he felt suddenly unsafe.

'Shall we?' he said in a nervous laugh, nodding at the lodge where the cafeteria waited, hoping he wasn't about to be pummelled. He'd wanted to go with Maury, but he'd already hurried off in his excitement.

Ennastasia dabbed at her face with her cloak, looking dazed, then pointedly walked on without him.

'All right, then,' said Oswin under his breath, progressing alone, his stomach rumbling. At least he now knew how Ennastasia reacted to snowball attacks. It was, rather puzzlingly, not to shout at him, which was what he'd expected. He decided it had been worth the risk for that sliver of fascinating information.

Oswin took a seat at the back of the cafeteria, grabbing the promised fruit salad. There was hot tea to drink, but he decided on water with extra ice. Once he'd finished, a thin sheet of snowflakes formed in the air in front of him. The snowflakes grew, branching and solidifying into a sheet of paper that drifted onto the table. All the other apprentices had received their own, too: a timetable. With one read, Oswin memorized it.

'You got your timetable, then?' Zylo sat opposite him. 'What have you got first?'

'Scelving.'

Zylo beamed. 'Best subject. It teaches you cave delving, sure, but also the coolest thing ever: *scouting*.' He started to shovel a mountain of porridge into his mouth. 'I won't spoil the subject for you. My lips are sealed,' he said around his food. Oswin winced at the sight, wishing his brother's lips really *were* sealed.

Evidently finding the spoon too slow, Zylo drank his porridge in two impressive gulps. 'Just know it's the best thing ever.' He wiped his mouth then rushed to his own lesson, whistling jovially despite his hurry.

Scelving was in the Iceberg Cabin, which Oswin thought an apt name when he saw it was half embedded in a miniature mountain of ice. One side of the cabin was hidden inside the Iceberg, while the other stuck out, weighed with fresh snowfall and icicles hanging from its roof that were as long as Oswin was tall. Bladed boots hung above the door and wooden shutters cosied against the windows.

He joined the meandering apprentices heading for it, hearing the scrape of blade-shoed apprentices gliding on an ice rink, and the clunk of others sinking their climbing axes into the side of the Iceberg. He was so fixated on the climbers that when someone fell into step beside him and said a loud 'Hello!' he practically leaped out of his skin.

'Maury!'

Maury gave his exaggerated wink again. 'The one and only.' He turned to the two identical apprentices walking alongside him. 'This is Oswin.'

Oswin sent a silent thanks to Maury for not saying his surname, before recognizing one of the apprentices.

'Fate wants us to meet again, I see,' said Gale, a lot calmer now a sphere of ice wasn't threatening to crush him. The girl walking alongside him looked strikingly identical to Gale, from her narrow face to her black bob with a sharp fringe. She even had lilac orbs hovering around her shoulders like he did. The only difference between them was the turquoise scales on her cheekbones that Gale decidedly lacked.

'How come you have scales?' asked Oswin.

The girl exchanged a look with Gale.

Maury said, 'Oswin wasn't taught much growing up. He doesn't know that kind of question is rude.'

The girl visibly relaxed, while Oswin's eyes widened, horrified he'd apparently done something wrong. He was about to apologize when the girl said, 'You're the Fields stray, right? Cathy and Frank told everyone—'

Maury elbowed her. There was an awkward pause.

Oswin cleared his throat. 'What's your name?'

'Philomena Residuan of the Huts. I'm Gale's twin.' She reached out a hand. It took Oswin a second to remember what to do before giving it a tentative shake.

'Philly and I are children of prophecy workers,' Gale added.

Philomena mumbled, 'Yes, that, too. I *suppose*.' She gestured at the scales on her cheekbones, shimmering in the Thaw sunlight. 'This is a blessing from the ice. Some people are born with them, some not. It's usually not polite to ask about them.'

'Oh. Sorry.'

'You're forgiven.' Philomena wafted a hand. 'Some people think it's the same as monsters that have extra growths, but that couldn't be further from the truth. Beasts are wretched, after all.' Maury darted a frightened look at Philomena. Oswin guessed beasts were pretty scary if mentioning them could garner such a reaction.

Gale chimed in, 'Philomena's favourite skulls come from dead beasts. Of course, she didn't find them herself. They're gifts from cave delvers and scouters. Any bones Philomena sources herself are from the rodents she kills.'

Philomena puffed out her cheeks. 'I do not kill rodents!

I'd never hurt a living thing, not even *beasts*. I take the skulls from *already* dead mamats.'

While Philomena and Gale bickered over what was more important – having a sizeable collection of purple orbs or mamat ribs – Oswin leaned conspiratorially towards Maury.

'What's an oddity?'

Maury blinked a few times. 'What?'

'You mentioned an oddity earlier. Said it could have been behind the carnivorous trees.'

'Oddities aren't real, Oswin.'

'Why bring them up, then?'

'I was making an obscure joke based on an ancient theory inventors had. People used to believe that things like Philomena's scales were caused by oddity magic leaking into the world. Now we know that they're caused by a blessing from the ice. Honestly, oddities are nonsense.'

'But what *are* they?' Oswin used his pleading eyes again.

Maury looked at him reluctantly but, eventually, gave in. 'Supposedly, they're powerful relics that people could use or, in the weirdest cases, *merge* with. People believed they caused all sorts of interesting mayhem and dangerous crises.'

'Dangerous crises? Like carnivorous trees?' Oswin added darkly. 'Or shrinking spheres?'

Maury shook his head. *'Oddities. Aren't. Real.* Anytime something happened people couldn't explain, they'd say it was an oddity. Over the decades, Tundrans found answers to those mysteries, and the idea of oddities fell out of fashion. I was only joking when I mentioned them. Most people don't even know of them.'

'Right. Sure,' said Oswin as they reached the Iceberg Cabin. It was time for his first lesson, and he was armed with a thousand questions for whichever poor master was to teach them. But as he went to follow the others in, Secondmaster Rochelle appeared and pulled him to the side.

'I have a message for you,' she said in her rough voice, and Oswin's heart shot into his throat.

'I'm sorry.' He wasn't sure what he'd done but was certain he'd somehow made a mistake.

'Whatever for?'

Oswin didn't have an answer.

'I'm sure you're aware your situation at Corridor is unique,' said Rochelle delicately. She didn't say the word *stray*, but Oswin winced all the same. 'I have the unfortunate task of informing you that, when it comes to the Utility Provings, there will be more at stake for you than your peers.'

Oswin felt progressively colder as she spoke. Rochelle, looming as she was, was looking at him with sympathy, which meant she had bad news.

'When an apprentice fails a Utility Proving, they're given chores as punishment, and must pass at least half of them to graduate. If an apprentice were to fail their first five Utility Provings, they'd be kicked out in the middle of their third year, for instance. Unfortunately, we masters have been informed that if you fail even *one* Utility Proving, you won't be given chores as punishments.'

'What, then?' Oswin's voice came out squeaky with dread.

Rochelle grimaced. 'You'll be kicked out of Corridor for good.'

7

THE NO-READ AND CO.

As Oswin made his way into the Iceberg Cabin, Rochelle's words replayed painfully in his ears. There were two Utility Provings a year, he had no clue what they would be, but the next one would take place at the end of the Thaw. If he failed he'd be sent back to the produce field. He'd remain the useless, lonely stray he'd always been. Failing wasn't an option.

Oswin ducked into the Iceberg Cabin, trying not to think too much about his impending doom. The floor was buried in fluffy rugs, the fireplace smelled of soot, and climbing equipment was tied to the walls with aged rope. The master was a young-looking man with white skin, a stubbly chin and curly black hair that poked over his ears. Oswin thought he looked a bit like a ball of moss, wearing square glasses.

Sitting down, Oswin eyed a collection of items on the desk: climbing axes, spherical compasses and pins with arrows that moved when he raised or lowered them. Instructions on the blackboard asked them to guess what they were for, but he didn't feel like making guesses; he felt like panicking about the Utility Provings.

Maury was tinkering away, her tongue poking out in concentration as she deconstructed the objects and attached magnifying lenses to her monocle to examine their interiors. Gale was whispering to the orbs hovering around him, and Philomena was enthusiastically inspecting a climbing axe. Oswin started out with good intentions, looking the items over, but when a bit of metal broke off, he pocketed it to add to his eclectic collection. That made him feel a bit better, even if it didn't change the danger of the Utility Provings.

Philomena gently swung an axe. 'This equipment is for cave delvers and scouters. Imagine fending off monsters with this!' Her eagerness to sink the sharp end into a theoretical beast made Maury look up from her work with a queasy expression.

Gale said, 'Our dads work in prophecy, so we've seen plenty of stuff like this. They get lots of delvers and scouters seeking assurance that their expeditions will go smoothly.'

'Superstitious bunch,' muttered Philomena.

Gale leaned an ear to one of his orbs. 'Really?' He looked at Oswin. 'They've got a message for you.'

'The orbs?' said Oswin.

Philomena shifted uncomfortably. 'Yeah. They're how we ... um ... tell the future.'

Oswin nearly fell out of his chair. 'You can tell the future?'

Philomena averted her gaze, but Gale nodded eagerly. 'Sure can!'

'Can you tell me what the Utility Provings will be?'

Gale grimaced. 'We can't *ask* for specific information, only gratefully accept what we're given.'

Oswin's shoulders sagged in disappointment, while Philomena glared at one of the dusty orbs hovering around her.

Gale gestured at one of his own orbs, recently polished. 'This one wants you to know that you should *Steal The Ghost*, whatever that means.'

The clanking of the apprentices' working faded as Oswin's world focused on Gale. Those words again. They settled in his brain like silt in an underwater cave. 'It said *what*?'

Gale wriggled his fingers. 'We love it when they get spooked, don't we, Philomena?'

Philomena let out a quiet sigh, eyeing the climbing equipment enviously. 'Yep. Sure do. One hundred per cent . . .'

'Did your orbs say anything else?' said Oswin.

'Nothing else.' Gale lowered his voice to a harsh whisper. 'I'm curious: what was it like before Tundra took you in? Given you're a . . .' He widened his eyes meaningfully.

Oswin's throat felt rough. 'I don't remember.'

'How can you not remember? Were you a baby or something?'

'No.' Oswin wondered if this was how everyone else felt when he was firing off questions, then decided it couldn't be. His questions were too important. Everyone must realize that. 'I was seven when Tundra took me in.'

'Yet you don't remember what it was like being a stray? Do you even remember your birth parents?'

'Gale!' Philomena hissed.

'What?'

'That's rude.'

Oswin bit down on a retort as the young master with the moss-ball hair walked by, his flowing skirt sweeping the floor. Different shades of blue thread formed pictures of climbing axes, ropes, compasses and bladed shoes on his cloak. 'It's lovely to meet you all! I'm Master Stewart Kestcliff, your Scelving master. What do you think these objects are?'

Philomena put her hand up, waited for Kestcliff to nod at her, then said, 'Cave delving and scouting equipment.'

'Just so! They are used by scouters for scaling the Wice, and delvers for investigating the frost caves.' He reached into his skirt pocket and produced a small spellbook. Oswin watched in interest, one hand absently crinkling the material of his sleeve.

'*The Objects Return.*' The equipment shot neatly back onto the shelves. Kestcliff said, his voice low and ominous, 'Our first lesson is on the monsters who dwell in the frost caves below us.' He wrote 'The beasts below' on the blackboard. A shiver ran through the classroom.

Oswin's fidgeting ceased. 'What are the frost caves?'

'I'll politely request you raise your hand if you have a question,' said Kestcliff, to a smattering of giggles. 'Now, as I was saying—'

Oswin blurted, his hand now in the air, 'What are the frost caves?'

Kestcliff looked at his raised hand, fought a laugh, then adjusted his glasses once he'd composed himself. 'Apologies, I wasn't clear. You raise your hand *and wait* to be called upon.'

'Stray,' Cathy hissed quietly.

Oswin dropped his arm, his face heating.

'This is Tundra.' Kestcliff sketched the flat settlement. 'And below –' he drew a spiralling geometry like an insect nest – 'lie the frost caves. It's within these that the beasts below dwell.'

Oswin envisioned spectres of shadows or lumbering beasts. The other apprentices were just as silent in their imaginations. The only sound was the crackle of the fireplace.

Kestcliff looked at home in the terrified tension. 'We'll start with the no-read.' The apprentices flinched, but Oswin bit his lip to stop himself giggling. He couldn't imagine a less scary name than 'the no-read'.

Kestcliff nodded solemnly. 'The no-read is one of the sensory beasts. Like the no-see, its name is an instruction on how to survive it. Reading a description of the no-read's appearance summons it, which is why all new apprentices get one Scelving lesson before their first few weeks of learning to read and write. It reduces the pranking. Before, students would trick each other into thinking they'd read about the beast. A century before that, a student took notes while a master was describing the no-read. The student then read their own notes and ... well ...' He cleared his throat.

'What happened?' asked Oswin.

Kestcliff acted as if he hadn't heard. 'We treat the no-read with a healthy caution. Not only do we teach you about it before you learn to read, but we also do *not* teach you what it looks like. Ever.' Kestcliff moved to the board. 'Observe. The name of the no-read is, ironically, safe. It's what we call the monster, not its appearance.' He wrote 'No-read'. Oswin's previous amusement faded into anxiety. 'See? Nothing. No monster appearing from thin air.' A few apprentices turned to double-check. 'If I had written a description of the no-read, we would all be in trouble. Thankfully, what the no-read looks like is a closely guarded secret. Those who do know have strong magic and training prohibiting their ability to share the information.'

Oswin raised his hand and, with difficulty, battled his words back until he was called on to speak.

Kestcliff smiled. 'Thank you for waiting. What's your question?'

'What happens if you *do* read about the no-read?'

A silence fell over the class. Gale glanced at Oswin,

and Maury stiffened in his chair. Oswin felt a spike of frustration. He might have known the answer if Lullia had shared this kind of information with him. Then he felt guilty for the thought. Lullia had given him a home, which was more than a stray deserved.

Kestcliff said, 'If one reads a description of the no-read, the monster appears and ...' He sniffed, clasping his hands. '*Removes* your eyes.'

The room was so quiet Oswin could hear the creak of the iceberg leaning against the cabin. The way Kestcliff had said 'removes' felt too clinical for what he imagined was anything but.

Kestcliff continued: 'There is no known way to stop a no-read once you have read its appearance. Those who try end up dead. Once the reader's eyes are gone, the no-read vanishes, having ensured its victim will never be able to read in the same way again.'

Oswin's mouth went dry, picturing claws reaching for his eyes. 'Right,' he said, breathless. 'And how many monsters, besides the no-read, are there?'

A shadow fell over Kestcliff's face. 'Many.' He added, hastily, 'But don't worry. A powerful magic, coming from the Watchtower in Central Tundra, protects the settlement. Monsters rarely breach Tundra. The only exceptions are the no-reads when read about, and other thought-activated beasts, *whom I shall not name for obvious reasons.* Now, before the end of the lesson, I'd like to squeeze in three more beasts. The meersnof, the kikorka and the skelaard.'

Oswin's brain only felt content with learning once it had been filled with information on monsters with spindly legs, jaws that shot out of their mouths or with fireplaces for faces. At the end of the class, the apprentices rushed out into the snow, theorizing about what other sorts of monsters existed, but Oswin hung back.

Kestcliff, cleaning his glasses on his tie, watched him. 'I've a feeling you have more questions.'

Oswin gripped his pack's strap, nodding.

'Ask away.'

'If you know anything about trees eating people, *I beg you*, please tell me.'

Kestcliff held back a laugh. 'I don't know anything about trees eating *people*, but the trees of Shemmia Woods eat ice.'

'*Ice?*'

'Why do you think they grow in ice instead of soil? That's their food.'

'But that doesn't make any sense ...' Oswin couldn't understand why the trees would swap from eating ice to trying to eat *him*, so he turned his mind to the conversation he'd overheard instead. 'Can you think of anything being planted?'

Kestcliff didn't hold back his laughter this time. 'Flowers. Trees. Lots of things.' Oswin's knuckles turned white from how tightly he gripped the strap of his pack. Another dead-end. 'What's your name?' asked Kestcliff suddenly.

'Oswin.' He knew not to say his surname by now, but it didn't seem to matter. He could practically hear Kestcliff thinking, *He's the stray*. He *had* to change the topic. 'What was the Great Freeze?'

Kestcliff frowned at the abrupt shift. 'It happened a decade ago. The longest Freeze ever recorded, which led to lethal famine.'

Oswin knew he was pushing his luck with his next question. 'And Michael Fields?'

Kestcliff's eyes narrowed from behind his square glasses. 'Michael Fields had his followers believing anyone who wasn't strong should be committed to the ice. He nearly destroyed Tundra in his pursuit of perfect survival. You'd do well to stay away from his memory. People will get the wrong idea.'

'But—'

'I have another class to prepare for. I appreciate your eagerness to learn, but for your own sake you should drop that particular curiosity.'

'Sure, but—'

'I'm telling you to leave.'

Oswin huffed, frustratedly leaving it there.

8

A BEAST FROM BELOW

Corridor usually gave their apprentices three lessons a day – two before lunch and one after – but as it was their first day they spent the rest of it having the rules and basic layout of Corridor drilled into them. Even so, by the time evening arrived, Oswin felt surprisingly energetic. Back on the produce field, work never ended until Lullia said so, which was often well into the night. Oswin was usually so exhausted by then that picking the lock on the cupboard for a dinner Lullia might have denied him if he'd worked poorly, or sneaking out in the comfort of night, was always a battle for his aching muscles.

At the end of the day here, though, he was buzzing with energy and plagued by questions. He didn't bother joining the other apprentices while they explored the common room. Instead, he settled into his own room and spread the map of Corridor on the windowsill. In a matter of moments, he had every detail memorized. All he had to do now was wait for sunset.

He paced *a lot*, nervous about what might lie ahead in the Utility Proving, and how he could show he belonged at Corridor. He wasn't *entirely* sure when the Thaw ended, and therefore when the first Utility Proving would occur, but he did know it was roughly halfway through the year. Back on the produce field, he'd notice the sky changing from a crisp blue to an overcast smog – what he now knew was the Thaw and the Freeze – so he'd have to keep a close eye on the weather. As soon as the wind cut into his skin instead of gently shoving his limbs, the first Utility Proving would begin.

To combat his nerves, Oswin practised picking the locks in his collection, the clinking of his tools comforting. His leg bounced, and when a question popped into his mind that he couldn't answer, he banished it with the scratching of lock picks.

He kept working until the sky waned to dusk. Then, with a clatter, he put the tools down. He fixed his trapper hat snugly on his head, pulled his neck scarf over his nose and clasped his uniform's cloak around his shoulders. Just as he'd done on the produce field, he was going to do here: sneak. Only this time, he was doing it to investigate.

Unlike Lullia's cabin, the dormitories' door didn't have padlocks, bolts and lock chains. Oswin scoffed at how easy getting out was compared to the silent struggle he'd always had back home.

Slipping outside, he sneaked down the steps and winced at the crunching sound of the snow below his boots. Snow made sneaking harder, but he'd learned that shuffling his feet *through* it was silent enough that even the many ears of a mamat wouldn't notice him.

The air was calm. On a colder Tundran night, his nose might have fallen off, but right then the quiet cold merely sank into his bones. A creeping but forgiving chill. He rather liked it.

He followed the river for a time, then peeled away from the gurgling water. With only moonlight to gleam on the world, his eyes stretched wide to see. Soon, he had reached what had been marked on the map as the healer's home. Smoke puffed from the chimney in soft snores: something about cabins in darkness was comforting to him. Inside, a healer mixed herbs with rock fragments. Oswin wanted to knock on the window and ask what he was doing, but then he'd be caught exploring. Besides, there was a lit candle on the windowsill. There was one thing Oswin liked less than heights, and that was fire, *especially* from a candle. The thought of its warm sensation made him queasy.

After passing a gazebo made from blunted axes melded together, and raised on stilts, he reached the Atrium. He was hoping he might find something that would explain the shrinking sphere. Maury had said oddities weren't real, but in his opinion, a powerful relic that someone could merge with, and that caused crises, could certainly make a sphere malfunction. Maybe, they *did* exist.

Unfortunately, unless he'd somehow missed an item conveniently labelled 'Oddity', there wasn't anything to be found. He checked footprints, sniffed for strange scents and listened for whispers. Nothing.

After a few hours of searching, he headed back, passing what the map had called 'the Battlefield' on his way. It was filled with ice walls, ditches and tunnels. Cluttered among them were prickly pines. His pin-drop-precise hearing could make out sniffing at the centre. Curious, he wove through the tunnels to see the rough shape of a girl sitting on a block of ice.

'Are you okay?' he asked. He was just able to see the

outline of her hair twists in the dark and realized who it was.

Ennastasia pushed off the ice, drying her eyes. 'Don't sneak up on me.' She shot him a look that could melt iron. 'You're in my personal space.'

'I'm nowhere near you.' Oswin took a step back regardless.

'You do realize with whom you're speaking, *right*?'

'Ennastasia Barkmoth.'

'Yes, but you don't seem to grasp my name's significance. Don't you know *who I am*?'

'I'm all ears. Who are you?'

Ennastasia's features scrunched up. In the dimness Oswin barely saw her half-flabbergasted and half-disgusted expression as she repeated his words. 'Who are you? *Who are you?*' Her face fell into blank realization. 'Who are *you*? I can hardly see you in the dark.'

'Oswin.'

There was a pause, in which Oswin felt Ennastasia's distaste. 'The stray. I used to think my grandfather was lying about your existence. Lullia kept you well hidden.'

'How do you know my mother's name?' snapped Oswin.

'My family knows who's who, and the guardian of the only stray in Tundra is a big deal. The fact you don't know that about *my* family is concerning. Didn't Lullia teach you the basics?'

Something ugly reared in Oswin at the tone Ennastasia was using for his mother. 'Why were you crying like a little toddler?'

Ennastasia's venomous expression sunk into apprehension. 'If you thought I was crying, you're an airhead.'

'Why did I hear sniffling, then?'

'Enough questions! Timber!' she cursed. 'You sure are insufferable.'

'I already told you my name's Oswin. Not timber.'

'It's an expression. Like "ice below" or "cindering coals". I'm not *actually* calling you timber.'

'Fine. But what upset you?'

'I said, enough questions.'

'Were you feeling homesick?'

Ennastasia took a step. 'I'm a Barkmoth. I could have your tongue cut out.'

'Then at least tell me what being a Barkmoth means—'

'You should already know!'

Oswin shrugged. 'Well, I don't.'

'Well, you should.'

'Well . . .'

Ennastasia snarled. 'You know what? Your time is worthless to me.'

'Wait,' he said as she left, the word *worthless* ringing in his ears. He glanced at the pine trees and ice tunnels. 'I may be worthless, but I bet I'm better at sneaking than you.'

Ennastasia turned, incredulous. 'So?'

'I'm useful. I can be . . . stealthy.'

Ennastasia made a face. 'You're challenging me to a *stealth-off*?'

'I guess I am.'

Ennastasia shook her head in disbelief.

'Come on. You know you want to. It'd cheer you up.'

'I *wasn't* crying.'

'Right. And *I'm* not a useless stray.'

There was a long pause. Oswin was starting to think Ennastasia really would storm off. Instead, she said, 'All right.'

'All right?' He could hardly believe it.

'But when I win, you leave me alone.'

Oswin smiled below his neck scarf. 'I think you mean *if* you win.'

'I know what I said.'

Oswin's smile grew. 'And if *I* win, you tell me exactly who you are.'

'You can't beat me – I'm a Barkmoth.'

'More like Annoyingmoth.'

Ennastasia scowled. 'That was dreadful.'

'Not my best line,' he admitted.

'Enough talk. Let's begin. Three, two—' Ennastasia cut off, her expression going slack as she stared past Oswin, fear igniting in her pupils.

Alarmed, Oswin peered into the darkness. 'What did you see?' He looked back, but Ennastasia was gone. He panicked, then saw footprints leading behind an ice wall. 'That's cheating,' he muttered, ducking into a tunnel, and realizing the world was a bit brighter than a second ago. Green lights danced through the sky, like dye in swirling water. The lights had always been his favourite distraction back on the produce field, however infrequently they appeared.

Putting his mind on the competition, he listened closely. He heard rustling pine needles, scuttling small creatures and there, on the other side of the Battlefield, he could hear ... A page turning. Why would Ennastasia be looking at a book in the dark?

A creak sounded behind him. He looked over his shoulder. He could have sworn a tree had inched closer. Memories of grabbing roots surged before his eyes. For the first time, he felt on edge in the darkness.

He fled through an ice tunnel and waited behind a wall, listening again. Before, there had been the quiet of midnight, but now the trees' swaying masked the noises he'd been using to track Ennastasia. He looked around with narrowed eyes, confused. The trees' movements didn't feel natural. It wasn't that they were trying to eat him, like in Shemmia Woods. It was more like they were being controlled.

He moved to where he'd last heard Ennastasia, found her footprints and followed them until they disappeared at the bottom of a block of ice. She must have climbed it. He would have followed but even reaching up had him feeling dizzy at the height.

'Nope,' he said to himself, his bravery fracturing. He ducked into a ditch, trying to pick up other tracks. He couldn't, and the trees were still swaying too much, bothering his sensitive ears. Then, in the middle of the Battlefield, he heard something. It was a tapping noise, like canes clicking against the ice.

'What in timber?' Ennastasia hissed, her voice deeply distressed.

Something was *very* wrong.

Forgetting the stealth-off, Oswin hurried over. He worried this was another of Ennastasia's tricks to win, but then he saw *it*.

Swathed in green from the dancing lights stood a creature as tall as the pine trees: a skull with antlers, perched on top of three spindly legs. Its jaw was like that of a human, teeth flat and wide, and tentacles squirmed within the skull, poking out through the eye sockets. The sound it made was worse than its appearance, its three feet tapping eerily, stuttering jaw clacking, tentacles squelching.

The creature turned, its empty eye sockets passing over Oswin. He held his breath. It didn't notice him. The skull pivoted again, looking at the hide from where Ennastasia's voice had come. One of its legs struck the hide, sending it flying. There was a thud in the darkness and a spray of snow burst from the impact.

Her hiding spot gone, Ennastasia stood slowly, green light shining on a book she opened. Oswin thought of the no-read and his stomach dropped to the depths of the frost caves. Had Ennastasia read a description of it? Was this that very beast? Was it going to take her eyes?

'Hey!' he shouted.

The creature stopped. The squelching noise ceased. It swivelled to look at him, and Oswin felt a pull at his elbows, as if something invisible was drawing him towards it.

He hadn't thought this through *at all*.

The creature scuttled for him, its skull perfectly level as it did.

Oswin ran. The tapping noise followed, growing closer as he darted around ice walls and through tunnels. He couldn't outrun it; his sickly lungs were already failing. Desperate, he dropped into a ditch, hurried along as silently as he could, then threw himself into a hollow below overhanging branches.

A drum beat thudded as the monster placed two legs on one side of the ditch and its third on the other. It balanced there, pivoting its skull back and forth like a broken mechanism.

Searching.

Its legs bent, lowering its skull as its human-like jaw clacked a steady rhythm. Its tentacles reached out from the eye sockets and under the jaw, feeling for life.

The beast moved closer to Oswin's hiding space. He flinched with every snap of its teeth. He didn't know when he'd stopped breathing, but the urge to gasp was clawing at the inside of his lungs. If this was it, at least he could make peace with the fact his sacrifice had kept Ennastasia, a *Tundran*, safe.

Oswin drew in air. He placed a hand over his mouth, forcing it to be a slow breath despite the pain squeezing at his oxygen-begging brain. The breath *was* quiet. But not quiet enough.

The skull jerked in his direction. Its jaw creaked open, its rancid breath frosting the air with mould. It lurched forward.

9

CANDLES OVER ANSWERS

The skull of the beast was upon Oswin. Its jaws stretched around his head. He could see the moist back of its throat, could smell its rotten breath warming his skin. Its teeth were a second from slamming closed on his neck.

'*The Timber Moves!*' Ennastasia's voice boomed.

The tree Oswin had been hiding below uprooted itself, spraying soil and snow. It speared the monster, throwing it away just as its jaw crunched shut, clipping fluff off his hat.

The green lights in the sky vanished. Darkness fell upon the Battlefield as the monster crashed into the ground in the distance.

'Oh, yes,' said Ennastasia sarcastically, sliding into the ditch to join him. 'Just sit there. Wait for it to come back. Brilliant idea.'

Oswin stared at where Ennastasia's voice was coming from, his eyes adjusting to the darker night, shaking with relief that his head was no longer in the beast's mouth. 'Did you just use magic?' Ennastasia skidded to a stop, looking as if she'd been caught slipping an ice cube down someone's back. He shifted his gaze to the spellbook in her hand. 'We don't get spellbooks until our second year.'

There was a tapping noise, accompanied by squelching, and it was growing closer.

'You want to discuss this now?' Ennastasia cried, grabbing the fabric of his doublet, forcing him to his feet. 'Run!'

'I can't! My lungs! I won't be able to breathe—' He felt it, rather than saw it. A presence above them. Two eye sockets staring.

'*The Timber Moves*,' Ennastasia cast again. Another tree whistled through the air, slamming into the monster. In the dimness, he saw the tripod beast hit the snow. It kicked its skeletal legs like an upturned insect, then struggled to its feet. It stared at them, then at the dark sky. Finally, it turned and ran.

Oswin frowned. 'Why is it leaving?'

Ennastasia put a hand to her forehead. 'Who cares?'

Oswin looked at her, breath misting in the air, then after the creature. Resolve hardened in his belly. He tried to follow it, but Ennastasia grabbed his cloak, so he simply squinted into the ink of night at the smudge of the retreating beast. He could have been seeing things – the lighting *was* dreadful – but before the monster was truly lost, he swore he saw it shrink into a human. Then it was gone.

'You have the worst survival instincts I've ever seen.' Ennastasia released him and walked in the opposite direction.

'Where are you going?'

'To tell a master. It seems I was right to imply you've only air in your head.'

'I think calling someone an airhead goes a tad beyond implying.' She ignored him, so Oswin added, 'You're welcome, by the way.'

Ennastasia halted. '*I* saved *you*.'

'I led the monster away. It was going to eat you.'

'And then it was going to eat *you*!' Ennastasia threw her hands up. 'Unbelievable ...' They walked in furious silence to the river, on the other side of which lay the masters' cabins. Ennastasia said, 'If you're expecting a thank you for complicating the situation, you're going to be disappointed.'

'That's very modest of you to admit.'

'Excuse me?'

'That you're good at disappointing people.' He probably shouldn't have said that while they were walking over the ice bridge. Ennastasia looked as if she might push him into the river. But if he didn't taunt her, the fear he should be feeling would overwhelm him.

'You can't talk to me like that. I'm a Barkmoth.'

'Does being a Barkmoth mean you get a spellbook early?'

Face flushing, Ennastasia slid her spellbook into her cloak's interior pocket. 'I don't have a spellbook.'

He pointed accusingly at her. 'I just saw it!'

'It's your word against mine.'

Oswin would have continued arguing, except he'd noticed the cabin they were nearing was the size of a doll's house. He frowned at it until, with a whooshing noise, it expanded to a normal size at their approaching.

'Do cabins usually do that?'

'Only ones with ancient enchantments,' said Ennastasia, 'which is not many. It's an outdated magic from when Tundrans thought being small hid you from beasts. Then the monsters started eating the cabins whole. Rather than sensibly removing the enchantments, Tundrans made the cabins grow when anything approached.'

'I thought magic from the Watchtower kept monsters out of Tundra?'

'Yes. But the Watchtower was only erected a couple of hundred years ago. Before then, it was a free–for-all. Besides, as we've *just seen*, there are exceptions to the Watchtower's protection – in ninety-nine per cent of cases they can't get in, but the odd one breaks through. Honestly, don't you know anything?' She wrapped her knuckles on the cabin door. 'It's Ennastasia Barkmoth,' she called, as if she wasn't about to announce a horrific attack. Oswin raised an eyebrow at her nonchalance. 'A beast is loose in Corridor.'

From beyond the frosted walls came the sound of movement. The ruffle of sheets, thud of footsteps and turn of a handle preceded the door opening, and the appearance of Secondmaster Rochelle. It was odd to see her without her fluffy grey hat, but even without it she was strikingly tall.

She loomed in the doorway, working her dark brown hair into a low ponytail. 'Why are you out of your beds? And what did you just say?' She grabbed a cloak from a rack overburdened with weighty garments.

Oswin said, 'There was a monster. In the Battlefield.'

Rochelle grumbled, pulled on gloves and her signature hat, and stomped outside. 'What kind of monster?'

111

Ennastasia beat Oswin to the description, so he followed silently while she outlined what had happened.

Rochelle led them past another cabin which, unlike the rest, *wasn't* shrunken. Rochelle cast the unshrunk cabin a look, as if it were breaking Corridor's rules and needed a detention.

'Who lives there?' asked Oswin.

'No one,' said Rochelle. 'That cabin's empty. Silence, now.' She led them to another cabin that *was* shrunken, marched up the front steps – not fazed by its expansion – knocked and loudly said, 'Get up. Get dressed. Go to Yarrow's.'

There was a dismayed groan, a *thunk* as someone fell out of bed, and then silence.

Rochelle tutted, then moved to the next expanding cabin.

The front door opened. 'Rochelle?' Yarrow put her spectacles on and pulled an extra scarf over the dozens she was already wearing. Her eyebrows rose at the sight of Oswin and Ennastasia. 'Come in.'

Yarrow's cabin was odd. The entrance room was an office, complete with an oak desk, book-laden shelves that, if they toppled over, could crush someone and three-dimensional paintings that felt as if they could suck you inside. The sitting room had easels and a brass chandelier that swayed ominously, its burning candles ready to light the place on fire. Oswin edged away from the flames.

Ennastasia grabbed his sleeve. 'Don't slink off.'

'I'm not *slinking off*, I'm just . . .' He gestured awkwardly at the chandelier. 'Keeping my distance.'

'Yes. Slinking off.'

But Ennastasia couldn't stop him standing in the corner furthest from the chandelier, his eyes never leaving the horrific little flames.

Yarrow opened a bureau and poured herself a glass of water. She took a sip and wiped sleep from her eyes. 'Well?'

Rochelle nodded at Ennastasia, before her eyes moved curiously to Oswin, who was trying his best to cower behind an armchair without being too obvious about it.

Ennastasia said, 'We were in the battlefield—'

'Why?' Rochelle ground out, but Yarrow held a hand up for Ennastasia to continue.

'A monster attacked us,' said Ennastasia. 'It ran away after a brief altercation and is currently at large.'

Yarrow nodded at Rochelle. 'Go.'

Rochelle turned to leave. As she did, Master Tybolt stumbled into the room, scratching their scruffy stubble. 'What'd you bang on my cabin for?' they asked.

'You took your time. Turn around.' Rochelle swung Tybolt about. 'We have a monster to find.'

'Delightful,' Tybolt muttered as they departed.

Yarrow said, 'Are either of you hurt?'

'No,' said Ennastasia.

Oswin peeked out from behind the armchair. 'What if it was a no-read?'

'What did it look like?' asked Yarrow. 'Did you both see it?'

'Unfortunately,' said Ennastasia.

'It was a skull with legs,' said Oswin. 'Long legs. Like twigs.'

'And tentacles inside the skull.'

'It almost ate her.'

Ennastasia scowled. 'It almost ate *you*.'

Yarrow closed her eyes, relieved. 'That's not a no-read. It was a meersnof.'

Oswin was about to ask what a no-read *did* look like, but Master Kestcliff's lesson replayed perfectly in his head. 'The Scelving Master taught us about meersnofs today.' He'd been so busy trying to survive the monster he'd only just realized he'd learned about the very thing that had been chasing him.

'What was it doing *here*?' Yarrow wondered.

Ennastasia glanced at her. 'I expected better of

Corridor's security. One near-death experience per day was *not* advertised on my invitation.'

'My deepest apologies, young Barkmoth,' said Yarrow. 'As you know, Tundra prefers Corridor to remain a dangerous place as a method of weeding out the weak.' She added dejectedly, 'Despite my efforts to the contrary.'

'The fact remains: facing beasts is not on the curriculum.'

'Nor is venturing out in the middle of the night. I'd politely ask what it was you were doing out of the safety of the dormitories?'

Ennastasia's nostrils flared. She was silent a moment, then averted her eyes and mumbled, 'We have a battlefield back home. My brother and I played there when we were younger. I was just . . .' She swallowed heavily.

Yarrow hummed, understanding. 'You missed home.'

Ennastasia glared furiously into the wall.

Oswin said, 'I followed her out. I was worried about her.'

'I don't need your worry,' Ennastasia snapped, then turned to Yarrow. 'Are you going to do anything but apologize about the beast that is *still at large*?'

Yarrow fixed a cold look on Ennastasia. 'Masters Rochelle and Tybolt will handle it.' She straightened in her chair. 'Your punishments will be decided when I am not exhausted. For the time being, allow me to escort the both of you back to your dorm, and to recommend you *remain* there, should you wish to avoid further incidents.'

'I know the way,' said Ennastasia. Then, clearly remembering Yarrow was the Grandmaster, added, 'Thank you for the offer,' before marching out of the room.

Yarrow watched her leave and gave her head a minute shake of disapproval, then turned to Oswin who was still huddled behind the armchair. 'Are you quite all right?'

He couldn't stop watching the candles. 'I'll be better once I'm back in my room.'

'Say no more.' Yarrow led him outside, where chains magically grew around her wheels to grip the snow. 'What's going on? Are you anxious about the Utility Provings?' Her voice was soft, as if Oswin would startle.

He very much did. 'Um! No ... not at all! I'm such a useful person; I'm sure I'll do great at proving that.' His nervous laugh couldn't have made his lie more obvious. He went quiet, glancing curiously at Yarrow who, quite inexplicably, had personally asked he attend Corridor.

'I sense you have a question,' said Yarrow.

'Why was I requested to train here?' he blurted out. 'I'm a stray. I thought strays weren't welcome, but then you specifically asked for me.'

They'd reached the dormitories by then, and Yarrow brought her wheelchair to a stop. 'Some people in Tundra don't welcome strays. I am not one of them. I wasn't going to let you miss the chance of training because of your birth, so I personally demanded you come to Corridor.'

Oswin stared, astounded. 'You did that? For me?'

'Yes.'

Oswin couldn't comprehend it. He was a stray, a drain on Tundra's resources, the one-log-too-many on the cart. Why would Yarrow want him here? 'I don't understand.'

Yarrow's lips pressed into a miserable line. 'I hope one day you will. Until then, have a good rest.'

'Wait – I have a few more questions—'

'And I have a beast to locate. Goodnight.' Into the softly falling snow, Yarrow departed. After a few moments of watching her leave, Oswin saw the figures of Rochelle and Tybolt running to meet her, and he couldn't resist stretching his hearing to their distant conversation.

'Nothing,' said Tybolt, Oswin just making out their voice as the three masters walked back to their cabins.

'Any tracks?' asked Yarrow.

Rochelle said, 'None visible in this light.'

Whatever Yarrow said in response, even Oswin couldn't hear over the distance. Clenching his jaw, he returned to his room, lay on the floor and stared at the ceiling. He was almost unsurprised when, squirming down his ear, distant and close at once, he heard the voice again.

'*Oswin Fields,*' it said. '*Steal The Ghost.*'

Exhausted, he fell asleep, the words echoing around him; he didn't have a clue what they meant.

The next morning, Oswin didn't immediately go to breakfast. Instead, he walked through the Battlefield, searching for signs of the monster. The only evidence of the two trees Ennastasia's magic had uprooted were slight hollows, though the creature's button-shaped footprints remained.

Oswin followed the small dots, visible in the morning light. By a cluster of trees at the edge of the Battlefield, the trail ended near some human footprints. The only trouble was, he couldn't be sure his eyes *hadn't* been mistaken in seeing its transformation last night. Maybe the tracks changed from a monster's to those of a human, or *maybe* the tracks had been scuffed over by the breakfast rush. No matter how carefully he inspected the ground, he couldn't be sure, and he wasn't going to tell someone without being certain.

Admitting defeat, he plodded to breakfast, where the other apprentices were alive with gossip. Someone had overheard two masters talking about setting up the Plughole for the first years' Thaw Utility Proving. Theories on what it could be ranged from diving into the falling water to climbing the icy walls of the chute. Oswin managed to ask what the Plughole was, and felt dread at the answer: a well-like shaft going deep into the ground in the north-east of Corridor. The river water tumbled down it into darkness.

Oswin felt sick at the thought. He knew he'd fail.

10

AN ENTIRELY
HYPOTHETICAL SPELLBOOK

As Master Kestcliff had told them, their first week at Corridor was to be spent learning to read and write. The first-year apprentices were sprawled out in the large cafeteria. Each of them had a practice book, and masters cast magic to speed up their learning. In Oswin's opinion, they were all being far too cavalier about the prospect of the approaching Utility Proving.

Running the sessions was Master Pin who, rather peculiarly, dragged a log behind her at all times. When Cathy asked her why, she said it was simply because she adored timber.

Master Pin gave instructions with a monotone voice and eyes staring into the distance. 'These are animate books. The magic that made them is infinitely difficult and thus they are highly valuable.' From her lack of enthusiasm, she could have been talking about harvest statistics. 'If you damage your book, your family will be responsible, financially, for replacing it. Work in silence.'

Without saying anything else, Pin dragged herself, and her log, to the side of the room, not paying the apprentices any more attention.

The apprentices spread out. Oswin could have sat with Maury, but she was already sitting with Philomena and Gale. He reckoned she wouldn't want to be bothered by him when she had Tundran company, so he found a secluded corner instead, settled into a chair and opened his book.

'Hello!' said the book.

Oswin almost fell out of his chair. 'You talk!'

The pages moved like a mouth. The cover shifted like eyebrows. 'Of course. I'm animate timber, like Reginald. Though my timber is a lot thinner, having been flattened into paper. And yes, there was that time when I didn't realize I was a book. One of the apprentices let the truth slip and I had a small breakdown over not being human. I'm over it now, so there's no need to bring it up, okay?'

Oswin nodded slowly. 'Okay . . .'

'I'm here to teach you to read and write. Have you ever read or written before?'

Oswin shook his head. Then, to his alarm, the book coughed up a pencil covered in scraps of paper: the book's equivalent of saliva.

'Use that,' the book said, then lay open.

'Before we begin, I was wondering, seeing as both you and trees are made of timber, do you know anything about ice-eating trees starting to eat humans instead?'

The book shot him an odd look. 'No?'

'What about shrinking spheres? Or oddities?'

The book's look worsened. 'No idea about spheres, but I know oddities aren't real. They were once popular in fables – anyone who merged with an oddity faced a grim fate.'

'Like what?'

'Are you going to learn to read and write or not?'

Gingerly, Oswin picked the pencil up. 'Yeah. Sorry.'

'To write, you want to—'

But Oswin's hand moved on muscle memory. Before he knew it, he was scribing entire sentences.

'You said you'd never written before,' the book murmured suspiciously.

Oswin stretched his aching fingers. 'I haven't. Not as far as I can remember, at least.'

'Try reading this.' Words appeared on the pages. Oswin dived through them, the story titled *The Dramatic Life of Jabidy Jorn*. It was full of unanswered questions. Why was Jabidy the chosen one? Why was her best friend not talking to her? He devoured the book in an hour.

'Can you show me the sequel? I have to know what happens next.'

The words on the page vanished. 'You've really never read or written before?'

'No!'

The book didn't look convinced.

Oswin tilted his head. 'What are you, exactly?'

'I'm a book. But I'm also a hive of thoughts. All of the practice books are one connected being. I hop from one to another to instruct new apprentices.'

'And what—' Oswin cut off when he heard his name. He fell silent and paid more attention to the nearby conversation. When he made out his name again, he picked up the animate book and crept towards the voices.

'What are you doing?' the book whispered.

'Shh,' said Oswin gently.

Glass shards chimed against each other, and Oswin realized it was Cathy and Frank.

'I still can't get over it,' said Frank as Oswin hid behind

a chair not too nearby, but close enough that his sensitive ears could eavesdrop. Frank and Cathy were reading by a crackling fireplace in a corner secluded from the other apprentices. Oswin was as unnerved by the fireplace as he was them.

'A Fields who's a stray,' said Frank. 'A *Fields* who's a *stray.*'

'It's an oxymoron. A Fields who's a *sickly* stray. You saw him – there's hardly any muscle on those bones, and those eyes ...'

'They're the eyes of the dead.' Frank was polishing the horns on his shoulders. 'Everyone and their snowman know what Michael thought of strays.'

Oswin's fingers dug into the back of the chair.

Cathy said, 'Not everyone. Some people think Michael was a fan of them.'

'Some people have their head in the snow.'

'In fairness, those in charge did their best to cover it up. They thought Michael's views were as dangerous as the beasts.'

Frank snorted. 'They probably thought Michael's views were *more* dangerous.'

Cathy's eyes drifted in Oswin's direction, who panicked that he wasn't fully hidden. 'Michael's ideas didn't go far enough. He thought that strays who survived on the

Endless Expanse, and stayed away from Tundra, deserved to be left in peace.'

'You think differently?'

'*All* strays must be put in their place, no matter where they—' Cathy cut off, having finally noticed Oswin. 'Had your fill of nosiness?'

Oswin froze in panic, which was more than enough time for Frank to dash over, seize his arm, and drag him back to Cathy, who snatched Oswin's animate book.

She said, 'I wonder – if the stray destroyed valuable property, would it get him kicked out?'

Oswin's heart stalled. 'No!'

Cathy tipped the book onto the fire, and Frank finally released the struggling Oswin. He rushed to the fireplace but the second he felt heat on his skin, he froze.

'Look here,' said Frank mockingly. 'The stray's afraid of fire.'

'How cute.'

Oswin stared as the book burned, unable to grab it. The scowl it shot him melted before his eyes. At least its mind could hop into another book, he consoled himself.

Laughing to themselves, Cathy and Frank walked off, reading their own undamaged books.

The book was ashes in a few minutes, and Oswin knew Lullia couldn't afford to replace something so valuable.

The thought of how she'd respond was terrifying, so he searched shelves, boxes and below the empty buffet table in the faint hope he would find a replacement.

'Stop buzzing around like a gadflyst,' Ennastasia snapped when Oswin peered below the chair where she was reading. 'I'm busy trying not to be bored out of my mind.'

'Sorry,' said Oswin, working hard not to cry. 'Cathy and Frank destroyed my book. I was seeing if there was a spare.'

Ennastasia narrowed her eyes. 'Not my problem.'

Oswin continued his doomed search. When Maury asked him what was wrong, he was too distressed to speak, so she told him to let her know if she could help, especially if helping involved building a ridiculous (and probably banned) contraption. He *could* tell her what had happened, but then he'd be dumping his stray problems on a Tundran. That wouldn't help his case at all.

When the lesson ended and the master collected the books, Oswin accepted his fate. He shuffled back to his seat to collect his backpack.

He stopped in his tracks. His animate book was waiting on his desk. Somehow, it had healed.

'Animate book,' the master said, holding out a hand.

Oswin's mouth hung open, astounded. 'Uh, right.

Yes. Of course.' He handed her the book, perplexed. He had half a foot out of the door when he heard a hushed conversation at the back, too far for the other apprentices to notice.

'I want to keep it.' Ennastasia held her backpack tightly.

'You must return the book,' the master insisted.

Ennastasia's nostrils flared. 'You do know who I am, right? If I want to keep the animate book, I very well can.'

The master decided it wasn't worth the fight and left, dragging her precious timber behind her. Ennastasia swung her backpack on, seemingly too light to contain a book, and marched to the exit. She looked Oswin up and down, then stepped into the snow.

'Wait!' He burst into motion after her.

'What?'

'Thank you.'

'Thank you?' Ennastasia crinkled her nose. 'Whatever for?'

Oswin's book hadn't healed after all. 'You left your animate book on my desk.'

'I did no such thing.'

'Then where's *your* animate book?'

'I gave it back to the master, obviously.'

Oswin shook his head. 'Nope. No. You did not. I heard your conversation – you told her you were keeping yours.'

Ennastasia glared. 'How in Tundra did you hear that? You were on the other side of the room.'

'You don't deny it, then?'

She huffed. 'Hasn't anyone taught you manners? Nosiness is not becoming.'

'I've mainly been taught how to shut up.'

'Yet you remain dreadful at it.'

'You sound like my mother.' That was a lie. Lullia would never have let him speak to her this way.

Ennastasia stared, aghast. 'I've already told you: you can't speak to me like that!'

'Why not?'

'Because I'm a Barkmo— No. I'm not having this conversation with you again.'

Oswin knew he was playing a dangerous game, but there was something hidden behind Ennastasia's disdain. He had to know what it was so, before he could think better of it, he snapped, 'I couldn't care less who you are.'

There was a lethal silence. Ennastasia's fiery eyes bore into him, but when he looked at her, *really* looked at her, he got his answer. She wasn't angry. Not really. She was surprised. That glint in her eyes was *hope*.

Oswin said, 'What I care about is that you helped me.' He paused, his curiosity bubbling. '*And* why you have a spellbook a year early.'

Ennastasia diverted her path from his.

'Okay, okay, I won't ask about the spellbook.' He changed his direction to follow her. 'You didn't have a spellbook, I never saw a spellbook, fine. But, *hypothetically*, if you did have a spellbook, and we faced a monster last night, how would you have stopped it?'

Ennastasia fumed but eventually she said, 'Let's say I had a spellbook.' She fixed him with a harsh glower. '*Hypothetically*.'

Oswin held his hands up. 'Hypothetically.'

'Then, *hypothetically*, if I was in the Battlefield, I would be able to stop it because I would be around trees.'

Oswin motioned at himself. 'Airhead, remember? I don't get why trees would matter.'

'Because I'd use what all Barkmoths are good at: timber magic. *Hypothetically*.'

'How does timber magic relate to trees?'

Ennastasia gestured at a pine. 'That is a tree. Must I explain that concept, too?'

'I think I've got that one down.'

'Fantastic. What are they made of?'

'Timber.'

'Wow! There *is* a brain among the air. I, *hypothetically*, used timber magic to fend off the beast and you're confused why being near timber was important?'

'Not any more. I think I get what happened now.'

'Which is that I watched in academic interest as the beast tried to tear you apart.'

'Of course. Except we both know you used a spellbook you're not meant to have.'

Ennastasia glared at him.

'Sorry! Sorry. All hypothetical. No spellbook. Absolutely nothing suspicious going on with you at all.'

Ennastasia continued to scowl but didn't throw him into the air with a tree-missile. Oswin took that as a win.

11

OPEN A DOOR OR A RIBCAGE?

Oswin sat next to Ennastasia at breakfast the following day. Promptly, she moved to a different table. Wondering if something was wrong with the previous one, he followed. Ennastasia stood up again.

'I sense you're avoiding me.'

'You sense correctly.' She narrowed her eyes at him. 'We're not friends. Stay away from me.'

'But you helped me.'

'I'm starting to regret that.' She walked to an empty table and sat alone.

Disappointed, Oswin checked who else he could sit with. Maury and Philomena were together, examining a slingshot Maury had built, then hurriedly hiding a teacup when Maury broke it with a hugely inaccurate shot. Their table only had two seats, and Maury looked tired. He probably didn't want to be pestered. Zylo was laughing raucously with his friends, seeing who could eat porridge the fastest. *He* probably didn't want his little brother hovering around him.

In the end, he resigned himself to a lonely breakfast. After he'd eaten, Rochelle ducked inside the cafeteria, removing her fluffy hat to fit in the low room.

'Ah, Oswin.' She placed a hand on his shoulder. 'Due to your sneaking out, you're banned from extra-curricular activities until the Freeze.' Oswin thought ruefully that it didn't matter. When the Freeze began, he'd either die in the Plughole or fail the Utility Proving. 'You'll also need to clean the Alchemy bowls and catalogue Vinderation equipment this week.'

'That's it?'

Rochelle frowned. 'I *could* make it more severe, but Yarrow believes this is sufficient.'

Oswin flexed his hands. 'Sure. A few questions: what extra-curriculars are there? And what are Alchemy and Vinderation?'

Rochelle's sympathetic smile returned. 'There isn't time to explain all that before your lessons.'

'Is Ennastasia getting the same punishment?'

Rochelle's smile dropped. 'She is not.'

'Because she's a Barkmoth? What does being a Barkmoth mean?'

Rochelle ducked out of the door, replacing her fluffy hat. 'I'm afraid I have to prepare for a lesson. Have a good day.'

Oswin sulked at the lack of answers.

For a week, his evenings were spent scrubbing bowls of sludge that dodged his sponge like a gadflyst did a swatter. At least when he catalogued Vinderation trinkets, *most* of them didn't run away, though he did have to stop himself from pocketing one. His inventory skills weren't sharp enough to get away with it.

Besides literacy, the apprentices learned the basic schedule of Corridor. Oswin was shocked that there was something called a 'week' with seven days: Firstday, Secondday, Thirdday, and so on. The first four were for lessons and the last three – something called 'the weekend' – were for relaxation. It was almost incomprehensible to Oswin, whose life until then had been a daily cycle of repetitive timber harvesting. The idea of getting three whole days to rest was boggling.

After three weeks of reading and writing, Oswin still

had no good answers and felt unprepared for the Utility Provings. Despite his best efforts, the animate book refused to entertain his questions. It was annoyed about the whole *didn't-pull-the-first-book-out-of-a-fireplace* debacle. When Oswin broached the subject of Michael Fields, it outright screamed until he promised to stop asking questions. At least, during his late-night excursions, he hadn't encountered any more monsters.

He'd kept sneaking out, of course. He couldn't be punished again if he wasn't caught, and he was skilled at not getting caught. It helped that there hadn't been any more dancing lights in the sky. The darker the night, the more bountiful his hiding.

On Firstday of the fourth week, Zylo joined Oswin for breakfast. His older brother swapped between having breakfast with his friends and him.

'You know you can hang with them, too,' said Zylo as he ate an apple in two bites, core and all. 'Then we could eat together *every* day.'

Oswin knew he could try to make friends, but he was a stray among Tundrans. They all had better, non-strays to sit with. He shouldn't take advantage of their politeness. 'I'd prefer to keep myself to myself.'

'I'm still going to pester you every other day. Can't get rid of me that easily. Besides, I've got to make sure you're safe.'

Oswin felt guilty. He hadn't told his brother about the monster, nor what Cathy and Frank had done, because Zylo would refuse to leave his side – or worse, forbid him from exploring at night.

Zylo downed his tea then ruffled Oswin's hair. 'Don't take any risks, okay?'

'I won't,' he lied.

'I'd better be off, Ozzy.' Zylo hurried away, while Oswin thought about how, the second he'd told Zylo he was a boy, his brother had swapped from the girlie nickname he'd once used for him to Ozzy. It didn't matter how cold Tundra grew, being called 'Ozzy' made Oswin feel indescribably warm.

By that week, those who'd never touched a book before could evaluate literature classics – like *Pieter and the Vine Giant* – so they moved back on to proper training, and their usual timetable. Cloak on, Oswin trekked to Scelving, excited to do something besides read and write, but as he sat down, Master Kestcliff told everyone to stand; they were going outside to skate. Apprentices rushed to put on the provided shoes. Oswin, who didn't know what skates were, watched Philomena as she confidently selected a pair of bladed shoes, then copied her. He couldn't help noting her floating orbs were gone, and that her hair had grown messy. Her brother's orbs gleamed, and *his* hair was immaculately groomed. But unlike Philomena, Gale looked glum as he picked out his skates.

Oswin soon understood why. Skating was dreadful. Kestcliff cast a spell so that the ice rink had loop-de-loops and spirals. Philomena skated upside down without a thought, while others wobbled along a flat track. Frank tripped and pulled Cathy with him, both laughing, while Maury just yawned fiercely.

Oswin was abysmal at skating and struggled over to Ennastasia. 'I bet I can skate faster than you,' he joked, his legs' panicked movements making his declaration an obvious lie.

'I was skating before Tundra took you in, you know.'

'So ... you're scared of my challenge.'

'*Scared?* I bet I could skate three laps before you've even finished one.'

Ennastasia was right. Oswin barely got halfway around before she was circling him, skating backwards.

'Fine, I suck at skating.' Oswin managed to point at Ennastasia without falling. 'Best of three? I'll beat you in our next lesson.'

'At what?'

'Taking notes. Bet I write twice as much as you.'

Ennastasia's eyebrows rose, bewildered. 'Have it your way.'

Their next lesson, Basic Spellbookery, was in the Classroom Treehouse. Thankfully, the classroom was in one of the lower-down cabins of the tree, nestled in the oak's branches. Oswin was only mildly hyperventilating when he reached it.

He and Ennastasia settled at the back, surrounded by the scent of old books. They feverishly wrote everything the badger-haired and beady-eyed Master Crull said about the three types of magic: fog, timber and coal. Crull explained most spells could be cast with any of the three magics powering them, but that each magic had areas they were better suited for. Fog magic loved the realm of future seeing and food growth, which Oswin thought a funny combination. Timber magic encompassed all things transmutation or timber, and fog-timber combination magic was in the business of healing. Crull was brief and stilted with his description of coal magic, saying nothing more than that it related to heat, light and fire, and that they *weren't* to use it. Ever. Oswin was about to ask why, before noticing Ennastasia was way ahead of him in their notetaking race.

To catch up, he shamelessly copied Ennastasia's notes. It was only after Crull told him off for being silly, having stopped by Oswin's desk and looked over his shoulder, that he realized that what Ennastasia had been writing was gibberish.

'Hilarious,' said Oswin.

Ennastasia smugly erased her words. 'Serves you right.'

She wasn't smug when the master took the register, realized she was a Barkmoth and promptly complimented her every breath. Oswin was confused why Crull's reverence didn't please her, but he was pulled from his thoughts when it was *his* surname being called. At least now he knew why his surname made the class go deathly quiet. It wasn't just that he was the only stray in Corridor; he was also Michael Fields' nephew.

Frank, balancing on the back legs of his chair with his feet on the table, whispered to Cathy, 'I hope he falls down the Plughole.' Cathy snickered, and a doomy dread filled Oswin.

When Frank wasn't looking, Maury splatted gloop, which congealed instantly, onto his laces, then gave Oswin an over-exaggerated wink. Oswin smiled in return, but quickly dropped the expression when Frank glanced his way.

Oswin and Ennastasia continued their note-taking – elbowing each other in sabotage – until Gale's hand rose.

'Isn't coal magic evil?' he asked.

Ennastasia's scribbling stopped. Oswin shot her a questioning look, but her eyes were glued to Gale.

Master Crull inclined his head. 'Coal magic will always try to destroy you.'

Ennastasia walked out, slamming the door. It had been so sudden that Oswin almost missed it. Needing to know what had upset her, he put his hand up.

Crull looked grateful for the distraction. 'Yes?'

'What do you mean: coal will try to destroy you? Does it have a mind?'

'In a way, yes. The magics can misunderstand what your spell is asking *or* deliberately misconstrue your words. Take the spell *Open*. The magic could think I mean a window, *or* my ribcage.'

A horrified shudder ran through the class.

'The spell *The Door Opens* is safe to use with timber and fog. The magic knows what I want to open. Namely, *not* my ribcage. But coal magic always looks for a way to twist your words, even when you're being clear. If you used coal magic for *The Door Opens*, the door would burst into flames and burn to ashes, which would *technically* open it. But the fire would take the rest of your home and potentially even your life. It's why only a handful of Tundrans have permission to use coal magic. Whatever risks you've heard about using timber and fog magic, times those by a hundred for coal. You don't receive a spellbook until your second year precisely because it is frighteningly easy to injure, even *kill*, with poorly cast spells.'

The rest of the lesson was dampened by the sombre start. Oswin took notes no longer to best Ennastasia, but to catch her up.

When the lesson finished, he enjoyed watching Frank fall on his face, finding out the hard way that his laces were congealed.

'Nice one,' Oswin whispered, giving Maury a low five.

Maury smiled. 'Any time.'

12

ETYMAGERY

Ennastasia was in her usual isolated seat in the cafeteria. She wouldn't thank Oswin for giving her his notes, but still, he liked having the excuse to approach her. Unlike Maury or Zylo, Ennastasia didn't have other friends, so Oswin wasn't keeping her from better company. Ennastasia certainly wouldn't put up with him out of politeness. She didn't know the word.

He hovered by her table.

Ennastasia took an angry bite of her potato and sweetcorn pasty.

Oswin slid the notes to her. 'You can have these.'

She dabbed her mouth with a napkin, her eyes narrowed. 'Why?'

'To prove I won the bet.'

She gave him her full attention. 'I'm being serious. What do you want?'

'Nothing.'

Ennastasia inspected the notes. 'Won't you need these?'

Oswin tapped his head. 'Already memorized.'

'Likely story.'

'I remember everything. I could tell you the room number of every first-year apprentice.'

'How in Tundra would you know that?'

'They were on the noticeboard.'

Ennastasia made a face. 'Nonsense. That was only up for one morning.' She pointed at Gale. 'What's his room, then?'

'Twenty. His sister's in twenty-one.'

'You picked random numbers.'

'Want to bet? This could be our tie-breaker.'

'I'm not betting again. I won our skate-off, yet you still pester me, which was not the deal.'

'It was best out of three, and you lost the note-taking.'

Ennastasia stood, chair scraping, and marched to Gale. 'You.' Gale startled, his orbs hiding behind him. 'What's your room number.'

'Twenty,' he squeaked.

Ennastasia walked to Maury and Philomena, cutting into their conversation. 'Your room number. Quickly.'

Philomena, facing away from her, said, 'None of your business.'

Maury kicked her under the table. 'That's Ennastasia Barkmoth!'

Philomena whirled, her eyes wide. 'Twenty-one. Sorry for my rudeness.'

Without a thank you, Ennastasia sulked back to her table.

Oswin followed. 'I told you. I remember everything.'

'Then remember to leave me alone. You can have your illegible notes. We're not friends.' She scrunched up the paper and threw it at him. It bounced off his front and landed on the floor. His hope dwindling to cold embers, Oswin nodded in resignation and left her alone.

The day's final lesson was Etymagery. Horrifically for Oswin, it was at the top of the Classroom Treehouse. He stared up at its treacherous steps, the cabins precariously balanced on branches. Walkways criss-crossed above each other, making his head spin. The wood was slippery, and he feared he'd fall between the rungs. He was sure the air held less oxygen at the top, and when he reached the Etymagery classroom, it was little relief. The cabin was half-rotten, its patchwork roof buckling below snow and decaying leaves. Inside, dust lined every surface. The drawers were so stuffed they couldn't close and the blackboard was a mess of chalk marks. Oswin sat and gripped his stomach, trying not to hurl.

Ennastasia sat next to him. 'This was the only remaining seat,' she said by way of an excuse. 'You being near it is an unfortunate side effect.'

'Would you prefer I sit on the floor?' He tried to sound sarcastic, but his wheeziness stole its power.

'Yes. Chop, chop.' She shooed him, and Oswin laughed quietly, forgetting his nausea for a second.

Ennastasia crinkled her nose. 'Does this room smell off to you?'

'Since you arrived, you mean?'

'You know that's not what I meant.'

Oswin had been so nauseous he only then noticed the scent of trampled leaves.

After twenty minutes, Frank whispered to Cathy, 'I heard if a master is more than fifteen minutes late, we're allowed to leave—'

The door banged open. Leaning against the door-frame, looking done with the lesson before it had begun, was Master Tybolt. They shuffled into the room, a mess of leaf-covered cloak. 'Good mornin', little brats.'

'"Morning"?' said Ennastasia.

'"Little brats"?' said Oswin.

With a spell, books zoomed onto every desk. 'Read,' said Tybolt, then stared out of a window, ignoring them.

Oswin swore a gadflyst buzzed between the pages of his book. Ennastasia took a finger and thumb and lifted the cover of her own. A loud crinkle greeted her.

Oswin whispered, 'What are we meant to be learning?'

'You really know nothing.' Ennastasia eyed Tybolt. 'Etymagery is the theory behind spell creation; how word choice affects spells.' She glared at Tybolt, now dozing. 'It demands focus, which that person does not possess.'

Oswin flicked through his book, skimming paragraphs on how spells were granted by one of the three magics. 'This is a textbook.'

'It's children's content. My tutor explained this when I was four. Everyone knows spells have three words or less, and that they're carefully worded requests to the magics. Or that –' she jabbed one particular paragraph – 'the fewer words a spell has, the stronger but riskier it is. This is painfully basic.'

'You had a tutor?'

'Of course. I'm a Ba—'

'Barkmoth. You might have mentioned that.'

While Ennastasia restrained herself from admonishing his insolence, Oswin read. His head swam with

Etymagery principles: rhymes sabotaged magic; 'Z' had a habit of turning hair black and white. He was wondering if that was what had happened to Master Crull and his badger-coloured hair when he heard murmurs.

'Are you sure it's wise to use a spellbook?' whispered Philomena.

Maury whispered back, 'You said it's your older brother's, right?'

'Yeah. He's back in the Huts. Hasn't even realized I've taken it. But you're not meant to use any spellbook except your own, remember? Or the spell goes horrifically wrong.'

'But surely if it works for him, and he's your family, it'll work for you? Please, I need help fitting the wooden spoke between the chains for the invention to resist enough force.'

'All right, hold on.'

Oswin saw Maury's contraption of chains and Philomena holding a spellbook. Dread sank in his stomach.

Philomena read, *'The Timber Slots.'*

When nothing happened, Maury frowned at his invention. 'What—?'

The cabin classroom, made from timber, tilted.

Oswin gripped his desk. Gravity claimed dust and cobwebs. Workbooks slid off tables. Floorboards splintered. Apprentices screamed.

Tybolt just snored.

The branches supporting the cabin started snapping. Ennastasia tried to run to Tybolt, but fell from the tilt.

Tybolt startled, finally noticing the issue. Oswin closed his eyes, wishing it were a dream. Tybolt lunged for their spellbook as the cabin broke loose, tumbling towards the ground.

'*The Timber Floats*,' Tybolt boomed.

Their fall slowed. The force pushed Oswin out of his chair as the cabin righted itself. It hovered back onto the thicker branches, the planks mending and cobwebs crawling back home. Once the danger had passed, Tybolt closed their spellbook, threw it onto a pile of clothes and fell back to sleep.

Philomena sheepishly pocketed her brother's spellbook. No one else had noticed it was her who'd caused the disaster.

Ennastasia went back to her chair. 'Honestly,' she said, unbothered. She looked at Oswin, curled on the floor. 'Are you quite all right?'

'No!'

'Hm.' She went back to reading.

After the lesson, and once he was back on the ground, Oswin collapsed into the snow, cold seeping between his fingers. He wondered briefly if the shrinking sphere could have been one of Yarrow's spells going wrong, like a ribcage being opened by a miscast spell or Philomena making the cabin fall. The next opportunity Oswin got, he'd ask the Spellbookery master, Crull. He *could* ask Master Tybolt, but he reckoned they were more likely to insult him than help.

Either way, he never wanted to go up to the Classroom Treehouse again.

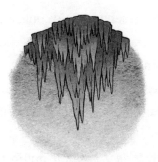

13

WORDS AND WATCHES

The next morning, Oswin told Master Crull his concern that the shrinking sphere could have been a mistake from Yarrow's spell.

'You're still harping on about that sphere?'

'I nearly died!' protested Oswin. 'It must have been a mistake. Why else would it have happened?'

'Yarrow? Make a mistake? She's one of the strongest spellcasters alive.'

'But surely it's possible that *one* of her spells could go awry?'

'It's utterly *im*possible.'

'At least can we agree there should be no more lessons

in the Classroom Treehouse? An entire class almost fell to their deaths.'

'Grow thicker skin,' snapped Crull.

'You won't increase the safety precautions?'

'Tundra wants the strong. Corridor won't coddle you, boy.'

Oswin wanted to tear his hair out in frustration, even if he was begrudgingly happy about the 'boy' comment. 'What if someone dies, though?'

Crull shrugged. 'Then they wouldn't have been much use as an adult.'

Oswin was floored by the callous sentiment.

Thankfully, none of his lessons on Secondday were in the suspended cabins of the Classroom Treehouse. AA&V – which his timetable said stood for Artificing, Alchemy and Vinderation – was going to be on the first floor of the Alchemy Lodge, in the room with the mountain-peak windows. He had to climb external stairs to get there, but it didn't scare him like the Etymagery cabin had. Besides, he was bursting to find out what Artificing, Alchemy and Vinderation actually *were*.

Inside, an interior balcony circled high above while the smell of singed wires and tangy potions drifted down. The weight of the air squashed talking into a soft murmur.

The walls were fitted with glass cabinets crammed with sludge and vapour, and ladders on rollers waited for some poor soul to plummet to their doom. Oswin couldn't look up as he approached the desks gathered around a blackboard.

When Ennastasia Barkmoth slid into the seat next to him, Oswin shot her a look.

The AA&V master tottered in, wearing a violet cloak and carrying boxes. She was a tiny woman with soot on her black skin, round glasses and bat-like ears that poked out of her short Afro, singed seemingly from some gone-wrong experiment.

As the bat-eared master – Jean Vervack according to the timetable – hefted her things onto the workstation, Oswin murmured, 'How come you're sitting next to me if we're not friends?'

'I hadn't noticed there were other seats.'

'They're right there—'

'Would you shut up? No one dares talk to me in the nosy manner you're so inclined.'

Holding his hands up, Oswin turned back to the master.

Ennastasia chewed her words with difficulty. 'I don't know how to do this,' she whispered, a helpless admittance. He realized with a bloom of sympathy that he might not be the only one new to making friends.

'Alchemy, Artificing and Vinderation,' Vervack said, excitement glinting in her eyes. 'Each a distinct branch of inventing but, for the sake of "simplicity",' she made a mocking tone as she said the word, 'we teach them as if they're the same until you're old enough to specialise. Frustrating, I know.' She smiled, clearly expecting them all to share her disapproval.

Vervack tasked the apprentices with taking apart and reconstructing citizen watches: pocket watches that always pointed to the Watchtower in Central Tundra. Scouters used them on the Endless Expanse so that, no matter how far they ventured in their search for metal, they could always return to Tundra. Vervack optimistically declared that she didn't care how many colleagues told her otherwise, *she* believed constructing citizen watches was a perfectly suitable task for first years. The apprentices nodded, not understanding what she was on about.

'Should we be teaching a stray this stuff?' Cathy asked, casting Oswin a glare. 'What if he goes onto the Endless Expanse and tells the other strays how to get here?'

Ennastasia snapped, 'Don't take us off-topic. Some of us are trying to learn.'

Cathy shut up, and Oswin felt a flush of gratitude.

'Continue,' Ennastasia prompted a wide-eyed Vervack, as if she were in charge.

As Oswin and Ennastasia worked on their citizen watches, a wordless challenge rose between them that each of theirs would be better than the other's. But it was clear no apprentice would be finishing their over-complex watch. Even Maury succumbed to an onset of shaking hands. At least he wasn't asking Philomena to cast cabin-ending spells with a stolen spellbook. Oswin wondered if Ennastasia had stolen her spellbook from a sibling like Philomena had. Ennastasia had mentioned a brother. Then again, her spellbook obeyed *without* disaster, and Philomena had mentioned that using someone else's spellbook always ended badly. The incident with the Etymagery cabin was proof enough of that for Oswin.

Vervack was so saddened by their 'shoddy watches' that she ended the lesson early, begged they pay attention next time and gestured at equations that looked as if they came from another millennium. Oswin swore he saw her wipe tears from her eyes, she was so upset by their failure.

'I think I did better than you,' said Oswin, nodding at Ennastasia's watch that was somehow gargling. 'Guess being a Barkmoth isn't everything.'

'You're a petulant wyrm. A trifling little gadflyst.'

'Wyrm?'

'Pink legless things that squirm in the dirt. *Airhead*.'

Oswin kept smiling. It was refreshing how Ennastasia bristled to hide her amusement. 'I need to ask Vervack a few questions,' he said as the other apprentices filed out.

Ennastasia crinkled her nose. 'Fine. I'll be outside.'

Oswin felt a happy rush. 'You'll wait for me?'

Ennastasia's mouth hung open. 'No . . . I just . . . want to admire the architecture of the lodge.'

He grinned.

'If that happens to take however long *you* take, then that's an unfortunate coincidence.'

He grinned wider.

'Oh . . . shut up,' she said, without malice, before storming outside.

This time, Oswin wasn't the only apprentice staying behind. Maury showed Vervack something before turning to leave, but then he spotted Oswin and approached, frowning seriously. Oswin worried he'd somehow upset him.

'I think I figured something out,' Maury whispered, taking Oswin to the side.

Oswin's heart leaped. 'What?'

'You were trapped in the shrinking sphere at the start of the year, right? Well . . .' He held out what he'd shown Vervack: a clear box containing a pebble. Carefully, he opened it and indicated Oswin pick it up. It was so smooth, it felt unnatural against his skin, and he couldn't place its colour. It was somewhere between blue and orange, or both, or neither. Its edges blurred.

'Put it in your pocket,' said Maury.

Curious, Oswin did, and his pocket shrank. Alarmed, he pulled the pebble out. His pocket returned to normal. Maury put the pebble in the box, sealing it tightly.

'How did it do that?' breathed Oswin.

'According to Vervack, it's a krimpsteen. They're really old, enchanted stones. They make stuff shrink and grow. It's how the masters' cabins change sizes: each one has a krimpsteen embedded in its timber.' Maury leaned closer. 'This is my best theory on how the sphere shrank.'

Oswin felt a weird jealousy that someone had found out more than him, then realized that was foolish. Maury had every right to wonder what had happened. He'd fainted as a result, after all.

If Maury had been investigating, Oswin *needed* to know what he'd discovered. 'Did you find anything else?'

'This is all I've got. A theory. Whatever happened with the sphere, intentional or accident, a krimpsteen caused it.'

Oswin's eyes flew wide. 'One of the masters' cabins wasn't shrunken.'

'What?'

'I walked by a masters' cabin one night. No one lives in it and, unlike the others, it wasn't shrunken.' Oswin didn't explain that he'd been there after a monster attack. Maybe that was unfair, given how much he wanted Maury to tell him everything he knew.

Maury looked thoughtful. 'So either the cabin's krimpsteen was broken or someone could have stolen it to shrink the sphere.' They exchanged an ominous look. 'I'm going to tell Grandmaster Yarrow. See you around. Don't be a stranger.'

Oswin waited until Maury was gone before walking to the front desk, feeling alive at understanding the shrinking sphere incident a little more. Maybe, if he was lucky, he could get more answers. 'Excuse me, I was wondering—'

'Sorry. No questions. I have an experiment to check on.' Vervack turned, balancing the boxes of broken citizen watches, and Oswin saw his chance of getting information melting between his fingers.

'It's not a question, but a concern!' he rushed out. 'I overheard apprentices saying they stole information on oddities from your office. I didn't see their faces, though.' *What's a lie when there's information to be gained?*

Vervack looked mildly horrified. 'On oddities?' Without

another word, she hurried further into the Alchemy Lodge. Oswin waited for the door to swing shut behind her before following. He peeked into the corridor beyond, glad the wall's torches were unlit, and spotted the end of Vervack's violet cloak disappear around a corner.

Ducking into small cloakrooms any time another master crossed his path, Oswin traced Vervack's steps. He was spying from the end of a low-roofed corridor when he saw her dart into her office and heard her heft some boxes onto a desk. Padding silently, he crouched by the closed door and peeped through the keyhole.

He saw a stuffy room filled with alarming contraptions: what he imagined Maury's room looked like, only ten times more crammed. Silver and bronze needles glinted in frames. Glass baubles with swirling powders hovered by the ceiling. Stacks of dusty tomes were shoved into every crevice, including splintered dents in the wooden walls.

Vervack ran her hand along one shelf, her fingers stopping against an unloved file. She hummed in confusion, clearly surprised to find that the report Oswin had claimed was stolen was very much *not* stolen.

Oswin, though, felt alight with victory. The report wasn't stolen *for now*, because he knew it existed, and where it was.

Vervack returned to the door and Oswin's victory

became a stab of panic. He glanced at the hinges, seeing the door swung outwards, and pressed against the wall. With a creak, Vervack pushed it open, and Oswin gulped back a yelp when it bumped against his nose. Putting his hand to the aching sensation, he held his breath as Vervack walked off, the door keeping him mercifully hidden as it slowly swung shut.

Before it closed fully, Oswin darted inside, letting it clack loudly at the right moment, *just in case* Vervack's bat-like ears would notice it taking too long.

He rushed to grab the file – all ten yellowed pages of it – and snatched it from the shelf. He flicked through, imprinting everything into his memory before properly reading it. It waffled a *lot*, talking about dozens of ancient theories. Nothing interested him until the final page. According to the report, in the early days of Tundra, people believed in more than just timber, fog and coal magic. Some theorized there was ice, shadow, glass or even *ghost* magic.

Oswin stared at the word. 'Steal The Ghost?' he echoed, reading on. Ancient alchemists had claimed an oddity – a sort of relic – existed for every type of magic. Some suggested humans could fuse with them. Oswin squinted at Vervack's scrawls in the margins. She thought it was 'pseudo-Alchemy nonsense'.

Answers started to piece together. The voice had told him to 'Steal The Ghost'. If one of the sorts of magic was ghost magic, and a ghost oddity or relic existed, maybe he had to steal it. Of course, Oswin had no idea what the oddity for ghost magic could be, or if it existed.

To his crushing disappointment, the report had nothing else of use. He shoved it back onto the shelf and glared around the room. He tried to console himself that, between this and the revelation of the krimpsteen, he was closer to understanding what was going on. Consoling himself even further, he rummaged through the boxes and pocketed the citizen watch he'd worked on. Arranging the delicate cogs felt like picking a lock. He wanted to spend more time examining it, even if its complexity befuddled him.

Finished, he reached for the handle to leave, but before he could, the door flew open.

'You *overheard apprentices had stolen from my office*?' said Vervack softly, an eyebrow raised. 'Do you think I've a mamat's mind?'

Oswin's heart thudded so hard it held his tongue. Vervack stepped into the room and Oswin, in a panic, threw open a window and scrambled onto the sill in some desperate attempt at escape. He froze, seeing the gap between himself and the snow below. This was the first floor, after all.

'Don't!' Vervack cried in alarm, but before she could stop him, he had slipped on the icy ledge. A yelp ripped out of Oswin as he fell.

14

THE ONE WHO CAME BACK

O swin couldn't think; he could only feel cold fear as he fell. It wasn't for long, but his panic still dazed him, even well after he'd landed with a spray of white in the snow. He stared at the sky, hyperventilating until Vervack rushed outside, first to worriedly check on him, then to glare.

'Get up, young man,' she said. Oswin couldn't, so she hauled him to his feet. 'You're lucky you aren't hurt. Fog above, what *were* you doing?'

Oswin opened and closed his mouth, scrambling for an excuse as Vervack led him towards the masters' cabins. His mind latched on to the only thing he could think of.

'I wanted to keep working on my citizen watch. I was miserable I didn't finish it in the lesson.'

'Cry me a stalactite. That doesn't mean you can use some half-melted lie to break into my office.' Her eyes narrowed. 'You weren't thinking of using a citizen watch to go into the Teeth That Snatch, were you? You wouldn't be the first. Citizen watches don't work in there. Nothing does. You wouldn't have come back.'

'That's not what I was doing at all!' He resisted Vervack's pulling for a second. 'How can you know citizen watches don't work in the Teeth That Snatch if no one who goes in comes back?'

'One person did,' Vervack let slip, then came to a sudden halt. They both stood still, apprentice and master staring at each other.

Oswin stained the silence first. 'One person did?'

'I didn't say that.'

'You did.'

'I was making an educated guess. If citizen watches worked in the Teeth, Tundrans would simply follow them back out.'

Oswin's eyes searched her face. 'Who came out of the Teeth?'

'No one.' Vervack started leading him again, the masters' cabins growing closer. Oswin *was* horrified he'd be kicked out of Corridor for his second offence, but he was mainly angry Vervack wasn't answering his questions.

'What's going on?' came a voice.

Oswin and Vervack stopped, looking behind to see Ennastasia scowling.

'Run along now,' said Vervack politely.

'Let him go,' countered Ennastasia.

'This doesn't concern you—'

'I can make it concern me. I can make it concern my *grandfather.*'

Vervack's eyes shot wide. After a glower from Ennastasia, she let Oswin go. To Oswin, she said, 'If I catch you somewhere you shouldn't be again, I'll use you as a test subject for my degeneration potion.' Vervack's glare was so intense, her large round glasses magnifying it, that Oswin didn't doubt the threat. 'You're lucky you have a powerful friend,' she added, Ennastasia flinching at the word. With a bow of reluctant respect to Ennastasia, Vervack walked away.

Oswin turned to Ennastasia. 'Thank you. I owe you—'

'You have to stop talking to me.' Her voice was small. Frightened. She didn't meet his gaze. 'I told you, we're not going to be friends. We *can't* be. Stop getting yourself in trouble and ...' She pursed her lips. 'Leave me alone.'

She turned sharply, stomping through the snow. Oswin watched her, feeling frustrated, then quickly reminded himself that he was a stray. He didn't get to be frustrated with a Tundran.

Next was Preparation for the Worst, or 'Pufftow', taught by Rochelle. The worst was facing monsters, the best was avoiding them, and the compromise was fleeing. After an hour of running, hiding and sparring, Oswin's chest compressor was uncomfortably sweaty, but at least – as he gathered his things at the end of the lesson – he realized it had distracted him from thinking about Ennastasia.

'Don't touch that!' Maury snapped. Oswin looked up. Maury was hiding a paper-wrapped book below her arm, glaring at Philomena, but then her expression turned to shame. 'Sorry. I shouldn't snap. I'm just tired. What were you saying?'

'Before I reached for your *precious* book, you mean?' teased Philomena as they both walked to lunch. 'Just that I'll become as strong as High Watcher Greyheart.'

Oswin wanted a closer look at this mysterious book. Besides, Maury *had* told him not to be a stranger, so he decided to catch up to them. 'Why do you want to be like Greyheart?' he asked.

Philomena smiled welcomingly at him. 'Because he's a war hero.'

'He is?' His eyes flicked down to the book.

Maury shifted it so it was out of sight. 'He leads the Watcher's Ring now, but back in the day, it was *him* who stopped Michael Fiel—' She swallowed her words, and Oswin clenched his teeth as if he'd got a splinter, thoughts of the mysterious book vanishing. He gave a resigned shrug and slowed his pace, feeling foolish for trying to speak to them. Maury went to say something, but a wailing made everyone freeze.

Rochelle was unperturbed. 'That would be the toothoot.' A bird – large and thin, with a stretched-out face and turquoise feathers – swooped down to land on Rochelle's head. Oswin abruptly realized Rochelle's hat didn't just look like a bird's nest. It *was* one.

Apprentices tried to pet the bird, but Rochelle shooed them towards the cafeteria. Oswin endured a lonely lunch of hiding from Maury and Philomena before going to his next lesson: Culture. It was taught by Yarrow in the trunk of the Classroom Treehouse, which was mercifully on the ground floor in a hollowed-out room within the tree. After the lesson Oswin happily repeated to himself every Tundran tradition he'd learned as he walked back out onto the snow.

Ennastasia appeared at his side.

He scowled at her. 'If you don't want to be friends, why do you keep coming near me?' He tried to keep irritation out of his voice. He was a stray. Ennastasia was a Tundran. He shouldn't be annoyed with her, but he was losing his patience.

Ennastasia leaned past him, nodding towards the distance. 'My grandfather. He's come to visit me.'

On the horizon was an aged man in impressive-looking attire, his white skin wrinkled.

'So?'

'I'm using you to hide from him.' Ennastasia kept low.

'Oh. Why didn't you say so?' Oswin held his cloak to make sure she was out of sight. 'And you're hiding from him because . . . ?'

'None of your business.'

'I'm helping you, here.'

Ennastasia puffed her cheeks, then said, reluctantly, 'I don't particularly like him.'

Oswin was about to ask why when he saw the distant man's gaze sink to the base of Oswin's cloak; he'd spotted Ennastasia's boots peeking out below. He sped towards them. 'We've been found out. You'll have to re-hide.'

But fear seemed to strangle Ennastasia's words. Even in the shrinking sphere, she hadn't looked so worried.

Oswin glanced around for someone to help, and spotted Yarrow wheeling towards a large mound of snow behind the Classroom Treehouse. He shoved Ennastasia ahead of him, guiding them both in her direction, but her grandfather was gaining on them.

'He's fast for his age,' said Oswin. The man looked as if he'd seen countless Freezes.

'And cruel.' Ennastasia's lips pressed into a thin line. 'What's your plan?'

'Ask Yarrow for help.'

Ennastasia groaned. 'Re-hiding would have been better.'

They reached Yarrow, who turned to peer through her spectacles at them. 'How can I help?'

Oswin, out of breath, said, 'We need to be busy. So busy we can't talk.'

Yarrow looked beyond them, seeing what had concerned them. 'As it happens, I was about to attend to a vital chore. I *could* entertain two helpers, but I don't need to.'

'Please,' said Ennastasia, and Oswin did a double-take. 'What?'

'I didn't know you knew that word.'

She glared. 'Ha ha.'

Crunching footsteps announced her grandfather's

arrival. His cold eyes took them in, lips pressed firmly in a way that reminded Oswin of Ennastasia. For a pause, no one said anything.

'Harnan Barkmoth,' Yarrow greeted with all the friendliness of an icicle to the eye.

'I'm here to speak to my granddaughter,' Harnan responded in just as cool a voice. Ennastasia edged away from him.

Yarrow gestured behind her. 'I'm afraid she's helping me with Reusie. Of course, you may remain as we wake her for feeding if you would like to speak to Ennastasia. Though, I'd advise caution. You were nearly crushed by Reusie when you were an apprentice, correct?'

Oswin looked over his shoulder at the snow mound, finally noticing how it rose and fell. *Something* was buried there, breathing. Something *huge*.

Harnan's head twitched in a stifled movement. When he spoke it was with a cold, crawling speed. 'Another time, perhaps.' He looked at Ennastasia, and Oswin was grateful it wasn't him under that lethal gaze. 'We *will* speak soon.'

He marched away and Ennastasia's shoulders collapsed in relief.

'I've helped you.' Yarrow turned to the miniature mountain of snow. 'Now, you help me.'

15

REUSIE THE OBSIDIAN

Oswin and Ennastasia craned their necks to take in the hill of white. Fragments of snow ghosted off the top, spinning through the air. Yarrow pulled something silver from a pocket.

Oswin pointed, surprised. 'That's a citizen watch.'

Yarrow sighed. 'Vervack tried to get your class to construct citizen watches, didn't she?'

Ennastasia crossed her arms. 'It was ridiculously difficult.'

'She never learns.' Yarrow sounded more fond than annoyed. She popped off the back panel of the watch, then handed a small tool to Oswin and tweezers to Ennastasia. Holding the citizen watch flat, Yarrow directed Oswin to hold a cog still and told Ennastasia to move a small metal cube to it. But Ennastasia moved it too enthusiastically, and it smashed into the cog. It let out a petrifying screech and Oswin thrust his hands over his ears. He bent in agony, seeing the air shaking like pond ripples. The noise increased, and his vision blurred, a silent cry falling from his mouth. The earth shook and he fell to his side, his balance failing.

With a sudden snap, Yarrow silenced the watch, and every muscle in Oswin's body slackened. He removed his hands cautiously, feeling as if the world was spinning. A nasty headache chewed his brain. Dizzy, he looked around. Ennastasia was on the ground as well, looking both unwell and furious, while Yarrow calmly took out a set of ear plugs.

'I hadn't expected you to move the signal regulator so harshly,' Yarrow admitted, 'but at least I'm certain that will have done the job.' She indicated the hill, which was getting taller, snow breaking off in clumps. Oswin flipped onto his back and shuffled away as the snow continued to rise. With a growling rumble, the white flakes flung off as the creature shook herself clean.

A three-metre-tall giant stood above them, her dark grey beard knotted with ice, her obsidian stone body jagged at the edges and gleaming in the sunlight.

'Good morning, Reusie.' Yarrow beamed at the giant. Reusie leaned down so her humongous head hovered above Yarrow, large enough that, if she tipped forward a bit more, Yarrow would be crushed.

Reusie opened her mouth and a low bellow rumbled out of her. A hundred small insects of the same dark obsidian, and a handful of feathered sticelings, fluttered off her back. Her grumble wasn't as loud as the citizen watch had been, but it shuddered through Oswin's flesh with its deeper tone. He realized the ground shaking hadn't been from the watch, but the force of Reusie moving.

'Care for breakfast?' Yarrow clicked a box open. Oswin got shakily to his feet, wanting to move away from Reusie, but desperate enough to know what was in the box that he leaned forward instead. He saw a dense cube of ice. With two fingers, and an incredibly slow movement, Reusie popped it into her mouth. With one crunch, the ice was devoured, and Reusie lumbered back to her sleeping spot. She curled up and fell right back to sleep.

Yarrow closed the box and patted it contentedly. 'I'll be back to give her lunch in two years.'

Oswin's eyes bulged. 'Two years?'

'She's very sleepy.'

Ennastasia, who had returned to her own feet quicker than Oswin, looked at Reusie. 'Evidently.' Snow was already dusting onto Reusie as the gentle rise and fall of her chest grew imperceptible.

'It's good to see the both of you making friends,' added Yarrow, turning her chair to depart. Oswin wrinkled his nose in anticipation, glancing at Ennastasia, who had the expression of someone who'd just been slapped.

'I'm not making friends,' Ennastasia said. 'We're not ... I'm not ...' She threw her hands up. 'Whatever. Have a good day, Yarrow. Thank you for your help.'

Oswin felt the bite of tears and then frustration. He berated himself. He was a stray. Ennastasia was Tundran. So on, so forth.

Ennastasia stormed off, in much the same manner her grandfather had minutes before. Oswin wondered, if his own uncle were still alive and in Tundra, if he'd be as intimidating as Harnan Barkmoth.

'Do you need anything?' Yarrow asked him.

He wanted to ask questions – because of course he did; there was little else that could make him feel better after another Ennastasia abandonment – and decided not to beat around the bush. 'I want to know about Michael Fields.'

Yarrow fell still. 'I understand you didn't learn Tundran customs growing up, so let me make one thing clear: in Tundra, your family is who you share your last name with.

Michael Fields is your uncle and he was abhorrent. You are his nephew. You cannot be seen investigating him. People will get the wrong idea.'

'Can't I at least know why Michael did those horrid things?'

'Because he'd sacrifice everything on the altar of survival.' Yarrow gestured towards the dormitories. 'The chore is over. You may go.'

'One more thing. Do you know anything about oddities?'

Yarrow fixed him with a harsh look from behind her spectacles. 'I said not to investigate Michael Fields.'

Prickles formed along Oswin's back. That question *hadn't* been about Michael. So how was his uncle connected to oddities? He opened his mouth to ask as much, then decided he didn't want Yarrow to know what she'd let slip. 'Right. Thanks. Bye.'

Yarrow watched him go, brow furrowed.

16

A HEIST IS BORN

At night, when no one else would be around, Oswin traipsed down the curved-enough-to-mess-with-your-head corridor, which was also not-curved-enough-to-notice. He fiddled with his citizen watch as he went. He'd got in the habit of taking it everywhere with him. When his nerves about the Utility Proving grew unmanageable, he tinkered with it.

The corridor opened onto the common room. An interior tree was twined with orbs of light, gleaming like scales that, unlike candles, didn't flicker or emit heat. Oswin much preferred them. There *was* a firepit further down, but thankfully it was nothing but soft embers. Roots spread over floorboards from the tree and hanging chairs swayed from branches. Paintings of mamats, their manes of ears listening for predators, hung on the walls.

Oswin braved steps to a mezzanine – because books waited at the top – and grabbed a handful before sitting by a globe. The air smelled of dusty paper, and the ceiling arched within reach of his fingertips.

None of the books explained oddities. One mentioned Huvect, a card game where miniature monsters battled each other. Another talked about survivalism, a view that anyone not ideal for survival should be committed to the ice. Supposedly, it had caused civil war during the Great Freeze. Oswin had a sneaking suspicion the following ripped-out pages would have spoken about Michael Fields.

He thumbed through a picture book, *Creatures of Tundra and Beyond*, which showed long-furred animals dashing between shrubs and ice snakes gripping swords with their tails. On its final page was a human with arrows pointing to a variety of creatures. He saw mamats, sticelings and vohoonts, which were furry four-legged creatures with bird-heads and wagging tails. Without words explaining the images, he was only annoyed.

When he'd exhausted the reading, he walked back to

the firepit, staring anxiously at the ashes. The embers stared back.

The noise of footsteps pulled him from his trance.

'I thought everyone would be asleep,' said Ennastasia, looking as surprised to see him as he was her.

'Why were you waiting for everyone to be asleep?'

'Why aren't *you* asleep?'

They stared at each other, and an unspoken bet on who could hold their tongue the longest formed.

Without knowing why, Oswin blurted, 'My brother gave me my hat when Tundra took me in six years ago.'

Ennastasia leaned against the tree-trunk, her face shadowed.

'He left to become an ice apprentice. My mother told me I'd never get that chance because—'

'You're a stray.'

Oswin nodded shamefully. 'I thought I'd never come here, thought I'd hardly see my brother, but when I wore the hat it felt as if I had a piece of him with me. I felt just as rugged and grown up as him.' Oswin took his hat off, holding it tightly. 'There's the answer to your question from our first day. That's where I got this hat.' He gestured at her earring. 'Where did you get that?'

Ennastasia pushed off the tree. 'It's ...' She clenched her fists. 'We're not going to be friends. Not because you're a stray, to be clear,' she said, evidently noticing his miserable look. 'If I ever gave you the impression a stray shouldn't be here, then I was, well, not *wrong*, because I'm never *wrong*, but maybe I was being a tad unfair.' She looked as if she was trying to fit a square block into a circular gap, her words a struggle. 'I couldn't care less where you got the hat. I was just throwing a question back at you when you asked about my earring. If you have any sense, you'll stop bothering me, and stop trying to be my friend.'

His annoyance unleashed itself, so strong he couldn't restrain it any more. '*You* keep sitting next to *me*. *You* keep walking over to *me*.'

Ennastasia clenched her jaw. She didn't have a response.

Oswin made a split-second choice. 'What if I knew something interesting?' He hadn't shared what he'd found with anyone else, and though he felt as if Ennastasia was the least likely person to believe him, he knew she'd be brutally honest.

Ennastasia's glare intensified. 'As I said, I couldn't care less.' She turned on her heel.

'Not even about a mystery?'

Ennastasia kept walking.

Ignoring his brain screaming against sharing information, he said, 'When the monster fled, it shrank into a human.' He felt as if he'd stepped off the Wice and was plummeting. He was sure Ennastasia was about to tell him he'd lost his mind, then report him to Grandmaster Yarrow and get him kicked out.

Ennastasia stopped. Oswin could practically hear her arguing with herself on what to do. Decision made, she advanced on him. Oswin fell into a chair, pressing fearfully against its back.

Ennastasia stared with a fierce expression, then sat in the neighbouring chair. 'Expand.'

'Expand?'

'Yes. Expand on what you've just said. Unless your air-inclined skull has reached the conclusion that I want you to build an extension to Spruce Dorm.'

Oswin faltered for only a second. 'I checked the day after the attack. It was impossible to be certain, but the monster's footprints could have changed to human footprints.'

'Have you told the masters?'

'No. I could be mistaken.'

Ennastasia snorted. 'Your lack of common sense is astounding.'

'I'm already telling you all I know; there's no need to flatter me.'

Ennastasia lips turned into a snarl, but Oswin relaxed.

There was no doubt; there *was* an amused smirk below it. This was what he'd wanted every time he'd joked with Lullia. Or anyone, really: the fake annoyance that welcomed more teasing.

She leaned back in her chair and crossed her legs, her ruby earring catching the faint light from the embers. 'So long as you don't know what it means to be a Barkmoth, you'll keep being rude to me, won't you?'

'Oh, absolutely.' Oswin tried to snarl-smirk himself. From the amused look on Ennastasia's face, it wasn't working. He blamed his sad eyes. 'Especially if *you're* rude to *me.*'

'I get to be rude. I'm me. You, on the other hand—'

'*I* haven't finished my story.'

'Get on with it then, Os-*will-regret-the-way-he's-talking-to-me-one-day*-win.'

'Ridiculous name.'

'Ridiculous person.'

Oswin snorted, then steeled himself. He said, as if pulling out a tooth, 'I've been hearing a voice.'

'Always a good sign.' Ennastasia's eyes were oddly fixated on the ashes of the firepit.

'I've heard it twice – once in my room and again when that *thing*, the meersnof, appeared.'

'What did it say?'

'*Oswin Fields, Steal The Ghost.*'

The wind howled outside. Oswin swore it was louder than last week, and a sinking worry that the Freeze was drawing near gripped him. He pushed it aside and explained everything he'd found out, from the shrinking sphere, to the krimpsteen, to the potential existence of a ghost oddity. He failed to mention that everyone had, resoundingly, told him oddities didn't exist. 'What do you think?'

Ennastasia looked at the ceiling, exhaling. 'Sometimes hearing voices is a sign that you need support from the Icefirmary.'

'Icefirmary?'

'Correct.'

'As in "infirmary" but with "ice" at the front?'

Ennastasia shifted uncomfortably. 'Correct.'

Oswin snorted, amused.

'There are, however,' Ennastasia continued, 'rare occasions when a voice can originate from *beyond*.'

'Like ghosts?'

Ennastasia made an unimpressed face. 'No. Like magic, you dingbat.' She tutted. 'Ghosts, *honestly*.'

'But it *is* asking me to Steal The Ghost.'

'If this voice isn't the result of a condition of your mind, then it's from magic. If it's magic, it will be communicating in a way your tiny human brain wouldn't be able to understand. "Steal The Ghost" won't mean literally stealing a ghost.' She added, under her breath, 'They don't even exist.'

'They might.'

'Logic dictates they don't. A human is their physical composition. Take that away and there's no human and therefore no ghost. Claiming ghosts exist is like claiming you can have soup without any ingredients.'

Oswin held up his hands. 'If you say so.' He hesitated. 'Soup would be really nice right about now ...'

'If this voice is from magic and you heard it around the same time that monster appeared, I'd wager the two are linked. It's the best lead you have. You'll need to break into the research quarters in the Alchemy Lodge and look for books tangentially related to the phrase "Steal The Ghost".'

Excitement speared Oswin. 'Research quarters?' Then he frowned. '*Tangentially?*'

'Just ...' She pinched the bridge of her nose. 'Break into the Alchemy Lodge. See if you can find books that mention stealing ghosts.'

'Don't you mean *we*?'

Ennastasia stood, dusting her uniform. 'No. As I said, we're not going to be friends.'

'What if you came along for the ride? I'll do the sneaking; you just watch.'

'Why in Tundra would I do that?'

'For the same reason you claim to have stood by when that monster attacked me. Academic interest.'

She mulled it over, then grimaced as though she'd stepped on a pin. 'Oh, all right. I'll come along, but if you get into trouble, I'm not helping.'

'Great.' He jumped to his feet. 'Let's go.'

'Now?'

'Yes!' A bounce in his step, he jogged to the end of the common room. 'The day is far from born, the night far from old. Let's break into the Alchemy Lodge!'

Ennastasia followed, pulling gloves out of her cloak. 'Without any prep work?'

'Don't need it. No one can see me if I don't want them to.'

'The meersnof found you despicably easily.'

'Details.' Oswin wafted his hand as he pushed the door open, the cold night air blustering in. He didn't mention the odd pulling sensation he'd felt towards the beast.

They crunched through the snow to the Alchemy Lodge. Already, Oswin was envisioning every architectural feature of the lodge, figuring out the best way in. He was also trying to ignore how the snowfall was thicker, the snowflakes clustered in heavy clumps instead of soft droplets.

Unprompted, Ennastasia said, 'You clearly like asking questions and we have time before we reach the lodge.'

Oswin's mouth parted, the cold bite of the wind hitting the back of his throat as he was violently pulled from his scheming. 'Are you *inviting* me to ask questions?' He'd never liked Ennastasia more than right then.

Ennastasia scowled. 'Forget I said anything.' When the happy look on Oswin's face crumbled, she sighed. 'One question. You enjoy them, obviously.' She added, harshly, 'This isn't because we're friends, I just ... It's polite to offer something in return for getting to watch your shenanigans.'

Oswin thought *very* carefully. 'What does it mean to be a Barkmoth?'

A glower settled on Ennastasia's face. 'Let me make one thing clear. If you want to be frien— *acquaintances*, you must *never* look into my family.'

'But you've always gone on about how I should know what it means to be a Bark—'

'And now I'm telling you to leave it alone.' Her glower turned lethal. 'I'll answer any question, but not that. Promise me you won't look into Barkmoths.'

'All right.'

'*Promise me.*'

'I promise,' said Oswin sincerely.

'Good.'

Oswin thought some more. 'How about this instead: what are the lights that appear in the night sky?'

'They're the expressions of magic. Also known as eoms. When the lights appear, magic is at its strongest.'

Oswin smiled, content at having one mystery solved. 'Thank you.'

'I could answer another one,' said Ennastasia, her face flushing. 'Not because I'm being nice. Just to fill the time.'

'Of course, of course.' Oswin's mind raced through the hundreds of questions he was desperate to ask. 'What would be the best way to pass the Utility Proving?'

'Depends on what it is.' She glanced at Oswin, considering. At last, she said, 'The Watcher's Ring decide the trials. They're the most influential Tundrans. They tell Grandmaster Yarrow what the Utility Provings will be, and she has to do as they say, no matter how dangerous or impractical.'

Oswin's eyebrows shot up. 'Really?'

'Yes.' She looked as if she was chewing on her words. 'Which is why it's fortunate that I've, shall we say, *overheard* what the first Utility Proving is going to be. If you wanted to ask a question about it.' She held up a hand. 'About the Utility Proving. *Not* how I got the information.'

'What's it going to be?' he asked straight away.

'A team-versus-team battle on a bridge over the Plughole. One team has to get an object to the other side; the other has to steal it from them.' She shivered in the cold. 'In answer to your earlier question, on how to pass it, I'd recommend teaming up with someone highly competent.'

Oswin's eyes twinkled. 'Someone like you?'

Ennastasia averted her gaze. 'I never said that . . .'

'You're not highly competent, after all.'

Ennastasia gaped at him, then lightly punched his arm. 'Rude!'

Oswin grinned. 'Thank you.'

Ennastasia frowned at him.

'Annoying-moth,' Oswin said fondly.

'Stop calling me that.'

'I never called you "that".'

Ennastasia opened her mouth to say something, then groaned when she got his awful joke. 'I'm not speaking to you for the rest of the heist.'

'Ooh, it's a *heist* now. I've never been on a heist!'

'Shut up.' But she was smiling, too.

Taking her advice, as they had reached the Alchemy Lodge, he shut up.

17

THE BOOK OF ODDITIES

The doors to the cafeteria were shut tight and the key holes were X-shaped. Oswin had no clue how to pick them.

'Guess we'll have to try another night,' said Ennastasia.

'Nope. We won't.' Oswin ascended external stairs leading to the first-floor balcony. He found heights easier in the dark, when it was harder to see, but his heartbeat picked up all the same. 'Here.'

By the mountain-peak-shaped windows was the door to the AA&V classroom. The lock was normal. He pulled out his lock picks.

'What are you doing?'

'Shh,' said Oswin to an indignant look from Ennastasia as he listened to the movement of the pins. Once they were in place, the turning pressure clicked the lock open. He bowed victoriously.

Ennastasia rolled her eyes. 'Very impressive.' She walked in and lowered her voice. 'The research quarters are up there.' She gestured at the internal balcony.

Oswin craned his neck, his eyes trailing up glass cabinets and ladders on rollers. 'Is . . . there another way?'

'Further into the lodge, yes, but final-year apprentices will be there, working on their projects.' She looked flatly at Oswin. 'You'll be caught, and I don't think Vervack will listen to me a second time.'

'Maybe we shouldn't be doing this, after all. Let's just—'

'It's only a ladder.' Ennastasia stepped onto one. Oswin watched its rollers shift. 'So long as you don't let go, you'll be fine.' She was a quarter of the way up in a few breaths.

'Right.' Oswin put his hands on one of the ladder's rungs. 'Sure.' He stared at it, not moving.

Ennastasia hopped onto the balcony, crouched at the edge and peered down. 'Come on.'

Oswin looked, unblinking, at his hands. 'Am I halfway up?'

'Are you half— Oswin, you're on the floor.'

He saw both his feet firmly planted on a rug. He looked

back at Ennastasia, the height making him want to empty his stomach. 'I'm taking a different route.'

Ennastasia threw her arms up. 'You've got to be kidding me. For timber's sake, *climb*.'

'Wait there.' Oswin pushed away from the ladder, feeling as if his hands were burning from where they'd gripped the rungs.

Ennastasia put a hand to her face. 'Utterly useless.' As Oswin moved to the double doors at the back, he tried to ignore how hollow the word 'useless' made him feel.

In the corridor beyond, sounds were compressed by tapestries and curtains, and the air was blemished with the scent of smoke from the unlit torches. Oswin's eyes darted from one torch to another, worried they'd burst to life. He kept low and reached a turning point. Hearing shuffling feet and a yawn as someone flicked through crinkling pages, he waited until whoever it was moved on before he continued.

This new corridor had lit torches, creating a loathsome glow. He found a set of stairs leading up, just as the footsteps returned. He ducked into the stairwell, pressing against the wall.

Someone walked by, short and with pencils tucked behind her bat-like ears: Master Vervack. He held still, not daring to breathe.

Vervack didn't notice the shadow pressed against the wall, and Oswin's shoulders drooped in relief. Once she was out of sight, he continued up. He tracked every step, a three-dimensional map forming in his mind. Based on the height of each corridor, he'd need to ascend two more floors to reach Ennastasia.

He got to the third floor without incident, but as he sneaked to the fourth, rushed footsteps headed towards him. He didn't have time to hide, so he removed his trapper hat, pulled his neck scarf down and straightened, assuming the walk of someone who was meant to be there. He continued as if all was well with the world.

A final-year apprentice turned the corner, eyes snapping onto him.

Oswin gave them a smile. 'Long night, eh?'

'You're telling me.' They didn't question why he was there, just moved onto the floor below, out of sight.

Oswin's shoulders sagged. He flopped his hat back on.

The second he stepped onto the fourth floor, he saw the internal balcony of the AA&V classroom. To his frustration, it was empty. He didn't hiss Ennastasia's name – that could give him away – so he crept to a corridor on the other side. The shuffling of Master Vervack, who he realized was below in the AA&V classroom, grew distant.

The new corridor was dim and narrow, and he felt like a mamat rushing through its den. Every wall – even the ceiling, somehow – was lined with books. Eventually the corridor, though it felt more like a tunnel, reached a circular room. In the centre was Ennastasia.

'I told you to wait!' said Oswin.

'I had better things to do.' Ennastasia stared at an empty space in the shelf.

Oswin stood next to her. 'What is it?'

Ennastasia gestured at a logbook on a desk. 'I checked for the key words "Steal The Ghost" and it pointed me in the direction of one book.'

Oswin inspected the logbook. Curious, he picked up a pencil tied to it by a golden chain and wrote 'Steal The Ghost'. The words swirled, giving him the number '205'. Moving back to Ennastasia, he saw '205' was written in gold below the empty spot on the shelf. 'It's gone.'

Ennastasia looked at him, mystified. 'No ... Really? I hadn't noticed.'

Oswin pointed to prove his point, then realized she was being sarcastic. 'Very funny.'

'Here's the thing.' Ennastasia went back to the logbook. She wrote '205' and the words swirled into '*The Book of Oddities*'. Oswin hovered at her shoulder. At the sight of 'oddities', his pulse electrified.

Ennastasia wrote '*The Book of Oddities*' and the words shifted again: 'Not on loan.' 'No one's taken it out.'

'But someone must have. It's not here.'

'Because it was *stolen*.'

His eyes widened. 'The exact book the voice led us to has been stolen?'

'Led *you* to. As I said before, this isn't a coincidence.' She went quiet, her eyes fixed on the empty space.

'What?'

She reached inside, pulling out a dark hair the length of her forearm.

'Why was that there?'

Ennastasia made a face. 'Because our thief has dark hair, *obviously*. You're marvellous with memory but dreadful at deduction.'

Oswin returned to the logbook, trying different phrases. 'Oddities' only listed the missing book, 'Shrinking spheres' took him to a tome on melting boulders, 'I'll be there when you plant it' a manual on gardening, and 'Fuse with magic' a romance novel.

Ennastasia looked over his shoulder. 'Fuse with magic,' she echoed.

'People used to think certain humans could fuse with oddities.'

Ennastasia took the pencil, changing the words to

'Merge with magic'. The letters reformed into *'Obscure Theories and Obscurer Theorisers'*.

Oswin's eyebrows rose. 'That looks promising.'

'We'll see.' Ennastasia walked to where the book was meant to be: slot fifty. Thankfully, it hadn't been stolen. She tugged it with difficulty out of the tight fit, then rifled through. 'No, no, no, no . . .' She stopped. 'Here. Does this look familiar?'

Oswin peered at the passage. It explained how a theme of merging with powerful relics was found throughout Tundran myths, from Kaldine the Ice Charmer to Ovi the Oblivious. More often than not, merging led to disastrous consequences for the human, including experiencing time stopping, creating uncontrollable fire, and losing control of their body. Humans were, apparently, too different and frail to withstand the objects' effects.

'A bit familiar,' said Oswin.

'It *sounds* like people merging with oddities.' Ennastasia checked the rest of the book, but it had nothing. She put it back, her hands inexplicably trembling.

'You okay?'

'Fine,' she said sharply, so Oswin left it there.

He tried a few more words in the logbook, but to no avail. When Ennastasia had had enough, she marched to the exit and Oswin had to grab her cloak to stop her before her loud walking alerted Master Vervack.

'Wait,' he whispered as Ennastasia shook him off. He pointed down. When Ennastasia saw why he'd grabbed her, her anger cooled. They waited, Ennastasia peeking over the balcony because doing so made Oswin queasy, until Vervack tottered out of the room.

The coast clear, Ennastasia descended the ladder while Oswin took the stairs. This time, no final-year apprentices crossed his path, and wherever Master Vervack had gone it was far enough away that he didn't encounter her. He did spot Master Pin dragging a timber log behind her, but she was so enamoured with it, she didn't notice him creep by.

'Come on,' said Ennastasia, waiting outside. 'I need to tell Grandmaster Yarrow.'

Oswin let out an alarmed noise. 'What? Why?'

'Because something deeply wrong is going on. The monster, the voice, the missing book, the changing footprints . . . I need to inform the faculty.'

'Don't you mean *we*?'

Ennastasia stomped through the snow in the direction of the masters' cabins. 'If I'd meant "we" that's what I would have said. *I* need to tell them because I'm a Barkmoth. *I* won't get in trouble. But if they know you've been snooping—' She cut off, cleared her throat, then said, 'I meant to say, I'll be the one telling them, because we're not friends. I'd rather not be associated with you.'

Oswin would have felt sad, but the sky had started to glow. He smiled at the lights, the cold barely registering as he enjoyed the bliss of understanding what he was seeing. Violet lights flowed in the air. With sharp movements they snapped to green and then red. An eom. Despite what Ennastasia had just said, he felt like hugging her for giving him knowledge.

There was a prickle on the back of Oswin's neck, like a puff of warm breath. His sense of bliss vanished. Goose bumps tingled his arms, and he felt a pulling sensation on his limbs. He stopped walking, his boots sinking into the snow as a noise reverberated in his ears, both near and far. It crescendoed into a voice.

'Oswin Fields, Steal The Ghost.'

He grabbed Ennastasia's arm. 'The voice. *It's back.* Can't you hear it?'

'I didn't hear anything.' Ennastasia glanced up and then back to Oswin, cogs turning in her irises.

Someone screamed. Oswin and Ennastasia looked in its direction: the dormitories by the Atrium. The screaming continued.

Ennastasia broke into a run, heading for the sound.

'Wait!' Oswin hurried after her, hoping his lungs would postpone their collapsing until later. Ennastasia wasn't the fastest, and he managed to keep pace all the way to the furthest section of the dormitories. Ennastasia took the steps two at a time, threw the door open, unhooked the spellbook she denied having from a belt clasp her cloak had hidden, and disappeared inside.

Almost tripping on the stairs, Oswin rushed into Hazel Dorm after her. The screaming came from a common room filled with lush greenery and dangling clay ornaments. There were even a handful of wheelbarrows filled with potted plants.

Towering in the middle like a giant frog was a beast.

Oswin gawked at it. It was as if someone had combined an orca and a frog, its skin slimy, the gums of its sharp-toothed jaw protruding from its mouth. Two tongues squirmed within: one wide, the other long and thin. It swung its bulging frog eyes, sitting above two beadier ones, in their direction. Below it – trapped beneath its webbed feet and wide fins, and crying in pain – was Zylo.

'Zylo!' said Oswin, horrified.

'Get out of here!' his brother cried back.

The beast took a step towards Oswin and Ennastasia, its elbows bent outwards, its moist black and white skin catching the light. The tips of its dorsal fins brushed the ceiling as it approached. It had taken its weight off Zylo, which was good, but it was charging them, which was *not* so good. Oswin froze.

Ennastasia didn't, a spell on her lips. With twangs, floorboards rushed the beast. They wrapped around its limbs, then clamped to the floor. The beast opened its needle-toothed jaw and screeched, something halfway between clicking and croaking. It thrashed, slime speckling the walls. Oswin held back a gag at the smell of rotten apples.

'Get Zylo!' Ennastasia shoved him. 'I'll keep it distracted.'

'*What?*'

The monster ripped one limb free from the floorboards, splinters stabbing the air.

Ennastasia levelled Oswin with a calm stare. 'We can't beat this. We have to run. *Get. Zylo.*'

Oswin took in a few breaths, filling his body with oxygen, and nodded.

Ennastasia turned the pages of her spellbook. '*The Windows Open!*' With bangs, the windows, including the floor-to-ceiling ones overlooking the Teeth That Snatch, snapped open. The monster freed itself a bit more, but recoiled, swinging its head as it tried to make sense of the movement. '*The Windows Close!*' With more bangs, the windows slammed shut. Some of them shattered, glass clattering onto the floor.

Not thinking too hard about what he was doing, Oswin sneaked underneath the distracted beast's sludgy belly. It was so busy with the windows, it didn't look down.

One of Zylo's legs was twisted, blood soaking his trousers. There was a gouge in his side and Oswin went cold at the realization his brother had been picked up by the monster's jaws. Zylo clearly couldn't walk, and Oswin couldn't lift him.

The beast snapped free. It slashed its two-pronged tail, breaking beams, smashing clay ornaments and knocking one of the wheelbarrows over. The pots within went flying, shattering with explosions of soil. With a clicking, croaking roar, it hopped towards Ennastasia.

Oswin grabbed the wheelbarrow and righted it. 'Get in!' he hissed, and Zylo managed to haul himself into it. Huffing with effort, he pushed Zylo into the corridor at the other end. Apprentices poked their heads out of their rooms, wondering what all the noise was. Oswin shoved Zylo towards one of them, yelled at them to take him and run, then turned back around.

'Ozzy!' Zylo shouted. 'It's too dangerous!'

Oswin didn't listen. Ennastasia was on the ground, spellbook knocked out of her hand. The beast loomed over her, baring its toothy gums. Its thin tongue shot out, saliva-lathered, and grabbed the front of her uniform like a suction cup. Ennastasia was lifted off the ground. Though she didn't scream, she certainly didn't look fond of what was happening.

Oswin picked up a plant pot. 'Hey!' He threw it at its tongue. Soil and broken clay splashed over the fleshy, pink appendage. The monster dropped Ennastasia and hopped back with clicks and croaks of disgust, running webbed feet over its tongue while its side fins quivered in revulsion.

Ennastasia picked up her spellbook, grabbed Oswin and hauled him after her. They fled the dorm and rushed through the snow. Oswin felt a tugging sensation on his limbs again and heard a crash, followed by thuds of wood. In the glow of the eom, he looked back.

The monster had burst out of the dormitory and was hopping after them, gaining ground. In one massive leap, it soared, opened its mouth and shot its long tongue at them.

'Get down!' came Rochelle's voice. Oswin didn't react in time, but Ennastasia grabbed his neck scarf and yanked him to the ground. '*The Air Cuts*.' From Rochelle's slashing hand, a scythe of wind whistled through the air. There was a slicing noise, an anguished croak and heavy hops of retreat.

Rochelle strode over, kicking up snow, and dragged them to their feet by the backs of their cloaks. There was a distant clicking and Rochelle, spellbook ready, braced herself. With a reverberating wail, a long bird with a stretched-out face glided to them.

Rochelle didn't look at the toothoot as she spoke. 'Follow it.' The toothoot wailed again, swooping into the dark from where the beast had vanished. Rochelle fixed them both with an intimidating stare. 'Was anyone hurt?'

Oswin looked back at the decimated wall of the dormitories. 'My brother.'

18

A THREAT FROM WITHIN

It was morning before Zylo was well enough to talk. Oswin was sitting in an uncomfortable chair in the waiting room of the healer's cabin, replaying events in his head.

'He's stable,' the healer said, walking in.

Thanking them, Oswin hurried into the other room. Zylo was on a bed filled with pillows. 'How are you feeling?'

'Terrible,' said Zylo.

'Did it hurt you badly?'

'Yeah, but it's all right. I'm tough.'

'Why were you there in the first place?' said Oswin. 'It was really late.'

'I was trying to help—' Zylo cut off, chewed his words, then shook his head, clearly frustrated. 'I was trying to help myself improve.' For a second, Oswin thought his tone was forced, but it was back to normal so quickly that it was probably the aftershock. 'I was trying to complete a one thousand push-ups challenge in the common room when that thing came out of nowhere and ruined my streak!'

Oswin stared. 'You care about a push-up streak? You almost died!'

'Yeah, but I didn't.' He was holding back tears. 'I was ten push-ups away from a thousand when it attacked.'

Fighting a laugh, Oswin put his hand on Zylo's shoulder in commiseration. 'That's rough.'

'I suppose I can try again once I'm healed.' He moved his legs. 'The healer plastered on this stinky ointment and said a few enchantments. Now I just have to rest for a couple of days and I'll be good as new.' Zylo indicated the chair by his bed. 'I'm saying I've got time to pass. Tell me what's going on with you.'

Oswin shifted guiltily. 'I'm meant to report to Yarrow the second you're in the clear.'

Zylo made a dramatic face. 'Oh, no! I'm at death's door! You'll have to stay, at least until I say I'm feeling better.'

Smiling, Oswin sat, and talked about how his lessons

had been going and how, come the Freeze, he intended to join the Huvect club.

'You can have my old set of cards,' said Zylo. 'I tried Huvect once, but it was too complicated.'

'Really? I don't deserve them. I'm just a stra—'

'You're my little brother. They're yours.'

Oswin's eyes misted. 'Thank you. And, listen, if you ever want to talk about what happened, I'm always here.'

Zylo wiped an eye. 'Thanks, Ozzy. I'm ... dealing with stuff, in all honesty, but it's nothing I can't handle. Don't go worrying. That's *my* job.'

Oswin smiled weakly. 'No promises.'

They tried to talk more, but the healer ushered Oswin to where Rochelle was waiting to escort him.

'To keep you safe,' Rochelle said, but Oswin reckoned it was to make sure he reported to Yarrow. As they walked to the masters' cabins, he glanced up, gulping at the overcast morning sky. Each day, Tundra slid further into a Freeze.

The inside of Yarrow's cabin still contained the unfortunately lit chandelier, though this time the paintings on the easels were further along in their production. Rochelle led him to one of the sofas and motioned for him to sit. Ennastasia was a few seats over. She didn't bother looking at him.

Yarrow wheeled into the room, her straw-coloured hair wind-tousled. She considered them while Rochelle stood in the corner, like a grandfather clock ticking ominously away.

'Once again we have an incident with a monster.' Yarrow looked suspiciously through her spectacles. 'Once again, the both of you are involved.'

Ennastasia said, 'I heard something and convinced Oswin to check it out with me.' Her eyes slid towards him. 'I thought he'd make good cannon fodder if anything went wrong. He didn't have a say in the matter. It was all my idea.'

Oswin frowned. He tried to say that wasn't what had happened, but Ennastasia's eyes widened into a meaningful look he didn't understand, so he held his tongue. Yarrow raised an eyebrow.

Ennastasia said, 'We've uncovered some concerning things.'

Yarrow raised her other eyebrow. 'Go on.'

'After the first attack, Oswin saw the monster shift into a human. It's possible its footprints changed into a human's.' Ennastasia looked at Oswin expectantly, making a subtle movement towards her throat. To Yarrow and Rochelle, it must have looked natural, but Oswin couldn't recall Ennastasia ever making such a mannerism. He checked his memory and grew certain of it.

'Was there anything else?' Yarrow prompted.

Ennastasia kept looking at Oswin, moving her hands as if opening a book, but flowing the movement into another as if straightening her trousers.

'Uh . . .' Oswin's mind scrambled to figure out the secret message Ennastasia was sending. There *was* more they could say. There was the voice Oswin kept hearing and the missing oddity book. Ennastasia's message clicked into place. She was asking if he wanted to mention the voice and book.

'No.' Oswin looked to Yarrow. 'There's nothing else.'

Yarrow narrowed her eyes. 'A monster hasn't breached Tundra for over a decade, let alone got into Corridor, *let alone* two in one Thaw.' She looked to Rochelle. 'Something is going on.'

'Agreed. Oswin, Ennastasia, whatever nosing around you've been doing –' Rochelle *loomed* for silence as Oswin began to protest – 'you've clearly been sneaking around, don't deny it. Whatever you're doing, stop. For your own safety. We'll look into the matter ourselves.'

Oswin finally realized what they'd faced. 'That thing was a kikorka.'

Rochelle stared stormily ahead. 'Indeed. Named after the sound it makes.'

Oswin held back a shudder.

Yarrow said, 'That will be all. I'm sure you both have important training to get to.' They were dismissed. In a strop, Ennastasia thudded out of the cabin, Oswin close behind. They crossed the icy bridge, bound for an early breakfast.

'A kikorka,' said Oswin.

'And a meersnof,' said Ennastasia. 'Two monster attacks, and both by beasts we learned of in our first lesson with Master Kestcliff. The coincidences keep piling up.' She looked back at him, curious. 'Why didn't you want them to know about the book and voice?'

Oswin shrugged. 'It doesn't feel normal that I can hear this voice. I want to keep it to myself, and we couldn't explain the book without explaining the voice.'

'Keeping quiet about it could sabotage their ability to stop the monsters.'

'But we're not even sure the voice, book and monsters *are* connected.'

Ennastasia let out a breath. 'In all honesty, I doubt they'd be able to solve it, even with the added information. At least, not as quickly as I'm going to.' She picked up her pace. 'I'll join the dots. I'll work out what's happening.'

'You sound confident.' Oswin hoped he was hiding his eagerness at the prospect of having someone to investigate with. He'd been doing terribly on his own.

'Because I'm me. Ennastasia Barkmoth. There's nothing I can't do.'

'Could you try being humble?'

'I'm actually very humble.'

'You said you could do anything.'

'For someone like me, that's extreme humility.' They reached the Alchemy Lodge and Ennastasia walked past it.

Oswin looked from the cafeteria to Ennastasia, then followed. 'Where are we going? Don't you want breakfast?'

Ennastasia tucked her hands below her cloak for warmth. '*I'm* going to speak with Reginald. Unfortunately, you're following me.'

'Too right I am. We're both caught in this mess, if you hadn't realized.'

'Believe me. I had.'

The fence was having a heated argument when they reached him. Ennastasia waited patiently while Oswin looked on, bewildered.

'Sometimes I forget things!' Reginald protested, not speaking to either Oswin or Ennastasia.

'Reginald?' said Oswin.

'Ah, if it isn't the stray,' said Reginald, his wooden spokes pursed like a frustrated mouth. 'I'm afraid I'm busy.'

Oswin looked the fence up and down. 'You're a fence.'

'Can't I be busy?'

Oswin shrugged. 'How busy can a fence get?'

'I have a heart for romance, all right?'

Ennastasia crinkled her nose.

Oswin stifled a laugh. 'Romance?'

The fence swayed, as if swooning. 'See that gate over there?' To the left was a beautifully carved wooden gate.

'That's Ferdinand, isn't it?' said Oswin.

'Ferdinand is my one true love. I'm trying to resolve our lovers' quarrel.'

The gate opened and shut like a mouth. 'You forgot to lock me! I was almost blown off my hinges by the wind.'

'I'm so sorry, my love,' said Reginald. 'I wasn't expecting the weather to be so harsh at this time of year.'

The gate slammed shut. 'Sorry won't neaten my hinges.'

Ennastasia said, 'As interesting as your trouble in paradise is, I have a question.'

Reginald bowed, the spokes leaning forward. 'Anything for a Barkmoth.'

Rolling her eyes, Ennastasia said, 'Earlier this year a meersnof attacked, and last night a kikorka struck Hazel Dorm.'

Oswin said, 'You're asking *Reginald* about the monsters?'

'Do keep up. Reginald, I need to know if anyone passed

through, over or under you on either of those nights. Anyone suspicious, or carrying a large package, or even the beasts themselves.'

Reginald hummed thoughtfully. 'No one.'

Oswin said, 'Not even an apprentice?'

'Ask Ferdinand if you don't believe me.'

Ferdinand said, 'He's right about that at least.'

Reginald huffed. 'What do you mean: "at least"?'

'Don't worry,' Ennastasia said, turning. 'We believe you.'

As they walked away from Reginald and Ferdinand's resuming argument, Oswin said, 'We?'

Ennastasia looked confused before she realized what she'd said. 'I meant "I".'

'Sure you did.'

'Stop smiling or I'll make you.' She shifted her cloak, revealing the spellbook she maintained she didn't own hooked on her belt.

'Sure you will.'

Ennastasia groaned. 'Stop being annoying! We've just figured out something major.'

'That's another "we"!'

'Focus!'

'All right. What did *we* figure out?' He beamed as if he'd just enjoyed a glass of icy water.

'The chance of two different monsters attacking in

quick succession after years of peace is astronomically small.'

'So?'

'*So*, someone or *something* must be causing these attacks. They can't be random. It's too unlikely.'

'But we have no clue who or what it is. We gained nothing from Reginald.'

'That's where you're wrong.' Ennastasia once again led them past the Alchemy Lodge. Oswin was starting to think they'd never get breakfast.

'I don't follow.'

Ennastasia gestured at him, following at her side. 'Clearly you do.'

'Now who's making silly jokes?'

'You're a bad influence,' she grunted. 'Think about it. If Reginald didn't see anyone coming in and out, then the threat must originate either from within Corridor itself, or ...' As they reached the dormitories, Ennastasia ducked below them, weaving through the stilts that held the corridor-like building off the ground. They reached the other side and walked onto the break of snow before the looming line of stalagmites and stalactites.

She pointed at what Oswin was afraid she was speaking of. 'Or, they never had to cross Reginald to get to Corridor because they came from there. The Teeth That Snatch.'

'I thought no one came back from the Teeth.'

'No humans, but who's to say monsters haven't found a way through?'

Oswin's eyes shifted from one stalagmite to another. Something about their creaking, peeling ice made his skin feel itchy, as if it would start peeling, too. 'Should we be here?'

Ennastasia looked at him, surprised. 'I thought you were the most curious person in all of Tundra?'

'Yes, but I don't have a death wish.' He didn't mention that a small part of him thought walking into the Teeth and never returning, never having to deal with the fact he was a stray, *was* tempting. If he left, he'd never have to prove he belonged, or face a Utility Proving. He'd stop being a burden.

'We won't go into them,' said Ennastasia, walking forward. 'We'll walk alongside them. Any tracks should still be here. There hasn't been snowfall since yesterday, so if we don't find any tracks, we'll have ruled this option out.'

'Which means?'

'Timber, you really are terrible at this.' Ennastasia strode to the line of icy spikes, Oswin following apprehensively. 'If we find no tracks, it means that whoever or whatever is causing this must *already* be in Corridor.' Her eyes narrowed. 'My bets are on it being an apprentice.'

'And how are oddities involved with all this?'

'Probably not at all.' As Ennastasia walked, Oswin hung at her side. The air sucked at his limbs, trying to steal him into the Teeth.

After what felt like years but was only half an hour, they'd checked every millimetre of Corridor's border with the Teeth That Snatch.

Ennastasia gave a confident nod. 'As I suspected. No tracks. The monsters are coming from within.'

'We can leave, then?' Oswin inched away from the Teeth. He hated how every time he blinked, they moved a centimetre so instantaneously that he never saw them in motion. Or, worse still, how the second he thought about the fact they moved, they stopped doing it.

'Yes. Honestly, you're such a baby.'

Oswin tried not to be offended.

As brilliant as Ennastasia's deductions had been, it didn't progress the investigation, even if it did rule out some options. They had good reason to trust the culprit was within Corridor, but besides them having brown hair that reached past their ear, they had little to go on. And, as Ennastasia had pointed out as they'd walked back from the Teeth, they had no reason to assume the person who'd stolen the book was the person who'd left the hair behind or caused the attacks. They'd reached a dead-end.

Oswin felt uneasy not knowing who was behind the attacks; not so much because he was scared, but more because he hated not knowing. At least he had a torrent of lessons that would fill his mind.

Scelving was a good distraction, because half the time it was utterly terrifying. While the other apprentices improved at climbing the iceberg, Oswin could do little more than sink his tools into the ice and freeze. Pufftow was just as challenging, given Oswin's lungs had a habit of failing and his chest compressor made his ribs ache. In one lesson, Cathy gave him a black eye and Rochelle vowed Cathy would never spar with him again, giving her a detention that involved trimming the branches of the Classroom Treehouse.

Oswin had said, 'I'm sorry to be a nuisance. Thank you for sticking up for me.'

Rochelle had looked taken aback. 'It's my job. Besides, *you* weren't a nuisance. Cathyquizzia was.'

'Still, I'm just a stray—'

'*Just* a stray?' She'd muttered in a low voice, 'For timber's sake, Lullia.'

Oswin had felt as if he was plummeting at the mention of Lullia. He'd almost told Rochelle to keep his mother out of her mouth, before remembering Rochelle was a master and he an apprentice.

Rochelle had said, 'You're a human being surviving in a cold world like everyone else here. The ice doesn't care who you are when it tries to freeze you. You matter, stray or not.'

He'd looked up at Rochelle. He'd been so stunned, he hadn't asked a single question for the rest of the day.

Basic Spellbookery, Etymagery and AA&V didn't require heights or combat. In Basic Spellbookery, he memorized the twenty-two basic spells, which mainly cleaned and mended, and were the easiest to cast. None involved coal magic. In AA&V, he could recite all of Vervack's rambling theories, and in Etymagery he could write how a spell's power changed depending on consonant alliterations, but he was at a loss as to *why*.

Culture remained his favourite. In one lesson he'd been particularly shocked to learn that mamats, vohoonts, sticelings – in fact, every animal but humans – not only ate ice instead of food, but were ultimately made of ice, even if blood still flowed in their veins.

Every morning, the clouds were thicker, the snow heavier, and the wind stronger. Thoughts of the Freeze made him tremble. The end of the Thaw, and the first Utility Proving, was meant to be weeks away, but the weather hadn't received the memo.

One morning, as wind battered the cafeteria windows

at breakfast, Yarrow and Rochelle walked in. Even indoors it was hard not to shiver.

Yarrow waited until the chattering apprentices focused on her. It didn't take long, what with the unusualness of the visit, and Rochelle's *looming* demanding attention.

'The Freeze has begun,' announced Yarrow. Simple. To the point. Devastating.

Oswin's heart sank. He thought he'd have longer. He wasn't the only one alarmed. The other apprentices eyed their half-full bowls before rushing to the buffet for seconds, knowing the offerings would soon be thinner.

Oswin understood their concern. The Thaw was when food was grown, and Tundrans fattened themselves. The Freeze was when resources were rationed, and Tundra held out for the Thaw's return. The issue was that the Freeze had arrived *weeks* early.

Oswin was only a tad worried about the food running out. Growing up, he'd been lucky to get food if he worked hard. He could deal with rationing. He was more concerned about what Rochelle said next.

'Given the early arrival of the Freeze, the first Utility Proving has been moved to tomorrow. It will be a battle on a bridge over the Plughole. Rest well. You'll need your strength.' With that, Rochelle and Yarrow left, as if two terrifying announcements hadn't been made in quick succession.

Oswin spent the rest of the day in a dizzying panic, facing the thought of the end of his time at Corridor or, worse still, his death in the Plughole. Maybe Frank and Cathy would get their wish and he'd fall down the well to drown in the underwater caves.

The next morning arrived too quickly. Oswin trudged to his doom, the howls of blizzardous winds gushing at the dormitory walls and the dawn sky tinged with the dying light of an eom. He heard the mysterious voice again and couldn't contain a shiver as the sound whispered into his ear.

'Oswin Fields, Steal The Ghost.'

It didn't speak again, so Oswin pushed the echo from his mind. He set off for breakfast, trying to ignore the knots in his stomach at the thought of what was to happen that day.

He stopped in his tracks. Apprentices were clustered around a section of snow by the river, the white stained red. Oswin held his breath as he pushed through, desperate to see what the fuss was about.

Arranged on the ground in the outline of a hand were dozens of dead mamats. Their glassy eyes stared at the cloudy sky, red snowflakes blustering in a swirl around them.

Oswin couldn't think of a worse omen.

19

THE BATTLE OF
THE PLUGHOLE

Lessons were cancelled the day of the Thaw Utility Proving. Oswin tried to eat a healthy breakfast, but the selection was rationed, with only porridge and toast to choose between. It didn't matter; he was too nervous to eat.

'You'll be fine,' said Zylo, ruffling Oswin's hair before flopping his trapper hat back on. 'I believe in you.'

'That makes one of us,' said Oswin mournfully. 'What about you? You're too injured to take part in the Utility Proving.'

'Too injured?' Zylo said incredulously. 'I may be

limping, but I've had time to recover. Besides, if you can't survive while injured at Corridor, how can you hope to survive if you're injured on the Endless Expanse? I have to take part in the Utility Proving, whether I want to or not.'

'Do you know what it is you'll have to do?'

'Yeah – we fourth years have to navigate a maze at the top of the Vinderation tower. Master Vervack's set up a hoard of traps and poisons.' At Oswin's horrified expression, Zylo shrugged. 'It's not Scelving-themed, which I'd have preferred, but I've never failed a Proving so far. Anyway, stop worrying about me. I'll be fine. Focus on yourself. Stay calm, try hard and it'll work out.'

Oswin repeated Zylo's words like a mantra as Rochelle herded the first-year apprentices to the north-east of Corridor, the toothoot circling overhead as they followed the river to Shemmia Woods. Just beyond Reginald, who grumbled sleepily as they walked through him, was an open space of snow before the ice floor of Shemmia Woods began.

Oswin was consumed by fear as he stared at the gaping hole ahead. The Plughole was large enough to swallow a cabin, with water roaring as it tumbled from the river and down the ice walls of the vertical chute. Oswin backed away while other apprentices edged forward to peer down.

'I can't see the bottom,' exclaimed Maury, adjusting her monocle to check, revealing a deep bag below her eye. She looked as if she'd been up all night inventing.

Philomena was on tiptoes. 'Wish I'd brought my climbing gear.'

'*Step Back,*' Rochelle boomed, spellbook open. The apprentices closest to the Plughole were forced away by her magic. Rochelle closed her spellbook with an angry snap. 'In case it has slipped your attention, if you fall into that well, you *will* die.'

'But our Utility Proving is to go over it,' said Oswin, voice shaking.

Rochelle said, 'Not without safety precautions. *The Bridge Appears.*' With a spell, a rickety rope bridge burst into existence over the well. It swayed in the wind, snow catching on the rope banisters and thin rungs. '*The Safety Fortifies.*' A fence sprouted around the well. Tall poles grew, ropes falling down from the top like hair. 'You will have a safety harness,' explained Rochelle. 'If you fall, or do not contribute anything useful to your team, you will fail.' She held up a hand to stall incoming questions, mostly from Oswin. 'I said 'teams', yes. One team will be representing the Archivists, the other the Archaeologists.'

Oswin frowned. 'The what and the *what*?'

That was when Yarrow arrived, pushing her wheelchair to join Rochelle at the front. 'The Archivists and the Archaeologists,' she repeated. 'The two distinct groups of cave delvers we have in Tundra. Both scour the frost caves for splinters for timber production, or artefacts from civilizations long gone.'

Maury's hand shot up and Rochelle motioned for her to speak.

'Thanks to the artefacts,' Maury burst out, 'we've gained uncountable important materials for inventions. Not to mention repurposed medical equipment.'

Yarrow smiled. 'Quite so. Excellent knowledge, Maury.'

Maury beamed, and Oswin, despite feeling unwell with nerves, shot her an encouraging thumbs up. When Maury's return wink lacked her usual enthusiasm, Oswin worried she was tiring of him.

That was when Ennastasia sidled up to him at the back of the group. Having her there went a long way to calming his nerves.

Yarrow said, 'The Archivists believe only in storing artefacts; they never analyse them. They believe looking at the past through a Tundran lens will cause distortion.'

Rochelle chimed in, 'To put it another way, the Archivists think analysing the ancient artefacts is like finding footprints and walking over them with your own.'

'Conversely,' Yarrow picked up, 'the Archaeologists believe in investigating artefacts to understand what they are and put them to use. They think what the Archivists do is find footprints, put them in a pretty frame and refuse to call them footprints, lest they misinterpret them.'

Rochelle said, 'The Archivists and Archaeologists fight bitterly over artefacts. In one battle, a group of Archaeologists were carrying an artefact back to the surface. As they reached a chute in the cave, they were attacked by the Archivists, who tried to take the artefact. In the end, the Archivists won.' She gestured at the gaping well behind her, the roar of the falling water almost drowning her voice. 'Half of you will be trying to get an artefact safely across, the other will be trying to steal it.'

'Just like the Archaeologists and the Archivists,' said Yarrow grimly, holding up a curled glass ornament containing swirling snow. 'The artefact,' she clarified, before tossing it to the apprentices.

Gale caught it, squeaked, then chucked it at Philomena, who looked far too eager about the whole thing.

'I'll represent the Archaeologists!' Philomena hoisted the artefact for all to see. 'We'll defeat any Archivists who stand in our way. Who's with me?'

Quickly, two teams began to form.

'Why don't the masters put us into teams?' Oswin whispered to Ennastasia.

'Because knowing which team will have the easiest win, and acting quickly enough to get onto that team, is part of the challenge.' She pushed him to the Archaeologist side, taking the last spots and leaving two other apprentices to dejectedly join the Archivists.

'Why this team?' Oswin whispered as Rochelle led the Archaeologists to the other side of the well and hooked ropes to their belts, so every apprentice was secured to a pole. The ropes were slack enough to give them plenty of movement but would catch them if they fell. It didn't make Oswin feel *any* safer, though.

'Holding onto the artefact should be easier than trying to steal it,' said Ennastasia. 'The Archivists are at a distinct disadvantage. We just need to create a battering ram, maintain momentum and rush through the other team.'

'You sound awfully confident.' Oswin eyed the well, so close to him that droplets of cold water hit his face. They were all tied in now, as was the opposing team. His stomach flipped in fearful knots. This was it.

When he realized Cathy and Frank were *also* on the Archaeologist team, his stomach went from flipping to imploding. Cathy grinned at him, showing far too many teeth.

'Of course I'm confident,' said Ennastasia. 'With my leadership and tactics, the win is as good as—'

Philomena sprinted across the bridge, undeterred by its swaying, the artefact held tight in her hand. She bellowed a war cry.

Ennastasia sighed. 'Never mind.'

Chaos broke out on the bridge. The teams flooded the thin rungs, tackling each other into the rope banisters. Snow and splinters scuffed over the edge, tumbling into the darkness, and Oswin couldn't bring himself to step over the chasm.

'Come on,' Ennastasia urged him, hurrying onto the bridge herself.

'Yeah, stray,' said Cathy, grabbing Oswin's shoulders. 'Get a move on.'

'I'll help you,' said Frank, ripping the safety belt off Oswin, releasing him from the rope.

Ennastasia glared serrated daggers at Frank. 'What are you doing?'

Cathy shoved Oswin. He was flung over the banister, the world spinning, the rushing of the water changing direction in a swirl of sound. The bridge brushed his hands. He tried to grab it, but felt it slip away. He fell.

Someone wrapped their arms around his waist.

There was a horrific second where air and water rushed

by his ears and the darkness began to consume him. Then, with a sharp jerk, he was pulled to a stop. Oswin, and whoever was currently holding his waist for dear life, swung from a rope and hit the side of the Plughole, *hard*. Cold water rushed over them.

Ennastasia spluttered in the torrent, but her grip didn't give up.

She'd jumped after him.

She'd jumped after him.

Oswin couldn't understand it, but then mindless panic overtook him as he realized how precariously they were hanging.

'Stop wriggling!' Ennastasia snapped, and Oswin just managed to hold himself still. Slowly, he looked down. His entire body went rigid. Darkness yawned below his boots, the water tumbling into the nothingness. He couldn't even hear when the water hit the bottom. It truly seemed endless.

There was a jerk as the rope attached to Ennastasia started to fragment, individual twines snapping under their weight.

'Flickering fog,' Ennastasia cursed, looking up. Oswin followed her gaze, seeing the top of the rope fraying. It hadn't been designed to support two apprentices.

'I'm sorry,' Oswin choked around his fear. His uselessness was going to get them both killed.

'Don't be sorry – help me figure out a way out of this.' Ennastasia looked around, her eyes wide, then kicked a foot against the icy wall. It slipped on the slick surface.

There were shouts from the bridge above as apprentices leaned over to gape at their perilous situation. Cathy and Frank stared in horror at the danger they'd put Ennastasia in, and probably at the fact Oswin was still alive.

There was another jerk.

The rope snapped.

Cold panic rushed up Oswin's throat as they fell. He felt the yawning darkness of the endless chute they were falling into breathe against his neck, but then freezing talons grabbed their doublets. Powerful wings beat around them, feathers brushing their faces. The toothoot soared them out of the well, depositing them onto the safety of the snow.

Rochelle hurried over. 'Are you two all right?'

Ennastasia spat out some of the well's water. 'Utterly spiffing.'

Oswin, shivering, managed a nod as he sank his fingers into the snow to feel the hard press of the ground below. He kept telling himself he was no longer in danger, but his pulse pounded in his ears all the same.

Ennastasia scowled at Rochelle. 'The rescue could have come sooner.'

Rochelle quirked an eyebrow. 'Accept my apologies.'

Oswin glanced behind Rochelle to see that Philomena had managed to get the artefact to the other side. The Archivists had been too distracted watching the near-death incident to stop her.

Rochelle stood to her full *looming* height and rounded on Cathy and Frank. 'What in Tundra was that?' Clearly, she didn't want an answer because she cut over their blubbering. 'You are working *as a team*. You are meant to keep your teammates safe. Instead, you put their lives in grave danger.'

If Oswin was given a choice between dangling over the well again or facing Rochelle's wrath, he wasn't sure which he'd go with. (That was a lie. He'd take *anything* over the Plughole.) Even so, he felt an odd sympathy for Cathy and Frank.

Yarrow wheeled over. 'Such behaviour is entirely at odds with Corridor's values.' She narrowed her eyes at Cathy and Frank. 'The other masters and I will need to think over your position here.'

Cathy and Frank stared at each other and then at Yarrow, astounded.

Rochelle leaned towards Yarrow, her voice dropping to a whisper so that Oswin could barely hear it. 'You know the High Watcher won't tolerate us kicking out Tundrans for the mistreatment of a stray.'

'And I won't tolerate attempted murder,' Yarrow murmured, just as quietly. 'Against a stray or any other. But, remember, they endangered Ennastasia Barkmoth.'

Oswin forced himself to his feet. Cathy and Frank were children, like him. They weren't nice people, but they'd only grow worse if they were kicked out of Corridor. 'I was trying to make a distraction,' he said, his voice wavering.

Ennastasia got to her feet, dusting herself off. 'I beg your pardon?'

Oswin shot her a look. '*We* were making a distraction so Philomena could get the artefact across.'

Yarrow and Rochelle looked at him with raised eyebrows, but no one was more shocked than Cathy and Frank.

Cathy recovered first. 'Exactly. It was a distraction. Teamwork, even.' She narrowed her eyes suspiciously at Oswin. He wanted to glare back, but just looked at the snow.

Ennastasia rubbed her forehead, then grumbled, 'A distraction. Precisely.' She added to Oswin, under her breath, 'I'd never come up with such a ridiculous distraction, or such an obviously fake cover story.'

Oswin shot her a fond half-smile, his jitters slowly melting as the incident moved into the past.

Rochelle looked at Yarrow, at a loss. 'A distraction,' she said, evidently *not* believing it.

Yarrow tilted her head. 'If it was a distraction, then, it must be said, it was successful. It would mean Oswin – and the others, of course – would pass this Utility Proving.'

Oswin's heart leaped. 'It was a distraction, I swear.'

Frank nodded. 'Definitely.'

There was a long-suffering silence as Yarrow and Rochelle had a wordless conversation of furrowed brows.

After a pause, Rochelle *loomed* at Cathy and Frank again. 'Don't think this will go unpunished. Both of you are to melt snow into cleaning and drinking water for the training grounds for the rest of the Freeze.'

Frank opened his mouth to complain, but Cathy elbowed him and smiled. 'Happily. Thank you for understanding.'

Rochelle glowered darkly at Cathy and Frank but left it at that.

As the apprentices moved away from the Plughole, and Philomena received a mountain of praise and high fives, Rochelle fell into step with Oswin.

'I'm sorry for what happened. I'll be keeping a close eye on Cathy and Frank – you have my word.'

Oswin couldn't grasp why she cared for a stray like

him. 'You've already done more than I could have hoped.'
He appreciated her sentiment, but he had a sinking dread
that, because he'd passed the first Utility Proving on luck
alone, the second would be even worse.

20

CARDS, SKATING AND DEAD RODENTS

The first lesson on Fourthday was Etymagery, and Oswin made sure he sat with Ennastasia. After hitting a dead-end in their investigation, Ennastasia had kept what she'd called an *appropriate distance*. Oswin understood, even if it made him feel lonely again. But after seeing more dead mamats that morning, arranged as disturbingly as the ones he'd seen on the day of the Thaw Utility Proving, he wanted someone to talk to. Someone who wouldn't worry about his safety, like Zylo, and didn't have better people to hang out with, like Maury.

'Did you see?' he asked as he got out his Etymagery

workbook. Master Tybolt was always late, so they had time to talk.

Ennastasia leaned back in her seat. 'Somehow, I missed the sacrificially arranged dead rodents.'

'But it was massive— You're being sarcastic again. Hilarious. Seriously, what was that?'

'How should I know? You and your questions.'

'Why doesn't Corridor send all the apprentices home? With the monster attacks and now this, aren't we all in danger?'

Ennastasia flicked through her workbook, with one hand spinning a pencil. 'No one will be sent home. The point of Corridor is to train ice apprentices to protect Tundra. The settlement has this idea that by being here for five years – even being in mortal danger – you become useful.'

'What if someone dies?'

Ennastasia caught her pencil. 'Some say it's good – saves on mouths to feed.' She was silent for a second, then murmured, 'My grandfather thinks so. It's one of the reasons I don't like him.'

Oswin felt shame clawing under his skin, trying to get out. That was what *he* was: an extra mouth. If he could solve the mystery of the monsters, he could prove, at least to himself, that Tundra wouldn't be better off if he left.

The cabin door was thrust open, and Master Tybolt trudged in. They collapsed into their chair at the front and indicated the students read their textbooks.

Gale put up his hand.

Tybolt rubbed their face, resigned. 'Yes?'

'Are you ever going to walk around the class and help us with our work? All the other masters do, but you don't.'

Tybolt wafted a hand, while the other scrunched leaves. 'I don't need to. Just read in silence.'

'But how will you know if we're learning correctly?'

Tybolt leaned their head back, letting out a long breath. 'Fine.' They rose unsteadily to their feet, and shambled around the class, barely glancing at the apprentices' writings before muttering, 'Write neater, your handwriting is like a half-cooked noodle' or, 'Write messier, those harsh lines are giving me a headache.'

As they were coming to Oswin and Ennastasia's table, they'd started murmuring 'brats', but stopped when they noticed the name on Ennastasia's workbook.

They blinked, then said, with barely any energy behind it, 'A Barkmoth. Oh, my, what an honour, pass my best to your grandfather, blah di blah di blah.' Their eyes shifted to Oswin's book, who moved his elbow to try and cover where he'd scrawled his surname, but from the sudden change in Tybolt's expression, he knew he'd been too slow.

Tybolt's gaze slowly raised to Oswin's face, uncharacteristically clear. *'Fields.'*

There was a tense silence. Even the piles of junk falling out of the cupboards seemed to shiver in anticipation.

Tybolt's shoulders pushed back. When they spoke, their voice was eerily steady. 'Get out of my classroom.'

Oswin's eyes widened. 'I ... What? Sorry? You want me to—'

Tybolt grabbed Oswin's workbook and slammed it down, the surname plain for all to see. 'Get out of my classroom!'

In a jerk, Oswin fled. Tybolt shambled after him, and the second Oswin made it outside, they slammed the door, yelling, 'Don't come back!'

On shaking legs, with his terror of heights joining his fear of Tybolt, Oswin descended to the trunk of the Classroom Treehouse. He sat in the shade, his breath frosting as his lungs ached from shock. He huddled against the wind, snow building on his hat.

He heeded Tybolt's warning. From then on, he waited in the common room during Etymagery. He was a stray; he shouldn't pester another master about Tybolt's outburst, especially when it was clearly about Oswin's relationship to Michael Fields.

With Etymagery off his timetable, Oswin had more

spare time. After receiving a set of Huvect cards from Zylo, for which he thanked him profusely while Zylo tried to give him a lung-crushing hug, he joined the Huvect club. The Freeze had started, so he was no longer banned from extra-curricular activities.

The Huvect club was in the gazebo every Fourthday evening, on tables made from shields with swords for legs. Secondmaster Rochelle ran the club, inspecting the matches and despairing at reckless strategies.

'Ah, Oswin.' Rochelle spotted him as he entered for the first time. 'Do you have Huvect cards or will you need some provided?'

Awkwardly, Oswin lifted the cards Zylo had gifted him.

'Good, good.' She pulled a chair out for him. Oswin sat and Rochelle gestured someone over. 'You and Ennastasia are friends, correct? You can play your first match against her.'

Ennastasia sat down opposite him, looking alarmed. 'We're not friends.'

Rochelle smiled tersely. 'I require apprentices to treat each other with respect.'

'I require masters remember who I am.'

Rochelle's pleasant expression grew taut. She walked away, not responding.

Ennastasia turned to Oswin. 'If you want a battle, I'll

need to challenge your top card. Here's mine.' She showed him a card depicting a spiked timber club. 'What's yours?'

Oswin grabbed a random card, which showed a snow pile. 'This one?'

Ennastasia wrinkled her nose. 'I suppose that will suffice.' She angled her top card at his. Oswin startled as his card buzzed. A hovering arrow of frost appeared. He moved the card; no matter where it was, the arrow pointed at Ennastasia.

'If you want to accept the battle, you need to press that arrow.'

Oswin did so, the arrow vanishing in a burst of snow, and the battle began.

His first time playing Huvect was a disaster. He didn't understand the game and Ennastasia had had lots of practice. Her timber-themed cards were superior to his mismatched ones. With each card placed, parts of the table curved up to form the card's depiction, but when Oswin summoned a soldier of fog, then a bird of coal, they quickly fell to Ennastasia's onslaught.

'I'm the reigning champion.' Ennastasia didn't sound happy. 'Everyone lets me win. Even in the skating club no one ever actually tries to beat me.'

Oswin peered at her curiously. 'There's a skating club?'

A defensive look crossed Ennastasia's face. 'Yes.'

'And you're in it.'

'Absolutely not. No. Not at all. I'm not in the skating club. Don't get any ideas.'

But Oswin was grinning. Ennastasia clearly *was* in the skating club, and no amount of lying could stop him from annoying her there, too.

The following week on Thirdday evening, Oswin skipped to the Iceberg Cabin for the skating club, unsurprised to see Ennastasia there. When she noticed him, she turned her eyes to the snow-flurried sky.

Oswin pulled on a pair of skates. 'Fancy seeing you here. I thought you were absolutely not, no way, *not at all* in the skating club?'

Ennastasia pinched the bridge of her nose. 'You're ruining my life.'

Oswin paused tying his laces. 'Just say the word and I'll leave you alone.'

Ennastasia was silent, the howl of the wind the only noise. 'We're not friends.'

Feeling foolish, Oswin started to untie his skates.

Ennastasia glared. 'I said we're not friends, not that I want you to leave.'

Oswin's face scrunched in confusion. 'You want me to stay?'

'No!'

'So, you *do* want me to leave?'

'Listen, just ...' She grimaced, forcing words through her teeth. 'I bet I can beat you at skating.'

Tying his skates in an instant, Oswin leaped to his feet. With a fond roll of her eyes, Ennastasia moved to the starting line.

Master Kestcliff blew a high-pitched horn and, like arrows from bows, the apprentices shot onto the ice. Oswin fell flat on his face. Ennastasia definitely won.

At dinner that evening, Ennastasia rubbed her victory in his face, but he was just happy he'd tricked her into eating with him. Whenever he claimed to have a card strategy Ennastasia couldn't overcome, or a skating technique she couldn't master, her 'appropriate distance' vanished so she could prove him wrong.

Oswin came close to beating Ennastasia one Thirdday when Ennastasia tripped on an ice lump and he'd almost crossed the finish line before her. Except, Ennastasia had then tripped him. Oswin still hadn't mastered getting up on his skates once he'd fallen, and had flopped about until Kestcliff had taken pity and helped him.

'You should try standing next time,' Ennastasia had taunted.

'But standing up once you've fallen on ice is impossible.'

'*I* manage.'

Oswin had said, in a simpering voice, 'Yeah, but you're a *Barkmoth*. The ground blooms below your holy feet and the sky cries at your genius.'

Ennastasia had laughed, but it hadn't been a mocking laugh, or even a half-hearted one. It had been genuine. Her unguarded expression had stuck in Oswin's mind.

The following day, after lessons finished, Oswin marched to the training gazebo for the Huvect club. He strode straight to Ennastasia and angled his top card – wisely changed to a defensive wall of ice – at her. He pressed his finger to it and Ennastasia's top card buzzed, an angry frozen arrow pointing at him. She accepted the challenge.

Many tense rounds later, they were down to their last cards and a small crowd had formed around them. Ennastasia's trump card, an ultimate avalanche, would have won her the game, however a strong gust blustered through the gazebo, whipping it away. In Huvect, protecting your cards from the weather was part of the challenge. If one was blown away, it was out of the game.

Rochelle raised her eyebrows. 'Oswin wins.'

Ennastasia rifled desperately through her cards, but eventually she gave up searching and nodded in weak acceptance.

Oswin beamed. He'd won after *weeks* of disastrous losses. The students around him blabbered to Ennastasia that she should have won. Their incessant chatter made her angrier.

Ennastasia blanked Oswin for the rest of the day until, on Fifthday, she stopped him before breakfast. 'I can show you how to skate better. Your awful technique pains me, so you'd be doing me a favour.'

'Do you mean it?'

'I'll change my mind if you take too long saying yes.'

'Right. Yes! I'd love to.'

'And listen,' she said, so quietly he could barely hear. 'Well done on your win in Huvect. I guess.' She held her hand out.

Her hand was a paradox before his eyes. Before Ennastasia had a chance to retract it, he shook it, grinning. 'Thank you.'

Ennastasia inspected his face, and Oswin remembered how odd his smiles looked, thanks to his sad-looking eyes. Lullia had always said so.

'You have a nice smile,' said Ennastasia, letting go.

He couldn't comprehend someone thinking his smile was nice. He replayed her words in case he'd misheard. He was so filled with warmth that he didn't know how to respond.

'Let's go.' Ennastasia turned to the ice rink.

'What about breakfast?' he spluttered, still thrown by her compliment.

'We can eat after.'

Oswin followed, a spring in his step, but his joy dampened when they came across a heap of dead mamats. This time, they were joined by dead luppies – medium-sized animals with fur that trailed behind them to obscure their tracks – and a deersun, with its scaled tail, hooved front legs and circle of antlers. Both were fast animals. Anything that could catch them must have been formidable.

'Again?' Ennastasia said, annoyed. Dead animals had become commonplace. Finding any meant dropping what you were doing to report it to a master. Some apprentices found it a nuisance. Oswin always felt miserable seeing the fate of the poor animals.

Ennastasia said, 'Let's go tell Master Kestcliff.'

Master Kestcliff was in the Iceberg Cabin marking apprentices' workbooks, sketching smiley faces next to good work and leaving detailed feedback on those who'd failed.

He looked up, blinking from behind his square glasses. 'You realize today is Fifthday? We don't have lessons until we're back to Firstday.'

Ennastasia crossed her arms. 'While I can forgive you for thinking Oswin could make such a mistake, surely you realize I would never be so airheaded.'

'Of course. My deepest apologies.'

'We found more mamats.' Ennastasia pointed a thumb over her shoulder. 'Luppies and a deersun too.'

Kestcliff stood, his cloak and skirt trailing across the ground, and walked to the door. 'At this rate the Scelving expedition will be cancelled . . .'

Oswin's eyes widened. 'What's the Scelving expedition?'

Kestcliff paused, his hand on the door handle. 'I suppose it doesn't matter if I tell you, given everything going on. It's the second Utility Proving for the first years, before the new year starts. A mini expedition into Shemmia Woods in two weeks. It's got skating, camping and a midnight disorientation test.' He shook his head. 'But with dead animals turning up so frequently, who knows . . .' He departed into the freezing morning.

It occurred to Oswin that, if the second Utility Proving *didn't* go ahead, he would technically never pass it, and be kicked out of Corridor.

He turned to Ennastasia. 'We *need* to figure out what's happening and stop it. The Utility Proving can't be cancelled.'

Ennastasia huffed. 'The issue is, we've got the same

information as before, and we've been stumped for a while now.'

'You *have* been avoiding me. We can't theorize without talking.'

Ennastasia couldn't look him in the eyes. 'Because we're not friends.'

Oswin told himself *that* didn't hurt, but his hurt was growing unmanageable. He snapped, 'Why not?'

Ennastasia stewed in silence, her face drawn tight with a worry he didn't understand.

I'm just a stray, Oswin repeated to himself. *I don't get to be angry at her.* 'Fine. Even so, we could have spent that time trying to figure this out. Two heads are usually better than one.'

'Agreed. They *usually* are.' The joke was a peace offering, and just like that, Oswin's annoyance turned to mush. He pulled his face into mock offence, and Ennastasia snorted in amusement, walking out of the cabin. 'Skating practice. Hurry.'

Ennastasia stepped smoothly onto the rink. His legs wobbling, Oswin tried to move his feet.

'No, not like that.' Ennastasia made a disapproving face. 'What do you expect to happen by sliding your skates around?'

'I expect to move.'

'That's silly. Do this instead.' She set off at a measured pace.

Oswin looked at his own feet and mimicked her movements. The first few times he fell and, unable to stand, had to crawl to the edge. But, by the end of Ennastasia's tutoring, he could shakily skate laps.

As he skidded to a halt, and Ennastasia helped stop him falling, he smiled at her. 'Thanks.'

Ennastasia gave him a friendly shove. 'I did this so I don't have to look at your awful technique.'

Oswin's knowing smile didn't waver. 'If you say so.' His grin was thwacked away by a snowball. He gasped, wiping the cold from his face. 'What was that for?'

'*That* was for the snowball you threw at me at the start of the year.' Ennastasia was already preparing a second, hard-packing it *far* more than necessary. '*This* one's because I feel like it.'

'All right, you're on.' Oswin scooped up his own snowball, and soon they were embroiled in a fierce battle. The shocks of cold had no effect on his soaring happiness. He'd never felt more at home than he did right then.

But at breakfast the next day, when Cathy shot him a detesting look and mouthed, 'Stray,' his feeling of belonging vanished. Weighed with guilt, he took less than his rationed portion. Just Cathy's stare had been enough to remind him he was a drain. He vowed to himself that he'd only take the food he absolutely needed. Unfortunately, Zylo caught on quick.

'Zylo,' Oswin protested as his brother heaped some of his own food into Oswin's bowl.

'You're my little brother. I'm always going to look out for you. Make sure you're staying indoors and keeping your head down.' Zylo glanced around. 'And, between you and me, I would be careful about hanging out with Ennastasia.'

Oswin looked up sharply. 'Why?'

'Lullia never told you about the Barkmoths, did she?'

Oswin felt a painful splitting in his chest. Zylo sounded as if he knew who the Barkmoths were, but Ennastasia had made him promise *not* to look into her family. He could flee and not listen to whatever Zylo had to say, *or* he could get answers. A question boiled on his tongue.

He sucked his lips, trying to contain his words, then felt a wave of shame as he helplessly said, 'Who are the Barkmoths?'

'They're only in charge of *all* timber transmutation in Tundra. Who do you think gives Lullia tokens in exchange for logs? Who do you think provides clothing, equipment, building materials – *all of it* – for the settlement?'

The world stretched around Oswin as realization sank

in. It all made sense. Why everyone walked on tiptoes around Ennastasia; why the masters had to bow to her every whim. He'd been teasing someone who could have Lullia's livelihood taken away if he annoyed her too much.

'Harnan Barkmoth, Ennastasia's grandfather,' Zylo continued, 'is the most influential member of the Watcher's Ring. He's as important as a Tundran can get.'

'Thanks . . .' Oswin said quietly, letting the information soak in. On one hand, he always loved gaining knowledge. On the other, he was repulsed. He wanted to scrub his brain clean of the information. But he could never forget what he'd learned. His knowledge would always be proof of the promise he'd broken.

21

THE SHADOW OF A THEORY

After breakfast, Oswin walked straight to the Spruce common room to meet Ennastasia. Every muscle felt stiff from skating practice, but skating was a wonderful thing. It was both less energy and faster than running, and barely tired his lungs. The fact that Ennastasia had tutored him only for him to break his promise made him feel dreadful. And really, he deserved to.

The Spruce common room was mostly empty. The hanging chairs swayed from the tree, the firepit crackled and the floor-to-ceiling windows overlooking the Teeth That Snatch were crystal clear. Ennastasia was leaning against one of the walls, between a painting of an ice cave

246

and a tapestry of a battle between a lumbering beast and a dozen scouters. She pushed off the wall, expecting him to follow. He did, too ashamed to look at her.

In the mezzanine, Ennastasia settled into one armchair and Oswin the other, and they began their discussions. They met regularly, building a list of everything they knew. They crafted and discarded theories, Oswin refusing to mention that he now knew what being a Barkmoth meant.

By the time the weekend rolled around again, it felt as though they were a little closer to an answer, though Ennastasia had said that anything on Michael Fields, oddities and ghost magic was too unfounded to be considered in their theories. The entire time, Oswin wondered if he should come clean about what he knew about the Barkmoths. But as he sprawled in the armchair, absently spinning a globe, regret sealed his mouth.

Ennastasia's gaze turned thoughtful. 'What if they weren't two different monsters?'

Oswin regarded Ennastasia as he subtly adjusted his chest compressor, so it dug less into his skin. 'The meersnof and the kikorka? They looked pretty different to me.'

'You saw the first monster shift into a human. Who's

to say the kikorka wasn't the same human shifted again? The monsters could be forms of a shapeshifter.' Ennastasia leaned forward. 'Maybe a shapeshifter who's an apprentice. That would explain the frequency of the attacks and why Reginald didn't see anyone coming in and out: the shapeshifter would already be inside. And it would explain why they're only shifting into monsters we've learned about. I imagine it's difficult to shift into something you don't know exists.' She added, 'It would also explain why they haven't shapeshifted into a no-read. We weren't given its description, so the shapeshifter doesn't know what they look like.'

Cold realization spread down Oswin's arms. He shot to his feet.

'What?' Ennastasia glared at him. 'Speak. What is it?'

Oswin found *Creatures of Tundra and Beyond* in seconds, Ennastasia grumbling at his refusal to elaborate. He placed the book, open, on the coffee table. He tapped the wordless page, where the image of a human sat. Around it, arrows pointed to mamats, fluffy vohoonts and feathered sticelings. 'That looks like a human who can shapeshift.'

Ennastasia peered closely, then stood up, too. 'We should ask Master Kestcliff what shapeshifting monsters exist.'

It was already towards the end of the Freeze, but the conditions were only worsening, the days shorter and sunlight weak. The weather was inhospitably cold, the meals were quarter-sized and everyone's faces hung sunken and tired on their skulls. Through the snow they struggled, reaching the Iceberg Cabin with shuddering limbs and chattering teeth. Ennastasia reached for the door-handle, but Oswin grabbed her hand.

Ennastasia snapped, 'It's freezing. Let's get inside already.'

'Listen.' A heated conversation raged within. He pulled Ennastasia to one of the windows, crouching.

Candles were lit inside, so they could see in, while being swathed in shadows themselves. They peeked through the frosted window, snow crunching below their fingers as they gripped the ledge. It was with surprise that Oswin saw, standing by the blackboard, not just Master Kestcliff and Grandmaster Yarrow, but the mammoth man who'd been at the introductions at the very start of the year. The High Watcher himself: Greyheart.

Greyheart walked heavily, the few snowflakes that had weaselled into the cabin jumping with each step from his massive boots. He was very tall, and Oswin couldn't help but stare, not just for the yawning darkness of his purely black eyes or his harshly groomed beard, but for his soot-coloured hair that was so smoke-like it waved like tall grass.

'What are they saying?' Ennastasia asked.

Oswin strained his ears.

Greyheart was speaking, his voice low and rumbling. 'It will not be cancelled. Scelving expeditions are central to a proper Tundran education.'

Master Kestcliff nervously adjusted his tie. 'With all due respect, Greyheart, one cannot receive a proper Tundran education if one is dead.'

Greyheart let out an unsettling grumble, his tawny skin lit softly by the fireplace. 'That's High Watcher Greyheart to you, Stewart.'

Master Kestcliff everted his eyes. 'Of course, High Watcher Greyheart.'

'I must insist it is cancelled,' said Grandmaster Yarrow. 'We've had two monster attacks and countless dead rodents left in disturbing formations. Since you refused to send any of your watchers to help, I've had to stretch my staff thin trying to catch whatever is behind this. An expedition into Shemmia Woods would be a gross invitation of danger.'

'Which is why it must happen.' Greyheart crossed his arms, showing muscles upon muscles bulging below the thick layers of his clothes. 'When I was an apprentice,

Corridor was a respectable training ground that moulded enduring Tundrans. Now, see what you've made it: a culture of pity.'

Yarrow looked so furious, Oswin thought her scarves would jump off her torso and strangle Greyheart. 'Certainly, Corridor has changed from a toxic environment to a place that fosters happiness, if that's what you mean.'

Greyheart scoffed. 'Happiness isn't needed for survival.'

'There is little more important for survival than that.'

'You cannot ignore my wishes,' Greyheart pressed. 'I'm in charge. Besides, just look at how you dole out the food! I've been commanding you for *years* to adjust rations based on an apprentice's value, yet I've seen low-value apprentices fed as well as a high-value one.'

There was a horrific silence. Kestcliff looked scared, but not of Greyheart.

With a creak, Yarrow leaned forward in her wheelchair, hand on her spellbook. 'If you reduce my apprentices to their supposed value again, not even your title will spare you my fury.'

Greyheart looked cowed, then straightened his shoulders and marched to the door. 'We're getting off-topic. Let me make myself clear, Penny.' He returned

Yarrow's glare. 'Either this expedition goes ahead, or I cut off Corridor's food.'

'That would cause mass starvation.'

'Of the *weak*.'

Oswin's grip on the windowsill tightened. He thought about the other apprentices. None of them deserved to starve. Not even Cathy and Frank. (Well, maybe *they* deserved it a little, but he knew that was the vengeance in him talking.)

Greyheart grabbed the handle as if trying to choke it. 'I'll know if you enforce extra protections for the expedition. Don't think I don't have eyes here. If you make accommodations you haven't in previous years, you can kiss your food goodbye.' He left, slamming the door so hard the cabin shook.

Oswin and Ennastasia pressed against the wall, waiting in darkness as Greyheart strode away. Ennastasia scowled after him and Oswin felt a stab of validation that she shared his indignation.

Oswin stretched back up to the window, hearing Kestcliff say, 'We could have more masters on the expedition but keep them hidden?'

Yarrow shook her head. 'We can't risk it.'

'You can't mean to run the second Utility Proving without extra help. Not with what's going on.'

'If we don't, more will suffer. Greyheart will know if we don't follow his rules. We'll have to conduct the expedition with the traditional precautions.'

'He wouldn't cut the food supplies, would he? It must be a bluff.'

'He would,' said Yarrow, her expression dark. 'You don't know him as well as I do. He's done it before. Keep in mind that the current Freeze started earlier and is harsher than the one before. We need every resource the Greenhouses send if we're going to make it to the Thaw.'

Kestcliff put his face in his hands, letting out a shaky breath. 'I'm not sure how much more I can take. I don't think I've felt this anxious since that child went missing in the Teeth.'

Yarrow nodded solemnly. 'At least she came back.'

Interest tugged Oswin, pressing him against the glass. Theories struck him, his stomach dropping as his thoughts raced.

Ennastasia nudged him. 'What is it?'

'At the welcome assembly you said no one has ever come back from the Teeth That Snatch, right?'

'Correct.'

'Earlier this year, Master Vervack let something slip. She said there had been an exception; one person made it out of the Teeth. But when I asked her about it, she changed her story.'

'She must have been mistaken. People don't come back once they've gone into the Teeth. *Ever.*'

Oswin nodded at the window. 'But Kestcliff and Yarrow also just said a child went into the Teeth and came back. A girl.'

Her eyes widening, Ennastasia looked through the window. 'That can't be right ... Did they say *who* supposedly came back?'

Oswin tuned back into what Yarrow and Kestcliff were saying.

Kestcliff had taken off his square glasses to rub his eyes. 'Julious was inconsolable when he heard his son had gone missing.'

Oswin blinked, confused. *Son?*

Kestcliff said, 'Julious's face, Yarrow ... It made me want to quit. But his daughter came back in the end. If we run this expedition and someone gets hurt and they *don't* come back ...'

Daughter? Oswin was even more confused. Had *two* children gone missing? But they were talking as if it was just one.

Yarrow put a hand on Kestcliff's shoulders. 'If we don't follow Greyheart's rules and he finds out, the death toll will be higher. Starvation will claim many apprentices and all their loved ones will have to grieve.' She closed her eyes. 'It is not a decision I make lightly.'

Oswin whispered to Ennastasia, 'Who's Julious?'

She furrowed her brow. 'A man who works for the Watcher's Ring as a watcher. What does that have to do with this?'

'The apprentice who went missing is Julious' daughter—er . . . or son? I'm a bit confused, to be honest.'

Ennastasia took a sharp breath. 'Julious is Maury's dad.'

Oswin couldn't look away from Ennastasia. 'Maury? But he just started this year. Why would he have been at Corridor and gone into the Teeth That Snatch *before* he was even an apprentice?'

Ennastasia's brown eyes darted to the window, the cogs he'd once seen turning behind them back again. This time they snapped to a conclusion. 'I've figured it out.' Without explanation, she walked to the front of the cabin. Scrambling, Oswin did the same.

Not bothering to knock, Ennastasia burst inside. Oswin slunk in after, tensing at the sight of the candles. He was tempted to step back out – he preferred the cold and dark to the flickering flames – but he *had* to know what Ennastasia had realized.

Yarrow and Kestcliff looked up, surprised.

'This is a most unusual hour to visit,' said Yarrow.

Kestcliff was silent for a moment, seemingly lacking the energy to speak, before forcing out, 'How can we help?'

'I know who's behind it,' said Ennastasia. 'The dead animals and the monsters.'

Yarrow regarded her. 'Enlighten me.'

Ennastasia set *Creatures of Tundra and Beyond* on Kestcliff's desk, open to the page with the shapeshifter. 'What is this creature?'

Kestcliff, putting his glasses back on with shaking hands, peered at the book. 'A mimic. A type of human who live on the Endless Expanse. Exceedingly rare. Why?'

'They can shapeshift, can't they?'

'They can.'

Ennastasia paced. 'Two different monsters attack Tundra in quick succession with no clear explanation as to how they got in and no report from Reginald of anyone coming in and out on those nights. Dead animals turn up, yet finding the culprit is impossible. They are elusive. They blend in. They must already be in Corridor.' She stopped pacing and looked directly at Yarrow. 'The culprit is a mimic, shifting into monsters and causing chaos, sneaking out at night to foster terror with their gruesome displays of dead rodents.'

Kestcliff tried to interrupt, but Ennastasia silenced him

with a glare. Oswin now understood why no master stood up to her. Her family could ruin anyone by cutting them off from every vital supply except for food itself.

Oswin deeply wished that he *didn't* know that.

Ennastasia continued, 'How did this mimic come to be in Corridor? Simple: they took the place of someone who went missing a long time ago, assuming their identity for many years until, finally, they arrived at Corridor as an ice apprentice.' Ennastasia's eyes sparkled. Oswin thought she looked excited, and he supposed he felt it, too. A satisfaction at being on the cusp of answers. 'We overheard you talking about the child that returned from the Teeth That Snatch. About Maury. I'm guessing her mother came to Corridor for enchantment maintenance and brought a younger Maury with her, who must have wandered into the Teeth.'

'Yes, but she came back,' said Yarrow. 'She's the only Tundran to have ever survived the Teeth.'

Ennastasia snapped her fingers. 'But what if the person who returned wasn't Maury at all?'

Yarrow's expression was severe. 'Are you suggesting a mimic pretended to be Maury after she was lost to the Teeth?'

Ennastasia gestured out of the window, in the direction of the Teeth. 'No one comes back from the Teeth That

Snatch. *No one.* Maury never returned. A mimic stole her place.'

Kestcliff stood, leaning on his desk. 'It's an admirable theory, and I'm most grateful that you've put so much thought to this, but there's a reason we masters discounted the idea of a shapeshifter being involved long ago. Mimics cannot shapeshift into anything larger than a vohoont. Meersnofs and kikorkas are fearsome beasts. No mimic could become them.'

The sound of the wind outside filled the space.

Ennastasia shook her head. 'That can't be. My theory makes the most sense. It *has* to be a mimic.'

Oswin hated not to side with Ennastasia, but it did sound as if it *couldn't* be Maury. But he daren't say so. This was a conversation for Tundrans.

Kestcliff and Yarrow exchanged a look.

Yarrow said, 'Mimics aren't strong. It would be lovely if we had an explanation, but I'm afraid this isn't it. Maury is a hard-working apprentice. I find it hard to believe he could be behind this. Besides, don't you think Julious and Henreeza, Maury's parents, would notice if their son had been replaced? Mimics don't gain the memories and mannerisms of those they shift into, just their voice and appearance.'

Her shoulders sagging, Ennastasia looked from Yarrow

to Kestcliff. Oswin stood very still, not sure what she was going to do, but ready to support whatever it was.

Eventually, Ennastasia left, not saying another word.

Oswin glanced at Yarrow and Kestcliff. 'Thank you for your time,' he said, trying to sound polite, before walking back into the freezing evening.

22

THE SCELVING EXPEDITION

Alongside the howling wind that never let up, grumbling stomachs became a familiar noise. The day before the second Utility Proving, Oswin noticed how small everyone seemed without proper meals in their bellies. He felt somewhat happy he'd found a way to trick Zylo into not giving him his extra portion. Oswin would take his full ration, Zylo would nod approvingly, down his own breakfast and hurry from the cafeteria. Oswin would then place his bowl on a table and walk away. Within moments, another apprentice would devour it. They always looked so relieved that it helped Oswin not notice his own hunger. Hearing rumbling stomachs didn't hurt, knowing he'd tried his best not to drain resources; he refused to be the log that made the cart too heavy to roll. And though Cathy and Frank shot him glares any time he ventured near the buffet, they clearly hadn't forgotten how he'd covered for them in the first Utility Proving. They didn't say anything, just kept their distance.

Basic Spellbookery was the first lesson of the day, but between the roar of the wind and the anxiety of the apprentices, little learning took place. Master Crull peered at them with his beady eyes, his face red with frustration. At one point, he tried to explain the importance of shutting spellbooks to end the effects of standard spells, only for Philomena and Gale to have a spat about the safety of the second Utility Proving, the details of which had been announced that morning.

'My future-gazing orbs say it's going to be dangerous,' worried Gale.

'Tundrans needs to be tough,' snapped Philomena.

'Pay attention!' said Crull, grabbing his black and white hair. He looked as if he wanted to curl up and snooze, not deal with fidgeting apprentices.

Scelving, their second lesson, was focused on preparation for the second Utility Proving. Kestcliff assessed everyone's skating to ensure they could manage the ice of Shemmia Woods, allocated them equipment to test, then finally revealed the pairs for the tents.

Oswin elbowed Ennastasia. 'We're sharing!'

She didn't look up from the patch she was stitching onto a piece of tent fabric. 'I saw.'

'What are the chances?'

Ennastasia cleared her throat awkwardly. They were standing at the back of the Iceberg Cabin, a pile of camping equipment on the desk in front of them.

Oswin looked at her. 'What is it?'

'Nothing.'

'Something's clearly up.'

Ennastasia closed her eyes. 'I requested we share a tent.'

Oswin stared, astounded. 'I thought we weren't friends?'

Ennastasia's cheeks flushed. 'We're not! But I will admit that, out of all the options, you are the most tolerable.'

'I am?' He could hardly believe it. He asked too many questions, and though *he* enjoyed his silly bets, he knew they were bothersome.

'It says more about the other apprentices than it does you,' said Ennastasia stiffly as she rifled through two bed rolls. 'Stop questioning it. We have work to do.'

AA&V was their final lesson, and if the apprentices struggled to understand Vervack's over-complex instructions on a good day, they had no hope of managing to do so then. The mountain-peak windows of the classroom were entirely white from the snowy weather. It felt as though it hadn't stopped snowing since the Freeze had begun. Oswin struggled to remember what the sun looked like, let alone what its weak warmth felt like on his skin.

Vervack had them building rudimentary wind instruments that were used to communicate over great distances on the Endless Expanse, but the apprentices were so distracted that by the end, the classroom was plagued with the dying splutters of their grim creations.

Afterwards, the approaching expedition loomed in the apprentices' minds. The anxiety was palpable. Oswin would have hidden in his room so as not to bother anyone, but Ennastasia nodded towards the mezzanine expectantly.

'We need a plan,' she said, sitting in her usual armchair while Oswin took his. 'I *know* it's Maury.'

'But Kestcliff said mimics can't shift into something as large as the monsters we faced.' Besides, Oswin thought Maury was too nice to be the culprit.

Ennastasia rubbed her forehead in annoyance. 'Maybe Maury's found a way to gain enough power. It's the only answer that makes sense.'

'Maybe we should just *ask* Maury?'

'Oh, yes. Brilliant idea. Hello, shapeshifting monster who'd be killed by Tundra if they realized you're a mimic, please do tell us if it's you behind the nefarious attacks. What's that you say? It's not? I guess we'll have to take your word for it.'

Oswin gave Ennastasia an unimpressed look. 'It's *not* Maury.'

'It *is*.'

'It's *not*.'

'It—'

'We have no proof it's him.'

Ennastasia sulked, still rubbing her forehead. 'You don't need to remind me.'

'It wasn't a reminder,' he said, tone shifting. 'It was a suggestion.'

Ennastasia's hand fell. She regarded him. 'And what, precisely, are you suggesting, airhead?'

'Kestcliff mentioned a midnight disorientation test as part of the Freeze Utility Proving.'

Ennastasia nodded. 'Each pair is taken, one by one, into Shemmia Woods in the middle of the night, spun around and tasked with finding their way back on their own.'

Though it didn't seem as scary as the Plughole to Oswin, now they were properly into the Freeze, he understood how deadly being caught in the cold and dark was. There was a real risk of death from the elements in the disorientation test.

Oswin said, 'I'm suggesting we stake out Maury and her tent-mate's tent until they leave on their midnight disorientation test, then sneak in and go through her stuff.' He narrowed his eyes. 'We may find our answers *or*, more likely, vindicate Maury.'

Ennastasia's mouth parted. 'Oswin Fields, that is a deplorable idea, deeply immoral and a gross breach of privacy.' She grinned. 'It will work *perfectly*.'

The expedition started early the next morning. The apprentices stood outside the Iceberg Cabin, rubbing at their frosted eyelashes and huddling below cloaks, while snow built small civilizations on their shoulders.

Master Kestcliff was standing at the front doing a headcount while Secondmaster Rochelle stood at the rear. Ennastasia and Oswin had their packs on their backs, bed rolls attached to the tops and skates hanging by their laces around their necks.

Master Kestcliff called above the wind, 'We're heading out! Stay close.' He gave an uncertain nod, as if convincing himself this was a good idea, then led the expedition to the fence.

Reginald gave a gruff greeting before Ferdinand swung open. In pairs, the apprentices entered Shemmia Woods. Though there was a path of snow that cut through to Central Tundra, the rest of the woods' floor was compacted ice. The apprentices and masters stopped where the snow changed to ice and pulled on their skates, snow soaking their socks. Skates on, Oswin stepped onto the ice, checking the roots closest to him. They didn't move.

He was still wobbly on the ice, but he was much improved from his first outing. The expedition moved quicker now they were skating, the woods keeping them relatively sheltered. The pine trees stretched above, as tall as the Alchemy Lodge, their dark needles spiking into the clouds. The harsh snowfall clustered on the sharp leaves, only a few snowflakes breaking through to the ground. When they hit the ice, they vanished, never imperfecting the smooth surface.

The thick tree-trunks were easy to weave around as Oswin skated at the back of the group, the scrape of his skates a comforting noise. Even the creaking of the ice, like the distant twang of muffled thunder, was strangely pleasant. Being surrounded by so much cold felt oddly like snuggling below a duvet.

According to Kestcliff, if they'd skated in a straight line, they would have reached Central Tundra within the day, but for the expedition they were taking a twisting route around the sprawling woods. They stayed in one group until the first marker: a wooden carving of a deersun. It was twice the height of Oswin, standing regally with its front hooves raised and its snake tail coiled on the floor.

Master Kestcliff came to a stop, the edges of his long skirt dusted with frost. 'Remember, you need to visit every marker before reaching the campsite.'

Rochelle *loomed* over the apprentices, daring them to be incompetent enough to forget the instruction.

Kestcliff said, 'See you there.' Turning on his skates, he disappeared between the branches. Rochelle followed a few moments later, her *loomingness* retreating.

Some apprentices bubbled with excitement while others were terrified. Gale looked as if he was about to lose the small meal he'd had for breakfast.

Pair by pair, they set off. At first, the group still huddled with each other, but as they progressed, some pairs hurried ahead while others trailed behind.

Ennastasia, to Oswin's surprise, moved incredibly slowly, so that the others were far ahead in minutes.

'Don't you want to be the first to reach the camp?'

'As much as I enjoy competition, given how I always *win*, we're best served by hanging back. We can keep a better eye on everyone. Particularly Maury.'

Maury and Philomena were skating a bit ahead, figuring out which direction to take. If Oswin thought Maury had looked tired before, it was nothing compared to the trembling mess into which she'd descended. Her monocle was askew, her uniform was bunched and the shaking of her hands was intense.

In what Oswin thought might be companionable silence, he and Ennastasia skated. Sometimes the ice tilted up, sometimes it cracked or bent from fat roots growing through it and other times deep ditches stretched along it. He kept watching the roots. They *still* weren't moving, but the second they did, he'd make sure Ennastasia saw. Maybe she'd be able to figure out why they wanted to eat him.

Oswin edged away from a nearby ditch, trying not to imagine what would happen if he fell into it. 'Why are there so many ditches?'

'The roots leave gouges where they've feasted.'

Oswin almost fell over, envisioning parties of Tundrans being gorged on by roots. 'Feasted? I thought the trees didn't eat people?'

Ennastasia pulled a face. 'Of course they don't eat people. They eat *ice*. Hence the gouges. They excavate large valleys when they eat the ice there.'

'Oh. You meant where they've feasted on *ice*.' He eyed

one of the ditches. He didn't know what to think. The trees had definitely tried to eat *him* when he'd first travelled to Corridor, and *he* wasn't made of ice. 'How come there are no animals here?' he asked suddenly, creeped out by how empty Shemmia Woods was. There was no bird song, or scuffling rodents. Just the creaking trees.

'Because all living things, except for humans, are made from ice. Given the roots eat ice, animals – rather unsurprisingly – steer clear of Shemmia Woods. Or, if they're foolish enough to venture here, are soon dispatched.' Ennastasia seemed creeped out herself, eyeing their surroundings.

Oswin swallowed, looking from one tree to another. He tried to keep away from the ditches *and* the trees. Given he was in a wood, he wasn't very successful on the second account.

They reached the next marker, a timber statue of a frostie: a creature that looked like a snowball with frosty dragonfly wings.

'Ever been bitten by one?' asked Ennastasia.

Back when Oswin had hauled timber on the produce field, he'd received cold stings whenever tiny snowflake blurs buzzed near him. 'Are frosties this big?' He pinched his finger and thumb together.

'Yes.' Ennastasia scratched at her forearms absently.

'They hide below logs. Annoying little things. Almost as bad as gadflysts. At least they leave you alone if you don't disturb them.'

'I have to ask,' said Oswin suddenly. 'How did you find the second marker? We haven't been checking our map.'

She pointed to the ground. 'You truly are an airhead. Look.'

Oswin saw the skating tracks the other apprentices had left. His mind skidded to a halt. They were identical to the indents he'd noticed when he'd heard the mysterious conversation at the start of the year. Whoever had been talking *must* have been skating; that was how they'd got away before he'd sneaked close enough to eavesdrop.

'I'm following where everyone else went,' said Ennastasia, oblivious to the realization Oswin had been smacked with. 'Work smarter, not harder.' She set off again, following the tracks.

By then, even Maury and Philomena were out of sight. All Oswin could hear was the creaking ice. If *he* couldn't hear the other apprentices, they must have been very far away.

Oswin caught up with Ennastasia, managing to keep his balance with flailing arms. 'You don't think the others have been . . .'

Ennastasia glanced at him, skating as if it were as easy

270

as breathing. 'No. The monsters have only operated at night. It's barely midday right now.'

Oswin hadn't realized that, but Ennastasia was right. The monsters had only appeared at night, and the dead rodents had always been discovered first thing in the morning. He felt a bit relieved.

They reached the third marker, a mamat fleeing a vohoont, and then the fourth, a bird with five wings and a tail like a net. Ennastasia said it was a netgel, before promptly calling Oswin an airhead for not knowing that.

By the time they reached the fifth marker, the sun was sinking towards the Wice, ready to disappear below its towering cliff walls. Oswin's hands twitched as the woods darkened and what had once been a comforting noise of ruffling pine needles started to sound like distant whispers, making the hairs on his arms stand on end.

When he looked at Ennastasia, he saw his unease echoed in her scowl. He figured some conversation couldn't hurt.

'Greyheart talked about giving apprentices different amounts of food depending on how valuable they were,' said Oswin, watching his skates. Technically, he also found skating as easy as breathing; not because his skating was good, but because his lungs were terrible. 'Couldn't you use your influence to convince him otherwise?' In his peripheral, he saw Ennastasia cross her arms, her fingers digging into her sleeves. 'Maybe you could even use your influence to—' He cut off, noticing the fury on her features. 'Sorry,' he said, even though he didn't know what he'd done wrong. 'I know I have a habit of asking too many questions.'

'You do.' Her nostrils flared and Oswin wished he'd kept his mouth shut. 'Is that it, then?'

Oswin almost fell over, there was so much misery in her voice. She sounded as if she was trying not to cry. 'What?'

'Is that why you've been befriending me? So you could get me to stifle Greyheart's influence on Corridor?'

'No!'

'Then it's something else.' Ennastasia came to an abrupt stop, digging her skates into the ice. Oswin caught himself on a tree, stopping next to her, but then remembered the carnivorous roots and flailed ungracefully away from the trunk.

'Name it.' Ennastasia gestured between them. 'What's this really been about?'

Oswin stabilized on his skates, then shook his head. 'Nothing!'

She searched his face. After a long pause, she said, 'Barkmoths control the Greenhouses.'

Oswin frowned. 'No. They control timber transmutation.'
That was what Zylo had said, at least.

Ennastasia's voice was dangerous. 'They do. The
question is, after you *promised* not to look into my family,
how did you know I was lying about the Greenhouses?'

Oswin's mouth fell open. He tried to form an
explanation, or a lie, but nothing came out.

'You *know.*' Ennastasia shook her head ruefully. 'Maybe
you didn't know what it meant to be a Barkmoth at first,
but you do now. You *promised*, Oswin.'

'My brother told me. I'm sorry. I was curious.'

'Curious?' Ennastasia scoffed. 'I've been through this
enough times to know how it goes. You want something.
A favour in return for being nice. Just name what it is. I'll
do it, but then you leave me alone.'

Oswin held his hands up. 'I don't want anything! I just
wondered why you hadn't used your Barkmoth-ness to
force the High Watcher to shove off. You can make even
Rochelle listen to you. I figured you could do the same to
Greyheart.'

Her shoulders rising and falling heavily, Ennastasia
stared daggers at him.

'I'm sorry,' he said, his voice pitiful. He felt tears
stinging his eyes. Not only was he a stray, but now he'd
ruined the closest thing to a friendship he had. When he

squeezed his eyes shut, he heard his mother's voice, and saw the flickering of candles. He couldn't stand it. 'I'll go.' He pushed off the tree and skated away. Ennastasia didn't stop him.

He travelled on his own for a while, replaying his fight with Ennastasia in his head, trying to imagine what he could have said to make it go differently. If only he'd agreed to her lie about Barkmoth's controlling the Greenhouses . . .

If only he hadn't broken his promise in the first place.

Oswin continued on, trying to find the meeting spot, but he was hopelessly lost. Just as he was starting to think he'd never find the others, he heard the noise of apprentices. Spotting their Corridor uniforms between the trees, he followed them at a distance until they reached the campsite. If he noticed a few roots moving out of the corner of his eye, he was too dejected to care.

As he approached the campsite, one of his skates caught on something. He tumbled, his trapper hat flying off and sliding to a stop at Rochelle's feet. He looked back, heart racing, but the roots were still. It had just been a lump of ice.

Oswin tried to get to his feet, but recovering from a fall was the one thing about skating he still couldn't get right. 'Could I have some help?' He hoped his trembling voice wouldn't betray how upset he was. He kept thinking about a ruby earring and glaring eyes, and was trying not to.

Rochelle scooped up his hat, then Oswin himself.

On his feet, he dusted fractals of ice off his legs, before gratefully taking his hat back. 'Sorry,' he said. It seemed to be all he *could* say. The light was truly gone, darkness settling among the trees, a fog breathing over the ice floor.

'How come you're alone?' asked Rochelle as she led him to a circle of tents around a bonfire. The flames danced amber shades onto the tents, the shadows flooding back when the light darted away. 'We were worried. Ennastasia arrived a while ago.'

'We got separated.' It wasn't exactly a lie.

Rochelle hummed, clearly knowing he wasn't telling the whole truth, then nodded at Kestcliff. 'All present and accounted for.'

Kestcliff made a mark in a workbook, then addressed Oswin. 'Quickly, into your tent. Rest as much as you can before your disorientation test.'

Rochelle guided Oswin to the tent Ennastasia had already erected, then left to join Kestcliff.

'We can put our feet up and drink some tea once they've settled in,' Kestcliff murmured to Rochelle, who looked exhausted.

His heart sinking, Oswin ducked into the tent and saw Ennastasia at the back, swathed in shadows, her knees pulled to her chest. Not knowing what to say, he took off his pack and began setting up his bedroll. He glanced at Ennastasia, a knot forming in his stomach. When Lullia was upset with him, his best bet was to make himself small and hide, but there was nowhere to do that in a tent. But, then again, Ennastasia was ignoring him, which was not what Lullia had done when she was angry.

Oswin finished making his bed and lay down, wrapping the covers around himself. When all Ennastasia did was lie in her own bed, his hands slowly stopped shuddering and the tension in his muscles left.

Ennastasia whispered, 'We'll talk about what happened another time. I'll be a splintered log of timber if we're not going to break into Maury's tent and get to the bottom of this just because you've been a total prat.'

'Okay,' Oswin whispered, hope making his heart beat faster. She was still talking to him, at least.

'You have good hearing, don't you?'

'Yes.'

There was a ruffle as Ennastasia shifted. 'I set up our tent next to Maury and Philomena's. Listen out. When the masters wake them for their disorientation test, *that's* our shot to snoop through Maury's things. Don't talk to me unless it's about the investigation.'

'Okay.' Oswin felt as if every bit of conversation was a blessing he didn't deserve. As he lamented his shortcomings, he listened closely to the tent next door. After a few minutes, he sat up. In the darkness, Ennastasia did as well.

'What?' she whispered, her voice edged with anger.

Oswin put a finger to his lips. After another minute he looked, wide-eyed, at Ennastasia. 'I can't hear anything.'

'They're probably asleep.'

'I mean, I can't hear *breathing*.'

'Is your hearing good enough that you'd expect to be able to hear breathing?'

'Yes,' said Oswin seriously.

In the darkness they stared at each other, the faint light of the dying bonfire seeping through the tent fabric, mingling with a gentle green glow from above as an eom picked up.

Ennastasia pulled on her skates and cloak in a frenzy, rushing outside. Oswin pulled his own skates on and dashed after her, forgetting his cloak. By the time he was outside, Ennastasia was emerging from Maury and Philomena's tent.

'Empty.' Her expression was grim. She skated to

the bonfire, looking around. 'Where are Kestcliff and Rochelle? One of them should be standing guard. What utter incompetency.'

'Ennastasia.' Oswin had stayed far away from the bonfire and its flames, and in the shadows at the edge of the campsite he'd seen the slumped forms of the masters. Rochelle and Kestcliff were out cold.

Ennastasia skated over to them. 'Fantastic,' she said darkly, then checked their pulses. 'Alive. Something powerful put them to sleep, and without anyone noticing. Your ears included.' She cast her eyes about, then nudged Oswin. 'Can you hear anything?'

Oswin closed his eyes, ignoring the horrific dying splutters of the bonfire and turning his attention to the world beyond. There was the groan of the swaying trees, the creaking of the ice and there, in the distance, voices.

'People talking. That way.' He pointed.

Ennastasia set off.

'Shouldn't we wait for the masters to wake up? Or get help?' said Oswin, following.

Ennastasia pushed her cloak to the side, revealing a spellbook secured to her waist, the brown cover like bark. 'I don't need help.' The unspoken insult that she didn't need *him* made Oswin feel as if he'd been sucker-punched.

They moved through the darkness, the only noise their

skates scraping. The air smelled of pine needles and ice and Oswin tried not to shiver, regretting leaving his cloak behind. Every now and then he'd tap Ennastasia's arm and indicate they change their course, keeping them headed towards the panicked talking. Ennastasia didn't look at him the entire time, and Oswin wished he could unlearn what he knew about the Barkmoths.

As they drew nearer, the voices grew louder in alarm and then, abruptly, the conversation silenced. Oswin gripped Ennastasia's elbow to stop her, barely keeping from falling himself as he did. They stood, Oswin listening closely. He shook his head. He couldn't hear anything any more. Ennastasia snatched her elbow out of his grip.

They kept moving, until Oswin's skate caught on something. He lurched forward but Ennastasia caught him.

'Careful,' Ennastasia whispered, a hint of softness showing through her rage. She must have noticed the relief on Oswin's face, as she quickly hid her concern with a snarl. 'Don't be clumsy.'

'I tripped on something,' said Oswin. Stretching their eyes against the dark, they both looked at what it was. Oswin expected a lump of ice or *worse*, a root, but what he saw was a book. The cover was wrapped in paper, so he ripped it off. The title *The Book of Oddities* stared at him. Next to it was a bloodied, turquoise scale.

Oswin's veins turned to ice, thinking of cheekbones covered in shiny scales. 'That's one of Philomena's.' He also remembered *exactly* who'd had this paper-wrapped book before, but he didn't want to say it.

Ennastasia crouched. 'This page is bookmarked.' She opened it, the pages ruffling in the wind. Oswin sank next to her, his eyes memorizing the two dimly lit pages in the second he saw them. He would have looked longer, or tried to understand what they said, but then his breath caught in his throat as if someone had grabbed his vocal cords and squeezed. There was a whisper, a stab of ice straight to his eardrum, and a tugging on his elbows.

'*Oswin Fields,*' the voice said, and he was paralysed. The light from the eom above snuffed, the soft glow that had permeated the world now a sudden absence. '*Steal The Ghost.*'

He felt as if he'd been released from a choke hold, gasping in breaths. 'I heard it again.' He worked his vocal cords with difficulty. 'It's the voice—'

From the darkness, someone ran at them.

23

GREEN LIGHTS ON
FIERY FRIGHTS

The person ran full speed at them, distress trembling in their screams of 'No!'

Ennastasia got to her feet, helping Oswin out of his crouch. The person collided with Oswin, whose arms flailed, just managing to keep him standing. Whoever it was panicked, pushed off him, then stilled, drawing in staggered breaths.

Oswin's eyes adjusted to the dark. He saw the tear-ridden face of Maury, her eyebrows drawn together.

Ennastasia opened her spellbook, preparing to cast. 'We know it's you. You're the beast terrorizing Corridor. Admit it.'

Maury's misty eye shot wide, her monocle nearly falling off. She looked confused, then the confusion evaporated into panic. 'N-no. I'm not!'

Ennastasia gestured at the book and bloodied scale. 'How else do you explain this?'

'I . . . We . . . It's just that . . .' Maury gripped her hair, as if to pull it out.

'Why don't I explain, seeing as you're a stuttering mess?' Ennastasia skated around Maury. A circling predator. 'The *real* Maury Craftwright went missing in the Teeth That Snatch.'

Maury covered her face.

'And you, a mimic, replaced her, tricking her grieving parents into thinking their daughter had returned. Fooling the rest of Tundra along with them.'

Maury sobbed.

'And then you, a *mimic*,' Ennastasia spat the word, 'tormented Corridor the second you arrived.'

'Ennastasia,' Oswin cautioned, not liking the harshness of her tone.

She ignored him, evidently still furious about what he'd done. 'Were you aiming to merely scare apprentices? Or are you so incompetent that you wanted them dead but failed to kill them?' She came to a stop with a click of her skates.

Her hands trembling, Maury uncovered her face. 'You've got it all wrong,' she said, but she sounded like someone who wanted to give in. 'Mimics don't have enough power to shapeshift into monsters.'

Ennastasia's eyes flashed victoriously. She looked at Oswin, who stared back, puzzled as to why she was grinning so widely. Then her grin vanished as she clearly remembered she was meant to be angry with him.

She said, 'Oswin and I had to ask Master Kestcliff about mimics to find out they can't shift into monsters. We haven't been taught about them in Scelving yet. So, tell me, Maury Craftwright, how do *you* know what mimics can shift into so precisely? Your knowledge is in inventions. *Not* beasts.'

Maury floundered for a response, but none came.

Ennastasia pushed off one skate, inching towards Maury. 'I think I've finally figured out how you've been doing it.' She nodded upwards. 'Eoms. Whenever one is present, magic is at its strongest. I wonder if, when an eom shines, a mimic gains enough strength to shift into anything they want? Even a monster.' She glanced back at Oswin. 'You have perfect memory, don't you?'

Oswin nodded, but he couldn't take his eyes off Maury. Her expression made him pause. The fear, the averted gaze, the trembling. He knew that look. He wore it all the time. That *wasn't* the look of a villain.

Ennastasia said, 'Tell me, Oswin, were there eoms during the monster attacks and on the nights before dead animals were discovered?'

It took Oswin's memory less than a second to confirm it. 'Every single time.'

Ennastasia turned back to Maury. 'You stole the life of a missing boy, then waited for eoms to appear so you could tear Corridor apart from within.' She shook her head. 'Pathetic.'

Tears broke free from Maury's eye. 'Please, you're wrong. I promise.' She grabbed desperately onto Ennastasia. 'I'm a Tundran – just like you!'

While Ennastasia looked coldly at Maury, Oswin blinked rapidly as her words speared his chest. *A Tundran. Just like you …*

Ennastasia shook Maury off. 'A likely story.'

'I mean it!' Maury persisted. 'I'm me. I belong here. This is my home!'

Maury's begging felt like swords through Oswin's stomach. He knew exactly how she felt. He put a hand against a tree, leaning into the bark, not able to care about the risk of roots right then. He tried to breathe, but his lungs had shut themselves off from the rest of his body. He knew Maury was talking about herself, but it didn't feel that way. It felt like what he told himself when he remembered how little he belonged in Tundra.

He needed to calm down. Now was not the time to lose his sickly lungs to panic. Then, like a current of electricity through his body, he felt the voice again.

'*Steal The Ghost.*'

It hit him. Not only had an eom appeared the night before each monster attack, but the voice had, too.

His vocal cords weak, he gasped, 'Ennastasia.'

Her focus shot to Oswin, all thoughts of Maury seemingly gone. She grabbed his shoulder to steady him. 'Are you all right?'

He tried to speak as he sank towards the ground. The darkness weakened as a green light breathed above them. In unison, the three apprentices looked up. The eom had started again, brighter this time. The lights dived down and wove through the trees.

Maury stumbled, choking out a low groan and scratching at her face. Her groan grew, gargling into a deep bellow.

Ennastasia blinked. 'What is this?'

Maury let out another pained noise, then a stifled cough, as if holding back bile. 'I'm sorry.' Her voice modulated between that of a teenager and something *much* bigger. 'You were right. You were right—' She keeled over.

'Explain,' Ennastasia snapped. Oswin watched, his lungs slowly crawling back to normal.

'I *am* a mimic. I took the first Maury's place but—' She covered her mouth, choking. 'Julious and Henreeza – Mum and Dad – knew straight away. They agreed to keep me safe. My first family died on the ice. I had nowhere to go—' She fell to her knees, her skin growing.

Oswin said, 'Why did you attack us?'

'I didn't mean to!' It was as if the words were too big to come out of Maury's mouth. Spit flew between her lips. 'I woke up in random places with aches all over. I'd been shifting and forgetting. I tried to stop it! I made chains to lock me away at night, I tried to get Philomena to strengthen the invention with a spell. I never told her why, but it didn't matter: the spell made the Etymagery cabin fall, and did *nothing* to the chains. I never had these issues before that incident with the shrinking sphere! It was as if someone else was controlling me!' She shuddered as if about to be sick. 'I tried to understand why the sphere shrank, but after the krimpsteen, I hit a dead-end. And all your questions about oddities had me looking into them, but *The Book of Oddities* didn't tell me how to fix it, or why it had happened. And I couldn't tell anyone. You've heard what Philomena says about monsters. Tundra wouldn't hesitate to kill a mimic—' A crackling growl stole her words. Her form shuddered, pulsating as it grew. Her skin stretched. Her hair, matching the strand they'd found in the research quarters, shrank.

Horribly, it occurred to Oswin that this whole time Maury hadn't been being friendly to be polite. She'd wanted someone to help her. Every time Oswin hadn't sat with her, she must have thought he didn't *want* to be friends. And of course, she'd felt as if she couldn't turn to Philomena, what with everything she said about beasts.

At first there was guilt, but then a chill spread up Oswin's spine. 'Where *is* Philomena?'

Maury couldn't answer. Her body grew into a snake-like silhouette, her voice changing from gargling to the crackle of fire, and Oswin, with sinking dread, remembered the third and final monster Kestcliff had taught them about: the skelaard.

Oswin and Ennastasia moved back as Maury, transformed, towered above them, cast in green by the eom. Her body was long and thin, and void of flesh and skin. There were just the bones of a spine, with ribs jutting on each side all the way to the white point of the tail. She looked like a snake's skeleton except for the head, which was a crackling fireplace. The mantelpiece was a pair of frowning eyebrows above two dark eyes, and the grates opened and closed like multiple mouths, fire spitting out of hot coals. It reared, sending a flowerpot, blue hand ornament and owl statue teetering on top of the mantelpiece, and bellowed a roar. Fire spurted from the fireplace-face. The trees above caught alight, the angry red dancing with the green of the eom. Oswin shrank in fear.

Ennastasia shoved him. 'Run!'

He didn't, though. If he did, the skelaard would follow him and Ennastasia, which would put a *Tundran* in danger. If they fled for the tents, that'd put everyone else at risk.

Oswin snatched the spellbook from Ennastasia's hands and threw it through the trees before she could protest. Enraged and confused, Ennastasia darted to retrieve it.

'Get the others out of here!' he cried after her, then skated beneath the monster, leading it in the other direction. 'I bet you can't catch me!' he called to it, slapping his hand against one of its jutting ribs for good measure. He regretted it instantly; the monster's bones were warm, and the sensation of heat against his palm almost made his mind shut down with unpleasant memories.

He forced himself to push on. He had to be quick.

The skelaard slammed down, trying to catch him, but missed. With a thud and a crack, the beast sank to the ground, its ribs stabbing into the ice. It let out another roar, fire reaching for the retreating Oswin, and then it pushed off the ground. It slithered through the air in pursuit, decimating trees, the ice cracking and splitting when it clumsily crashed against it.

Oswin moved as fast as he could, leading it away from the campsite. He didn't care that it would eventually catch him; he was keeping everyone else safe. He was being useful.

Urged on by the roar of the creature, and the crackling of the fire gushing out of its mouth, Oswin rushed through the trees. His skates carved over the ice, his eyes working tirelessly in the green glow to pick out a path.

The skelaard slammed its head onto the ground next to him. He barely dodged, avoiding the eruption of fire that sizzled out, yet the push of heat still shot all the way through his flesh. The creature spun, swiping its tail at him. The white bone turned black and amber, like cindering coals. Oswin ducked, the tail cutting the air, leaving a trail of smoke that stung his tongue. What Oswin hadn't accounted for, but really *should* have, was his lungs. They'd been struggling *before* breathing in the smoke, but now, as he pushed off a tree to gain more speed, he felt their ability to function falling away.

The beast roared again, spewing fire and setting more

trees alight. The angry glow brightened the woods in a gruesome red. Oswin's skin itched from the heat, and he finally noticed the tears on his own face seconds before they evaporated.

He tried to keep skating, the monster's hot breath cooking the back of his neck, but his lungs gave out, as if tar were jammed in his throat. He only managed a few paces before his head felt light and his muscles tingled. The monster coiled above him, the heat from its fiery mouth boiling his clothes.

It was the warmth that did him in. It made his mind stall with the echoes of an angry voice. He fell onto the ice and lay still, feeling the wonderful cold of it against one side of his body, and painful warmth on the other.

A small opening formed in his throat, and he wheezed in a desperate gasp, pushing himself up with his hands. The monster rose above him, hissing sparks and flames, its fire grates opening wide, ready to strike. Oswin tried to get up, but he kept slipping. His hands flew away from him. His skates lost their grip.

He turned onto his back and saw the beast's face centimetres away, so close he could see the dents and bumps in the iron of its forehead. The smell of soot washed over him, his skin a second from melting. Even if he could get back up, he wasn't fast enough to outrun it, and even if he could, where would he run to? He'd been skating without thought. He had no idea where he was.

Then, he remembered his citizen watch, sitting in his pocket. The monster lurched, and he snapped it out.

As the beast's gaping mouth was about to crush him, Oswin moved the cube within the watch, smashing it against a cog just as Ennastasia had done to wake Reusie. A screech erupted. The watch vibrated as if angry frosties were trapped within. He dropped it and slammed his hands over his ears; it was such a painful sound that it took him a second to realize the skelaard was recoiling, too. It thrashed from side to side and spat fire in amber sprays as it tried to free itself from the wailing.

Wincing, Oswin shuffled to a tree. He grabbed one of its branches and tried to lift himself up, but fell. Adrenaline made his limbs unsteady and the watch's sharp noise threw his balance.

The monster slashed its tail into the ground, spearing the watch, which let out a final croak. Oswin sat against the tree, defeated. All things considered, this wasn't a terrible way to go. He deserved the pain from the flames for all the ways he'd failed. At least he'd led the monster away from the others. At least he'd been of use. And with one less mouth to feed, he would stop being a burden to Tundra.

'There you are!'

Oswin saw Ennastasia skating over, dashing through the smoke.

With the open spellbook in one hand, her other cut through the air. *'The Timber Moves!'*

There was a thunderous crack. Lines splintered the ice as the tree Oswin was leaning against jerked out of the ground. Ennastasia's face was lined with pained concentration. The tree collided with the beast, spearing it to the ground. There it writhed, trying to break free. Its ribs scoured the ice as it struggled, sending up clouds of frost.

Oswin looked at Ennastasia, then felt himself slipping. Behind the tree had been a ditch. Without the tree stopping him, he almost fell into it, but caught himself at the last second.

'Ennastasia! You need to warn the others.'

'I was right! Maury is the culprit. *I was right!'*

'Brilliant! I'm so happy for you! Can we focus on the fact we're in mortal danger?' Oswin dragged in a few pained breaths. 'Why'd you come back? You could have been safe!'

Ennastasia looked at him, painted gold by fire. 'I wasn't going to leave you to die.'

Broken branches hit the floor in small explosions of sparks and soot.

'But *why*?'

The skelaard had wrapped its skeleton tail around the tree to pull it out, struggling to break loose.

Ennastasia swallowed. She seemed more scared of Oswin than the monster. 'Because you *are* my friend.'

Oswin's breath left him, but not because of his lungs.

'And I'm going to keep you safe. *The Timber Moves.*'

A branch shoved Oswin into the ditch.

'Stay hidden!' Ennastasia's voice called as he rolled, the green light of the eom and the amber glow of the fire spinning around him. He came to a stop at the bottom of the ditch, winded. Lying on his back, he stared at the pine needles against the starry night sky. He saw a tree sail overhead, landing with a thud in the distance, and realized the monster had freed itself. There was the sound of skating, a roar and then the noise of battle.

He tried to get to his feet, but it was even harder in the ditch. The curve of the ground made standing impossible. He kept slipping onto his backside. He didn't give up – he refused to leave Ennastasia, his *friend* – but his efforts were hopeless. After what seemed like decades of exhausting attempts, he stilled, thinking. He wasn't going to get out by mindlessly scrambling for an eternity.

As he stared at the sky, he thought about *The Book of*

Oddities. Before Maury had shapeshifted, he'd seen the two bookmarked pages, and now he summoned the memory back to the front of his mind, reading the words he'd imprinted into his thoughts.

Chapter 3

THE ODDITIES

As we've learned in previous chapters, the layers separated. We only know of other layers, other 'worlds', because the closest one, the oddity layer, can leak into our own. Its 'leaks' are called oddities and around them the strangest occurrences take place, from gifting magical abilities to powering spellbooks.

The oddities are poorly understood, but there have been numerous theories about them. Some have argued that timber, fog and coal magic indicate the existence of timber, fog and coal oddities. Alternative oddities were suggested in ancient times, before the magics of timber, fog and coal had been identified. These ranged from ice, to blood, to ghost or iron. Evidence of these was lacking, so the theories fell by the wayside.

Just as the magic that results from the oddities is risky, so too are the oddities themselves. The prevalent view maintains that, if the oddities of timber, fog and coal exist, for safety's sake hidden is how they should remain. Only in obscure stories do we see

Tundrans merging with items that could be considered oddities and, when they do, it never ends well.

Oswin closed his eyes, focusing on the memory as hard as he could. There hadn't just been words on the page, but images, too. Guesses as to what the different oddities looked like, sketched by scholars long since reclaimed by the ice. He recalled orbs of fog, thin lines of coal, two ovals of ice and, in the corner of the page, a sketch of a spectral glove labelled 'The ghost hand'.

His eyes shot open.

'*Oswin Fields, Steal The Ghost.*'

Oswin sat up. 'Do you mean the ghost hand? I need to steal the ghost hand?' He felt alive with possible explanations, then a stab of vindication. All this time he'd been saying the oddities were linked to the beast attacks. It seemed he'd been right.

He tried to stand again but fell.

'*Oswin Fields . . .*'

He sat very still. 'Yes?'

'*Steal The Ghost.*'

Oswin gritted his teeth. 'Really? You've never mentioned that before.' Then, with a shock, he realized he *had* seen a spectral hand, and not just as a sketch. At the start of the year, after Maury had fainted, he'd noticed a blue glow around her right hand. Then, earlier that night, he'd seen a flowerpot, an owl statue and *a blue hand ornament* on the monster's mantelpiece. It hadn't been an ornament at all, but a spectral hand.

'The ghost hand,' he realized out loud. He tried to stand, a plan forming in his mind. He needed to steal the ghost hand from Maury's beast form. If the ghost hand was an oddity, and corrupting her, then separating her from it should resolve the issue.

But instead of rising triumphantly, he flopped back down, slipping on the ice. He kicked a heel against the ground, angered, and that was when he finally noticed something *very* bad.

Moving through the ice, like slithering wyrms, were dark lines. They wriggled from side to side, feeling for something. Surrounding him. They inched closer, rising to the surface.

Oswin's eyes widened as he followed the dark lines back to the trees, realizing just what was happening. The roots were coming for him again.

They looked ravenous.

24

STEALING THE GHOST

Oswin kept trying to climb out of the icy ditch, but each time he'd either fall or make it a few paces before sliding back down. When he'd last looked over his shoulder, the roots had been below the ice. Now, some of them were breaking through. Worming towards him.

Feverishly, he scrambled at the ditch. He took his gloves off and dug his nails into the ice, but they scraped uselessly against it.

'*Oswin Fields, Steal The Ghost.*'

'I'm a bit busy!' He slid back and one of his skates hit a root. Its reaction was immediate. It surged around his skate, wrapping tightly and squeezing. Oswin tried to pull his skate free, but the root was snugly in place. With shaking hands, he pulled his foot out of the skate. He untied the other, now just in his socks, and drove the sharp blade of the skate he'd removed into the roots, cutting them back. Another root grabbed *that* skate, and Oswin lost his grip. Two others seized the ends of his socks and he had to pull his feet out of those, standing barefoot on the ice.

Oswin froze in surprise because he was, in fact, on his feet. Barefooted, he had an unnaturally good grip. He wriggled his toes. The ice wasn't slippery against his skin, though he was sure it *should* be.

'*Oswin Fields!*'

Snapped out of his stupor by the voice, Oswin noticed the roots closing in. 'Yep,' he said, turning. 'I should get going.'

He grabbed at the ditch with his hands and pressed his bare feet against the ice, finding climbing far easier now. With only a few slips, and a fair bit of fear, he struggled to the top. He grabbed at a tree-trunk and hauled himself onto flat ground, hearing the cracking of the roots retreating. He didn't have time to rest, even if his lungs were burning again. At least the roots had given up their quarry for the time being.

He trudged aimlessly, listening for Ennastasia and the

beast, but there was no noise. He thought maybe he could follow the trail of destruction, but burning trees and cracked ice surrounded him on all sides. There was no clear direction to the chaos.

After a minute of wandering through the carnage, he heard crying and broke into as fast a run as his tired lungs could manage. Skidding to a halt by a hollow tree, he saw a girl huddled within. Her messy black hair covered her beige face and turquoise scales, speckled with blood. A handful were missing, angry red sores visible below.

'Philomena!' Oswin sagged with relief. 'You're okay!'

Philomena looked at him, shaking. 'Maury told me to hide before she ... It's ... It's her ... She told me ...' She squeezed her eyes shut. 'I ran. I *ran*. I should have stayed with her, but she shifted and—'

'It's okay.'

'No! You don't understand. It's Maury! She's the monster—'

'*I know*. Listen, stay here. I'll come back for you.'

'No. I can help. I'm not running again.' Philomena tried to get to her feet, but something was wrong with her ankle, and she flopped back down.

Oswin held her firmly. 'You're injured. Stay here. Don't move.' He gave her a solemn nod, then set off again. He *had* to find Ennastasia.

As he hurried he listened impatiently for the faintest hint of her or the monster, while his mind conjured images of what awful fate could befall Ennastasia. He was starting to lose hope; among all the trees his searching felt useless. There was no way he could figure out where she was.

Then he felt a buzzing in his trouser pocket. Pulling the object out, he found himself staring at his top card for Huvect. A frost arrow flashed above it, pointing to wherever she was – Ennastasia was challenging him to a battle.

'Ennastasia, you genius.' He half-jogged, half-limped through the trees, trying not to shudder at their – thankfully unmoving – roots. He started to notice noises. Shouting. Thuds of heavy objects. Rumbling roars. Flashes of fire through the trees, singeing the branches orange. Finally, he made out Ennastasia, spellbook in hand, hurling tree after tree. The giant skeleton struck at her, its fireplace grates trying to crush her hands, but a tree speared the side of its face. It was stunned, shaking its head and spluttering specks of flame.

Ennastasia's arms shook. She looked exhausted and wasn't putting any weight on her left leg.

Oswin turned his Huvect card's buzzing off; he needed to be silent for this. As Ennastasia and the skelaard duelled, fire and bark clashing, he skirted around them. He didn't make a sound, forcing his breathing to be inaudible.

The monster rushed Ennastasia, sending her flying. She landed against a tree and sank to the floor, gasping in pain as her spellbook shot out of her hand. She crawled towards it, her fingers brushing the cover.

The skelaard's tail flicked it away. The spellbook slid across the ice and Ennastasia stared at the spot where it had been. The monster loomed above her and she turned to it slowly.

Oswin reached the back of the beast, terrified at the thought of what he was about to do. He launched onto the spines of the skeletal body and climbed, tears stinging his eyes from both the height and the warmth of its bones against his hands.

The skelaard lowered its head, breathing clouds of soot over Ennastasia. She stared straight at it, shivering, but not breaking her gaze. For a second, Oswin swore her veins glowed a faint amber, shining through her skin, but then the monster jolted to the side.

It had noticed him.

'Oswin?' The brief colour of Ennastasia's veins vanished.

'Keep it distracted!' he yelled as the monster snapped at

him. He ducked, feeling its boiling fireplace mouth clack shut where his head had been. It shook from side to side and it was all he could do to hold onto its warm bones. He looked down, seeing how high off the ground he was. He squeezed his eyes closed. 'Oh, splinters.'

Someone else must have been casting magic, because a slash of air cut into the monster, breaking off the end of its tail. It reared, screeching flame into the sky. Oswin cringed at the heat and ducked as hot bites of cinder fell around him. But he could see the blue spectral hand attached to the top of the mantelpiece. Clenching his jaw, he forced his limbs to move, convincing himself he wasn't that high up, and that sharp jolts of boiling heat weren't hitting his limbs every few seconds, making him feel as if chunks of his body were melting.

As another slice of air cut into the skelaard, earning another screech, Oswin stretched his arm as much as he could, the muscles taut. The end of his fingertips brushed the spectral hand.

In a blink, the world was still. Spouts of flame froze in the air. The beast was motionless. Even sound had vanished. Oswin's ears felt as if they were in a bubble. He leaned back on his perch atop the beast, dazed.

'*Finally,*' said a voice, not distant at all. It was right next to his ear, whispering like a thief. Oswin whirled to look behind him. There was no one there. *'I'm a ghost. And you can be too.'*

'Are you the one who's been speaking to me?' Still nothing moved. It was as if the world had become one of the paintings in Yarrow's cabin, but when Oswin looked forward again he saw a spectral hand floating before him. He recoiled, but when it didn't attack, he calmed. 'Are you the ghost hand? An oddity?'

'Yes, and together, we could return home.'

'Return home?'

'Why do you think I've been calling you? Why do you think I wanted to break away from this mimic and merge with you? Why do you think I kept trying to tug you towards me?'

Oswin frowned. Was that what the odd pulling sensation he'd felt had been? 'The monsters were targeting me,' he realized.

'You're the only way home for me. Let's go home.'

'What do you mean, "home"?'

'I mean ... home.'

Oswin felt a push against his rib cage. A sensation of nothingness. Water that made you dry. Legs composed of sound. Shapes his brain couldn't make sense of. The taste of colours and texture of balance. It was utter confusion.

Home.

He couldn't understand it. He *loathed* that he couldn't understand it. But though he didn't know what this *home* was, he knew at least one thing: it would take him far from Tundra.

'Where there's no such thing as a stray. Where you'll never be a burden.'

Oswin went to reply, but his words lodged in his throat. The idea of not being a burden gripped him; it was a crushing weight on his skeleton. 'If I leave with you, if we go "home", what will happen to Ennastasia and Maury?'

'They'll be safe. I've departed from Maury. She'll return to normal.'

'Why did you make her turn into monsters in the first place?'

'I wasn't compatible with her. I had to motivate her to let me go, or else I'd never have got to you. When the eoms bolstered her shifting power, I took the opportunity.'

'But she didn't know how to get you out of her! You've been causing her all this heartache, and putting people in danger, for no reason. Why didn't you just tell me all this?' Oswin felt like screaming. Why couldn't anyone ever just explain things to him? This oddity included.

'You really know nothing of us, do you? I couldn't choose more than three words and your name through which to speak. Not until contact. You've pulled me from Maury like a thorn

from a vohoont's paw. You've been useful. You can come home with me and never feel anything. Never think about the fact you're a stray.'

Oswin swallowed thickly. He looked at the monster, at the fire frozen in its consumption of the trees, all perfectly still, his thoughts biting at his heels. Every scrap of food he'd ever eaten, every cup of water he'd drunk, every item of clothing or equipment he'd used – it all could have gone to someone deserving. To a Tundran. Even if only Cathy and Frank had said it out loud, everyone knew it was true.

'Take me away from here.' As soon as he said it, Oswin sensed the change. Cracks raced along his body, as if it were melting, or shattering, or both at once. Zylo would be better off without him. Tundra had its skilled Tundrans. There was no need for him. But then, as his body collapsed, chunks breaking off and turning into white frost, and his mind felt itself slipping somewhere far away, a memory crashed into the back of his eye sockets.

Because you're my friend.

The melting and shattering slowed. It was uncertain at first but, piece by piece, it sped up, reversing the damage until Oswin's body was healed.

'No! We must go!'

'I can't. I have a friend here.' Oswin glanced at the skeleton monster: Maury. *'Friends.* People who need me.'

His eyes moved to Ennastasia. 'There's someone who doesn't have anyone else but me.' He could feel the ghost hand's frustration.

'*You're really going to make me wait longer to return home, aren't you?*'

'I still have no clue what you mean by that,' admitted Oswin.

'*Fine. Goodbye, Oswin. I won't be able to speak to you once we merge.*'

'Why not?' he asked before his brain fully processed what the oddity had said. His heart clenched. 'Wait! *Merge?* No, no, no, no, I don't want to merge with you. I never said that! Don't merge with—!' His body seized. The ghost hand hovered forward, glowing. Oswin shielded his face from the glare, but then his arms locked in place, too.

Its last ominous words echoed, almost smug, '*Don't worry. We're compatible.*'

There was a burst of light. A spectral blue shone over Oswin's right hand like a ghostly glove. In a snap, the light vanished, and the world moved again, the clumps of fire tumbling to die a hissing death on the ice.

The skeletal monster shrank and Maury was hanging in the air next to him, eye wide in confusion. Then they were falling. Oswin tried to scream, but no noise came out. His eyes didn't have time to adjust to the sudden lack of light, but his tongue could taste the soot and ice of Shemmia Woods.

'*The Movement Slows!*' came Rochelle's voice.

The sensation of motion lessened. With a soft thud, Oswin landed on cold ground. He lay still as everything that had happened washed over him. He was still in Tundra, he was still a stray and he was still useless. But he had a friend. Maybe, if he stopped second-guessing Maury, he could even have *two*. Useful or not, he didn't want to leave Corridor.

'Oswin!' Stumbling, Ennastasia fell to her knees at his side. She hesitated there, then hugged him. It was awkward, as if she'd never hugged anyone before, but it made Oswin stop thinking about hurtful things. He hugged her back tightly, his fingers digging into the fabric of her cloak. She pulled away and Oswin listened to the sputter of burning trees and watched the dying eom, holding onto the sides of her cloak. The rough material below his fingers was a much-needed distraction.

Secondmaster Rochelle walked over. The bags below her eyes had never looked larger.

Philomena was there, too, limping. 'I got help,' she said. 'Even if I had to crawl to get it.'

Oswin looked at Rochelle, every muscle in his body hurting. 'You were unconscious.'

'I *was*,' Rochelle agreed. 'I woke up without a clue where you were. Philomena told me what happened. I had some assistance finding you.' She nodded upwards, and Oswin saw the toothoot circling. 'Kestcliff's still snoring.'

'You cast the air cuts that distracted the monster.'

'I was trying to kill it, in all honesty.' Rochelle knelt by Oswin and Maury, checking them over. Oswin felt as if his body was a statue. He stared ahead, not sure what to do. Maury was shuddering all over, wiping at his eye.

Philomena sat next to Maury, whose body went rigid. For a horrid second, Oswin thought Philomena would snarl at Maury for being a mimic, but in a rush of movement she was hugging him.

'Why didn't you tell me, you silly mamat? I could've helped.'

Tears formed in Maury's eye, then the tension in his body melted as he hugged Philomena back. 'You've always said monsters are horrid. That you want to kill them.'

'I meant the beasts that want to eat us, not my best friend! It's like I said: I'd never hurt a living thing unless I have to. If a monster is peaceful, I'll be their friend.'

Maury's eye darted fearfully from Philomena to Rochelle.

Philomena said, 'I told her. She knows.'

Words rushed out of Maury. 'Please don't kill me,

Rochelle. I'm not evil. I couldn't tell anyone I was a mimic; I would have been executed. Julious and Henreeza, my adoptive parents, know I'm a mimic. You can check with them. This *thing* controlled me. I would black out and when I'd wake up I'd be covered in injuries ...'

Rochelle held up a hand and Maury's rambling trailed off. 'I won't be telling anyone. Though I will be checking with Julious and Henreeza to confirm your story. Right now, we need to find a way to stop your transformations.'

Oswin finally let go of Ennastasia's cloak and flexed his hand. 'You won't need to, actually.'

Ennastasia's grip on his sleeve tightened. 'Why not?' she demanded, and he swallowed. 'Oswin, *why not*?'

'I "stole the ghost",' he joked weakly. He turned to Maury. 'You were corrupted by the ghost hand, an *oddity*, but it's gone now. You won't transform any more.' He didn't mention the fact it hadn't left, only hopped from Maury to him. Maury was too relieved at the news to realize what Oswin had left out.

'You're sure it's gone?' Rochelle asked.

'I saw it disintegrate,' Oswin lied, impressed with how convincing he sounded.

As Rochelle turned to check Maury over, Oswin gestured for Ennastasia to lean close. Making sure it was only visible to her, he commanded the spectral glove to

309

appear and disappear around his hand. He felt unsettled yet excited at the sight. Controlling the ghost hand was as easy as blinking.

Ennastasia's hand inched towards her spellbook, which she must have picked up off the floor. Her voice was a whisper, her eyes darting in the direction of Rochelle, who was still checking Maury. '*You're* infected?'

'I don't think so,' Oswin whispered back. 'I'm not infected by it. I'm *merged* with it.' He recalled the words the mysterious voice had used. 'Unlike Maury, I'm *compatible* with it.' He tried not to think about all the dire warnings he'd read about fusing with oddities. About how it always ended badly for the human.

Ennastasia said, 'Even so, we'll have to keep a close eye on you for a few days. At least until the next eom. The heightened magic is what triggered the transformations in Maury. If you're safely merged, we'll find out then.' She tutted. 'So risky. What an airhead.'

A wealth of tiredness fell over Oswin. He raised his voice, turning to Rochelle. 'Can I sleep soon?'

'Of course.' Rochelle stood – satisfied that Maury was no longer infected with an oddity – and helped Oswin to his feet. She gently dusted his shoulders, then looked at Maury, Philomena and Ennastasia. 'Can you all walk?'

Ennastasia struggled to her feet. 'I can limp.'

Philomena said, 'Me too.'

Rochelle gave a brisk nod. 'That will do.'

At a slow, wincing pace, they headed back to the campsite.

25

THE UN–USELESS STRAY

As they travelled to the campsite, time passed in a blur. For once, Oswin didn't remember any of it. All he could focus on was the roars of fire, the height he'd climbed to and the tingling sensation around his right hand, where the ghost oddity had settled.

They returned to find the others awake, Master Kestcliff standing with a spellbook at the ready. Oswin was dimly aware of Rochelle murmuring with Kestcliff, who showed Rochelle the cups they'd drunk their tea from, the remnants of a potent mixture congealed at the bottom. Kestcliff reckoned it was responsible for knocking them unconscious.

Gale hugged Philomena, teary-eyed as he welcomed his twin sister back. Maury stood to the side, looking nervous.

'What happened?' Kestcliff asked Rochelle.

Rochelle stood tall and stoic, face impassive, but Oswin knew she must be warring with decisions. Eventually, she said, 'We found the monster. It's been defeated.' She said nothing about mimics. Maury let out a relieved breath as Rochelle held true to her word, explaining how they'd bested the monster without implicating Maury. 'As far as I'm concerned,' Rochelle continued, 'all the apprentices who helped stop this fiasco have passed the Freeze Utility Proving. They've certainly proven their competency.'

Oswin thought it was rather ridiculous how lucky he'd been to somehow scrape through both the Utility Provings and thus his first year at Corridor.

He was given shoes to wear but, in all honesty, his feet weren't even slightly frostbitten. Staring blankly ahead, he was led back to Corridor and taken directly to the healer's cabin. The healer gave him something warm to drink, even though he'd have preferred something cool, and he lay on a pillow-filled bed. He would have gone to sleep sooner if there hadn't been candles lighting the room but, eventually, his exhaustion overcame his fear.

When Oswin awoke, it was morning and the room was lit by the friendly light of the sun, the candles snuffed. Ennastasia was sitting in a bed next to his, reading a book that was half burned.

Groggily, Oswin propped himself up. 'I bet I'm in more pain than you.'

Ennastasia turned a page. 'That can be arranged.' She glanced in his direction. A smile broke out on her face that she took a second to force into a frown.

Oswin sat up properly, grimacing. 'That's *The Book of Oddities.*'

'Observant. I picked it up on the way back to the campsite.' She gritted her teeth, considering something. After a few minutes she said, reluctantly, 'The book has a sheet on its front page where apprentices who took it out in years gone by signed their name.' Her grip on the book tightened. 'One was Michael Fields.'

'My uncle?'

'No, a different Michael Fields.'

Oswin's eyebrows shot up. 'There's more than one?'

'I was joking, you utter dingbat. Honestly.'

Yarrow *had* let slip that Michael Fields and oddities were related. 'What did my uncle want with *The Book of Oddities*?'

'Who knows.' Ennastasia showed him the pages she'd

been examining. Oswin squinted, but it was too far away to read. She put the book back in her lap. 'You merged with the ghost hand. With an oddity.'

'Yeah.'

Ennastasia looked at him, confused. 'How do *you* understand that? You haven't read this.'

'Actually, I've read two pages. I saw them in the woods. Before the roots tried to eat me, I read it in my mind.'

Ennastasia stared at him. 'You memorized both pages from a few seconds of looking at them, in the middle of everything else going on?'

Oswin shrugged. 'Yeah.'

She stared at him, mystified. He stared right back.

He said, 'The most important thing is that I was right about the oddities being linked to this whole mess.'

'And *I* was right about Maury,' Ennastasia added, 'which, if we're keeping score, should be worth a lot more points.'

'What? No, it shouldn't.'

'Yes, it should.'

'No, it—'

Ennastasia, clearly bored with bickering, cut over him. 'The eom returned last night, but you didn't transform. Maury was infected with the ghost hand, but you're safely merged with it. It doesn't *seem* as if you'll become a threat.'

'Then it's over. We solved it.'

'I knew I could do it,' said Ennastasia. Oswin narrowed his eyes at her. 'Fine. I knew *we* could do it.'

'Thank you.'

'And, before you get any ideas, don't ask me how you've merged safely with an oddity when Maury couldn't. I've no idea.'

Oswin looked at his hands, fiddling his fingers together. 'It said we were compatible.'

'What?'

'The ghost hand. It said it had been trying to leave Maury to get to me.'

'Why?'

'Because I'm its only way home.'

Ennastasia blinked, then blinked again. 'Sometimes you speak and it's as if nothing but nonsense comes out. What does that even mean: you're "its only way home"?'

Oswin shrugged. 'I've no clue what its home is or why it thinks I'm the only way there. But I do know it gave me an option. When I merged with it we could have . . . gone.'

Ennastasia looked at him expectantly. 'Are you going to explain what you mean by that or stretch your dramatic silence until it's night-time again?'

Oswin stared out of the window, snorting softly at Ennastasia's comment. 'Away from here. *Beyond.*' He saw

Ennastasia's fussed look only grow fussier. 'Also no idea what that means.'

'There seems to be a lot of that going around.'

Oswin shifted, tensing at the pain the movement sent up his limbs. 'Actually, I owe you a lot of thanks.'

'Of course you do.' Ennastasia shut the book, pulling the duvet over it. 'But what specifically are you referring to?'

Oswin was glad Maury and Philomena were in a different recovery room in the healer's cabin. He wanted privacy for this. His shoulders tensed. 'When the ghost hand suggested we leave this world, it said that, if I did go, I'd never have to deal with being a useless stray again. I could be free of, well ... all this.' He gestured around himself. 'Being a burden.'

Ennastasia's brows knitted together, her previous joking air vanishing.

Oswin gripped the duvet, running the fabric between his fingers. 'I said yes. But then, as I was shattering, travelling to whatever strange world the ghost hand came from, I thought about how you said we were friends, about all the games and bets we've had this year, and ...' He pursed his lips, letting out a shaky breath. He tried to explain, but his voice box stung with too many emotions to function.

Ennastasia unclasped her earring. The ruby rested

in her palm as she gazed at it. 'It was my mother's,' she said, and Oswin's pulse stuttered at the information. He could tell from the look on her face how private that fact was to her. Gingerly, she put the earring back on. 'Being a Barkmoth means no one treats you with authenticity. They either hate you, are scared of you or want something from you.' She looked straight at him. 'You were willing to give your life for me. You led the beast away after throwing my spellbook in the opposite direction. Which – let us be clear – was a profoundly airheaded, immeasurably dreadful, and *utterly absurd* strategy, which you're never again to repeat. I'd call throwing my spellbook out of my reach a laughable idea had it not almost single-handedly sabotaged our chances of survival—'

'Really laying on the compliments here.'

'But ...' She gestured between them, struggling with her next words. 'If this *friendship* was just to get something out of me, you wouldn't have done that. I guess I'm saying it doesn't matter if you know about who my family are, so long as you don't *care*.' She swung her legs over the side of the bed, one bandaged. Carefully, she limped to Oswin, putting her hand on his forearm. 'But this is the most important thing: you're not useless.'

Oswin stared at her. He blinked once, twice, then

smiled as his vision blurred. Her words repeated in his head. 'You mean it?'

'Completely. You're my friend.'

'Thank you.' Channelling Maury's energy, Oswin winked at her. '*Best* friend.'

Ennastasia hobbled back to her bed. 'Don't push it.'

After another blissful sleep, Oswin woke again. Judging from the light outside, it was afternoon, as the sky was growing dark and the howling winds sounded cold against his ears. The healer gave him permission to return to his dorm, so he did, finding Zylo waiting. His brother gave him a rib-crushing hug, apologized for the enthusiastic reunion, then forced him to spill everything that had happened.

Oswin left out Maury's involvement, and his merging with the ghost hand, but, even so, Zylo was biting his nails during the whole story, seemingly always a second from bursting into tears.

'I made it out alive,' said Oswin, trying to comfort his brother.

'You almost didn't!' said Zylo.

'You couldn't have known. It's not your fault.' Oswin held his brother's hand tightly, but his words seemed to make Zylo more upset. 'And, as I said, *I made it out alive.*'

'You did. You did ...' Zylo repeated it a few times and that seemed to calm him.

The cold of the Freeze stuck around as Oswin's first year as an ice apprentice drew to an end. When he wasn't eating with Ennastasia or Zylo, he made a point of sitting with Maury, who beamed every time, before proceeding to tell Oswin about his latest invention that had either exploded or nearly lopped off a finger. It was nice to see him back to his usual, reckless self, hands not shaking, no dark bag below his eye.

One morning, Maury lowered his voice and said, 'Rochelle checked with my parents. I was telling the truth: they knew I was a mimic and went along with the lie. You can ask her if you don't believe me.'

'I won't need to. I believe you.'

'Thank you,' he said. 'I ... just ... Thank you.'

'Anytime.'

When Philomena wasn't eating with Gale, she joined Maury, seeming just as close with him as she'd been before the catastrophic incident. Perhaps closer.

On the evening when the year's lessons had finally finished, Oswin sat with Ennastasia in the mezzanine.

'Have you finished reading the book?' he asked, spinning the ornate globe on the side table, taking in the endless map of ice.

Subtly, Ennastasia pulled *The Book of Oddities* out of her pack. 'I have.' She lowered her voice to a whisper. 'A lot of the information was destroyed by the fire, but I managed to piece a fair bit together.'

'And?' Oswin took the book and flicked through it.

'The oddities are supposedly the source of *all* magic, leaking into our world from another, incredibly strange, world. Somewhere, there could be a timber oddity or a fog oddity, and those oddities wouldn't just be linked to timber and fog magic, they would be the very reason it exists in the first place.'

'What about coal?' He paused his rifling to glance up.

Ennastasia stared, steely-eyed, into the distance. 'Oh, yes. A coal oddity was theorized, of course.' She wafted a hand dismissively.

Oswin frowned. 'What's with the odd reaction?'

'It wasn't odd.'

'It was—'

'Let's focus on the ghost hand for now,' Ennastasia insisted, so Oswin wrangled his questions back as best he could. 'It goes without saying, the theories of the oddities must hold some truth, seeing as we know the ghost hand isn't a myth.'

'The ghost hand *is* an oddity, then?' Confirming that he'd merged with something so peculiar – something that had slipped into this world from another – was alarming. Especially given how it had affected Maury. At least *he* hadn't turned into horrific monsters.

'It would seem so. By taking it off Maury, you spared her.' Ennastasia crossed her arms. 'But what I don't get, and what the book doesn't explain, is why you were compatible with the ghost hand when Maury wasn't.'

Oswin handed *The Book of Oddities* back to Ennastasia. 'Who can say what any of this means.'

'Can't you just ask it?' She pointed at his hand. 'It's right there.'

'I've tried. Nothing but silence.' He ground his teeth together in annoyance. 'Merging with me stopped whatever communication it could do. But, clearly, there's something about me that the ghost hand gelled with.'

Ennastasia's eyes fixed on his right hand. 'You said the roots tried to eat you.'

Oswin started. 'What?'

'Back in the healer's cabin, you said the roots tried to eat you.'

'They did. I *still* don't understand the reason. Why do you ask?'

Ennastasia put the book back into her bag, contemplating for a long time. After what felt like ages, she gave a small nod, as if she'd figured something out. Oswin leaned forward expectantly, but Ennastasia just shrugged. 'No reason.' Her voice was casual even though her posture was stiff.

'That's another odd reaction.'

'Nope. Still isn't.'

Frustrated that Ennastasia was being cagey, Oswin stood, stretched and went to the staircase leading down from the mezzanine.

'Where are you going?'

'Home,' said Oswin. 'We've got a few weeks until our second year of apprenticeship. I'm spending them with my mother.'

Ennastasia scowled at him. 'You realize that's not the done thing, right? Apprentices are meant to stay at Corridor for five years and only visit home rarely, if ever. It's how we grow into independent adults.'

'I know,' said Oswin. 'Zylo told me yesterday, but if he couldn't convince me to stay over the break, you definitely can't.' He gave her a wave, then left.

It didn't take Oswin long to prepare. His belongings easily fitted into his pack, while his lock picks, collection of odd items and Huvect cards slotted into his pockets. Before long, he was setting off into the harsh Freeze to journey home. The Freeze was meant to have stopped by now, but it was brashly continuing, and Oswin knew

Lullia would need help on the produce field. Besides, he needed to show his mother that, even though he was now an ice apprentice, he could also be a good son.

When Oswin, leaning against the strong wing, reached Reginald, he looked down at his hand. As the snow blustered, he pulled his right glove off and opened his fist, stretching and curling his fingers. With ease, he made the blue sheen of the ghost hand appear and vanish. It would make a neat party trick, he had to admit, but he wanted to keep it to himself, especially because he didn't know what being merged with an oddity truly meant. He was glad only he and Ennastasia knew he had the ghost hand.

Oswin heard footsteps and pulled his glove back on. He turned and saw Ennastasia's red cloak whipping behind her as she hurried over. She stopped in front of him, then grabbed his arm and led him away from Reginald.

'What is it?' said Oswin.

Ennastasia checked for eavesdroppers. 'I realized something.'

'What?'

'The mystery isn't wholly solved.'

Oswin's brow furrowed. 'But it is. The ghost hand possessed Maury, turning her into monsters. She was a mimic who took the first Maury's place after she went missing in the Teeth That Snatch.'

'Yes, *but*,' Ennastasia hissed, 'how did Maury end up infected with the ghost hand in the first place? And who spiked Rochelle's and Kestcliff's teas so they'd fall unconscious?'

Oswin's stomach dropped. 'Oh.'

'Exactly. *Oh*.' Ennastasia shook her head. 'The oddities are just a theory, one that no one believed in—'

'I believed in them.'

'No one *sensible* believed in. A theory from long ago that wasn't taken seriously at the time it was written, and definitely isn't taken seriously now by the shockingly few people who know about it. Yet someone *must* know they're real, and know *enough* to use them for their own ends.' She lowered her voice so that he could barely hear it above the snowstorm. 'Someone planted the ghost hand on Maury.'

'Planted ...' Oswin felt a cold that had nothing to do with the weather. 'The conversation. The conversation I overheard!'

'What in Tundra are you talking about?'

'At the start of the year, I overheard a conversation in Shemmia Woods: "I'll be there when you plant it. I'll ensure all goes according to plan."'

Ennastasia's eyes bulged. 'You overheard the people behind this. They must have been talking about the ghost hand; they must have planted it on Maury. I think I know when, too: at the start of the year when everyone was distracted by the shrinking sphere and Maury fainted.'

'I saw the ghost hand then. A blue glow around her hand.'

Ennastasia clicked her fingers. 'Whoever's behind this used a krimpsteen to make a distraction, then planted the oddity on Maury. But for what purpose? And how did they have knowledge about oddities, let alone possess an *actual* oddity?'

Oswin stepped towards the masters' cabins. 'We should tell someone.'

Ennastasia grabbed his arm. 'We absolutely should *not*.'

'But whoever planted the ghost hand is up to no good.'

'And they could be one of the very masters you want to warn.'

Oswin stood, frozen. 'Michael Fields was looking into oddities. Do you ... think he's come back?'

'He's dead,' said Ennastasia flatly. 'He was unceremoniously chucked onto the Endless Expanse to starve or freeze, unless he was lucky and a beast got him first. But who's to say a follower of Michael Fields hasn't picked up where he left off? Maybe, before he was exiled, Michael was planning something with oddities. Maybe that was part of his original plot to destroy Tundra.'

'You think one of his followers may be finishing what he started?'

Ennastasia nodded gravely. 'We need to go over the shrinking sphere incident. Whoever orchestrated this would have wanted to make sure the distraction and the planting of the oddity went smoothly. They must have been there. You've got your perfect memory. We can use it to figure out everyone present. That will give us a list of suspects.'

'Yes. We *can* do that, and we *will*,' he said as Ennastasia let go. 'But next year.'

'What?'

'I need to get home. I need to help my mother.' He clenched his jaw. 'I need to be a good son.' He didn't mention the letter Lullia had sent him. It had strongly implied that if he didn't go home to help, he would be a failure of a son. 'When I come back next year, we'll figure it out.'

'I can't convince you to stay even another day?'

Oswin shook his head. Lullia's letter was burning a hole in his pocket.

Ennastasia breathed out. 'All right.' For a second, Oswin thought she was going to leave it there. But, as she started to move away, she paused. 'Goodbye ... friend.' It was obvious she had trouble saying the word, yet forced herself to all the same. Somehow, that made it sound nicer.

Oswin smiled. 'See you in a few weeks. I promise.'

'I'd better,' Ennastasia grumbled, hunching against the wind as she returned to the dormitories. Oswin watched her for a bit, then walked back to Reginald, who let him pass without trouble.

He travelled the snowy path that ran through Shemmia Woods, steering clear of the roots. Within a few minutes, he saw his mother coming to meet him, just as her letter had instructed she would. Not caring if his lungs gave out on him, Oswin broke into a run.

Lullia saw him, her ginger hair an explosion of curls in the cold air. When Oswin reached her, he wrapped her in a tight hug that she barely tolerated.

'I've missed you,' said Oswin.

'Yet you didn't visit.' She pushed him off her. 'Come on. Long journey.'

Oswin walked alongside her, the cold weather of the Freeze cutting through his thick coat to his skin, but it didn't bother him at all. After a year at Corridor, his head buzzed with questions: about Michael Fields and his interest in oddities, why the roots had wanted to eat him and who had planted the ghost hand on Maury.

He glanced over his shoulder through the snowfall,

in the direction of Corridor, and felt excitement at the knowledge that he'd return. When he did, he'd find the answers.

EPILOGUE

'You said no one would get hurt.' The ice apprentice skated to where a tall man, hair flowing above his head, waited. Enraged, the apprentice threw a half-empty sachet of tea leaves at the man's feet.

'No one *was* hurt.'

The apprentice's mouth parted in shock. 'Are you kidding?'

'Not mortally. And don't go sulking about the kikorka incident; that was your own doing.'

'I had to at least try to help her!'

'You're lucky I had her memory altered. She could have

blabbed that you knew what was going on. Show some gratitude.'

'Gratitude? *Gratitude?* The only reason I agreed to do this was because you said it was the only way to keep him safe. But he wasn't safe, not in the slightest. This wasn't part of the deal.'

'It is now.'

'No.' The apprentice cut a hand through the air. 'I'm done. You said you'd leave me alone once I did my part. I've done my part. Leave me alone.'

'You're done when I say you are. What do you think would happen if people found out it was you who planted the ghost hand? Who swapped the masters' tea leaves? I could even say it was *you* who used the krimpsteen on the sphere, not me. With a blink, I could have this fiasco laid firmly upon your shoulders. Worst of all, I could tell everyone it was your fault little Maury wandered into the Teeth all those years ago. Both you and the mimic would be done for.'

'You said you'd keep that a secret if I did as you asked!'

'And I will. I simply have more to ask.'

'That *wasn't the deal*!'

The tall man tutted. 'Must I really explain blackmail?'

'Leave Maury out of this. You can drag my name

through the mud, turn me into a pariah, get me kicked out of Tundra. I don't care. But I'm not putting *Oswin* at risk any more.'

A smile twisted on the man's face, his pure black eyes watching the apprentice closely. 'But if your name is dragged through the mud, if you're committed to the ice, he'll be at even greater risk. If you're gone, who will protect poor Oswin?'

'Protect him from whom?'

'Me.'

The apprentice took a step, fists clenched. 'Don't you dare hurt him.'

'Break from my commands and I will ensure he perishes, and that your name is so degraded there will be little you can do about it. Stick with me, help me complete what Michael could not–'

The apprentice baulked. 'You were allies with Michael?'

'That little twig? Never. But you see, for all my muscle, Michael had something I did not: brains. So, when I had the chance, I stole the plans that roach never got to enact. If you stick the course with me for just a little longer, Oswin will be unharmed. I'll even keep Maury's mimic secret under wraps, if that's still of concern.'

The apprentice paced like a caged beast, mulling the options over. 'Fine. But the first sign Oswin's in real danger, I'm telling everyone what I know, blackmail be damned. Got it, Greyheart?'

'*High Watcher* Greyheart,' he corrected the apprentice, smiling. 'You are frightfully easy to manipulate . . .' The smile deepened. 'Zylo Fields.'

ACKNOWLEDGEMENTS

So many people leave fingerprints on a book, from those who've edited the words to those who've inspired the writer. There are so many fingerprints on *Ice Apprentices* that's it's impossible for me to thank everyone, but I'm sure going to try!

First, to Silvia Molteni – agent extraordinaire – who took Oswin to places I never dreamed he could go. I have no doubt that, without you, this story would never have made it to where it has.

I have endless gratitude for my phenomenal editor Michelle Misra, whose skills straightened Tundra's confusions, and brought this icy adventure into sharp focus. I will never be able to thank you enough.

To the whole team at Simon and Schuster: a massive thank you for being so welcoming to me when I was (and still am) utterly starstruck by you all. To Rachel Denwood,

Ali Dougal, Lucy Pearse, Laura Hough, Dani Wilson, Leanne Nulty, Emma Quick, Jess Dean, Maud Sepult, Emma Martinez, Tanya Hill, Theo Steen, Jesse Green and Sophie Storr for all your phenomenal work in making this a reality. And to the proof readers and copy editors, Leena Lane, Hanna Milner and Catherine Coe, and many more, who made sure this story was in the best shape possible.

To Nicole Ellul, my US editor, a heartfelt thank you for making the daunting task of picking out all the Britishisms I had no idea were Britishisms so smooth, and another thank you to Brian Luster, Kayley Hoffman, and the entire team across the pond.

I'd like to thank Petur Antonsson for the most magical, frosty, monstrous cover I could have imagined, and whose illustrations have brought the characters to life. Nothing else could have captured the soul of this story so perfectly.

I'd like to thank Annabel Steadman for helping me brave an intimidating world containing so many of my personal heroes, and for signing my Dutch copy of Skandar, which I believe makes it the only Dutch signed Skandar book *in de hele wereld!*

I also owe so much to all the people who supported me long before a snowy world had built itself inside my head. To the learning support department of my secondary school, and all the wonderful teachers there, without whom I would have forever believed my dyslexia was a permanent barrier to the written word. To my best bud, Janina Arndt, for sharing your stories with me, and letting me share mine with you. To Megan Woods – your character work is second to none and was irreplaceable in all this. To my critique group, Sharon Boyle, Kirsty Collinson, Helen Mackenzie, Elizabeth Fowler and Jo Verrill, for always giving me the guidance I need to improve my work. Without your vital advice, Oswin never would have found his home.

To all my friends, who fill my life with colour. To Martha, Lucy, Charlotte, Andy, Fran and Arianna, your confidence in me was the fuel behind this all. I cherish every moment I spend with you.

To Jacqui and Geoff, thank you for filling my childhood with ferocious dragons and brushes that could paint doorways into other worlds, and giving me a love for history and stories. To Mum, Dad, and Sophie, thank you for sound-boarding all my ridiculous ideas, and giving me countless inspirations. To everyone in my family, both those still with us, and those not, I credit my love of writing to you.

And finally, to you, the reader; thank you for going on this frosty adventure with Oswin. I hope you'll come along for a few more.

ICE APPRENTICES

BOOK TWO

Coming February 2026